P9-BYS-815

In the Forests of the Night

In the Forests of the Night

The Goblin Wars: Book Two

Kersten Hamilton

CLARION BOOKS
Houghton Mifflin Harcourt
New York • Boston
2011

Clarion Books
215 Park Avenue South
New York, New York 10003

Copyright © 2011 by Kersten Hamilton

All rights reserved. For information about permission to reproduce selections from this book, write to Permissions, Houghton Mifflin Harcourt Publishing Company, 215 Park Avenue South, New York, New York 10003.

Clarion Books is an imprint of Houghton Mifflin Harcourt Publishing Company.

www.hmhbooks.com

The text was set in FCaslon Twelve ITC.
Book design by Sharismar Rodriguez

Library of Congress Cataloging-in-Publication Data
Hamilton, K. R. (Kersten R.)
In the forests of the night / by Kersten Hamilton.
p. cm.–(The goblin wars ; bk. 2)
Summary: Teagan, Finn, and Aiden have made it out of Mag Mell alive, but the Dark Man's forces follow them to Chicago, where Tea's goblin cousins cause all sorts of trouble while she is torn between the life she wants and the future she is drawn to as a wild Stormrider, born to reign.
ISBN 978-0-547-43560-2
[1. Goblins–Fiction. 2. Magic–Fiction. 3. Imaginary creatures–Fiction. 4. People with mental disabilities–Fiction. 5. Irish Americans–Fiction. 6. Zoos–Fiction. 7. Finn MacCool–Fiction.] I. Title.
PZ7.H1824In 2011
[Fic]–dc22
2011009846

Manufactured in the United States of America
DOC 10 9 8 7 6 5 4 3 2 1
4500320671

This book is for Meghan, who is full of strength and courage.
I love you forever, m'dearie!

PROLOGUE

TEARS were spilling down Teagan's cheeks as she went up the stairs. She locked her bedroom door so no one could follow her in. If Aiden needed her, he could just bang on it and wake Abby, who was curled up on the bed, frowning in her sleep. Teagan tiptoed past her, careful not to let even one sniffle escape, climbed out the window, and slid it shut behind her.

She made it to the middle of the roof before she collapsed, hugging the roll of duct tape. It seemed like a million years since the day Finn had told Aiden that duct tape could fix anything. Well, it couldn't fix this.

Teagan pulled her knees up, put her head down on them, and let the sobs come. They'd turned to hiccups when something touched her shoulder.

"Tea? Are you all right?"

"Finn!" She whirled to look at the window. It was still closed. "Where did you come from?"

"Came up the drainpipe," he said. "I heard someone crying up here and wondered who it was."

"You climbed up the drainpipe with your hand like that?" It was still wrapped in gauze and tape to help his palm heal.

"I can use two fingers." He wiggled them at her to prove it.

"Here." She wiped her nose on her sleeve, hiccupped, and held out the duct tape.

Finn took it and turned it over a couple of times. "You climbed out on the roof to cry over duct tape?"

"No," Teagan said. "I climbed out on the roof to be alone."

Finn sat down beside her. "You can do that. In a bit. But if you're not crying over the duct tape, what are you crying over?"

"I don't want to—*hic*—tell you."

"If you won't talk about it, girl, I guess I'll have to. What Roisin said that night . . ."

Teagan put her chin on her knees again. "It's true."

"I told you, I knew it was the minute the words left her mouth. It changes a lot of things, doesn't it?"

Teagan nodded.

"I think so, too. There's a Travelers' prayer I learned when I was little: '*I do not ask for a path with no trouble or regret—*'"

"'*I ask instead for a friend who'll walk with me down any path,*'" Teagan finished his sentence for him.

"You know it, then!" Finn said. "That makes it all easier. So, do you get my meaning, girl?"

"No." He couldn't mean what she thought he meant. She couldn't let him.

"No?" Finn ran his good hand through his hair. "I thought it was plain enough. I'm the Mac Cumhaill, that's the thing, not a word man like your da."

"And I'm a Highborn," Teagan said flatly. "Go back to Mamieo and her Travelers' prayers and leave me alone with my goblin blood."

"Are you thickheaded?" Finn asked. "I know your blood, and the heart that pumps it. I'm saying I'll walk with you down any path, as long as I am able. I'd have told you as much that morning in Mag Mell, but you'd have thought it was my promise to Aiden talking, wouldn't you?"

"Maybe."

"I don't need magic to make me keep my promises."

"I know," Teagan whispered.

"I love you."

"You can't," Teagan said.

"Why not?"

"You want to know what I was crying about?"

"I said I did."

"It's because I'm not good like you, Finn. I *am* a goblin. I fed Ginny to the hellhounds. Horrible, nasty Ginny Greenteeth kept her promise, and I *used* her to save my own life. She begged me not to. But I did exactly what Fear Doirich would have wanted me to, didn't I? Killing her was *useful,* just like cousin Kyle said it would be. Will you walk with me down that path, goblin hunter?"

Finn took a deep breath and let it out slowly. "Is that why you've been avoiding me?"

"Yes."

Teagan studied her shoes, waiting for him to walk away.

"Look at me, girl."

She looked up.

"I said I love you. That's not changing, no matter what you've done. But I need to know. Is that the path you intend to walk?"

"No," Teagan admitted. "I hate it. I hate what I've done. But I've started down that path, haven't I? It's in my blood."

"You've got choices, like any other creature," Finn said. "You can stumble down that road, pretending you can't help it. You can curl up and die of regret and sorrow for what you've done. Or you can get up and fight, even though the battle might be lost."

"Did Mamieo teach you that?"

"The Boy Scouts," Finn said. "Nothing could take it out of those two old men, not the streets, hunger, rags, or curses. They *chose* their lives. They taught me to choose mine. If you start to walk down that path again, I'll do my best to bring you back."

"That's what I'm afraid of," Teagan said. "My family is *goblin*, Finn. I don't want to drag you into it. I can devolve into something like Kyle. Thomas—a guy who killed an angel—is probably my cousin. I won't let you love me."

Finn scratched his head, as if he were considering.

"I may need your permission to kiss you, girl. But I don't need anyone's permission to love you. I choose it of my own free will, and there's nothing you can do about it."

Teagan shook her head. "You still don't get it. I know you thought I was your *a gra ma* whatever—"

"*A ghrá mo chroí*," Finn said. "The love of my heart."

"—but I'm not. What I did in Mag Mell *broke* me inside."

"And isn't it a Fir Bolg's job to mend what's broken, then?"

He reached out and traced a line above her bare arm, his finger an inch from her skin. The electric arc from his fingertip raised goose bumps as it followed his finger down her arm. It made her whole body shiver. "I've been wondering if you felt it, too."

"Yes." It was impossible to argue when she could hardly breathe.

"That's good." Finn nodded. "I'm just not sure what I'm going to do about it."

"*What?* Why not?"

"Because of the talk your da gave me that first day."

"But you asked if you could kiss me after that talk!"

"That's true," Finn said. "I didn't think I needed your da's advice then. I know I need it now. The man's had experience in this sort of thing." A door slammed below them, and Finn stood up.

"In what sort of thing?" Teagan could feel the heat flush her face. "Wait. You didn't ask *me* if I loved *you!*"

"Didn't have to." Finn stepped toward the edge of the roof and looked over. "I'm the Mac Cumhaill, remember? I told you I was going to change that plan of yours."

Teagan flushed. "I haven't changed all of it. I'm still headed for Cornell, and I'm not giving that up for anyone. I'll just have to figure out how I can focus on my studies *and* work things out with you."

"This might not be the best time to negotiate the finer points of our relationship," Finn said. He offered her a hand, and pulled her to her feet. "There's matters that need looking after."

"What sort of matters?" Teagan turned to look.

Lennie was standing on the sidewalk, holding Aiden up above his head.

"I see her!" Aiden said, and started waving his arms. "*Tea-gan!*" he shouted. "*Come quick! Thomas is growing feathers!*"

PART I: LHIANNON-SÍDHE

ONE

TEAGAN Wylltson blinked and tried to focus on her five-year-old brother, Aiden. His best friend, Lennie—a pudgy, pimpled eighteen-year-old—was holding him up so that he could see Teagan's perch on the roof of the porch. Lucy, the sprite who had taken up residence in her brother's hair, was zipping excitedly around his head.

"Come quick! Thomas is growing feathers!" Aiden yelled again.

"The man's shape-shifting," Finn said. He had taken her hand to pull her to her feet, and he hadn't let go. Every molecule in her was suddenly vibrating at a higher rate, and webs of electricity spread over her entire body. It felt good. *Really* good. But it did make it hard to focus.

"Where's Mamieo, then?" Finn asked.

"She was sitting beside him when I went through the living room," Teagan said, dropping his hand and stepping away.

Focusing would be a good thing right now. Finn's grandmother hadn't been happy when they'd dragged a wounded shape shifter out of Mag Mell, but she'd promised not to harm the creature—so long as he didn't do anything unnatural.

"Do you think she'll consider this—"

"Unnatural? I'm sure of it."

"She wouldn't—"

"Do away with the creature?" Finn rubbed his chin with the two good fingers of his wounded hand. "I doubt it. But I'd best go check on them just the same. Thomas might be needing some help."

"Finn," Teagan said, as he turned away. She glanced over to make sure Lennie had put Aiden down. He had. "I do love you."

Finn turned back, grinning. "I know it."

"But I'm not sure what I'm going to do about it, either. I meant it when I said that I'm still headed for Cornell. I'm not giving that up."

"You didn't think I'd go along with you? That's why you were crying?"

Teagan shook her head. "I didn't believe you could love me. I was going to get over it, and get on with my plans."

"That's just like you. Sticking to the plan."

"Not this time. You turned my world upside down, Finn Mac Cumhaill. If Cindy hadn't fallen for Oscar at first sight, I wouldn't have been thinking about—"

"Why are you guys still talking?" Aiden yelled.

"Just one more minute, boyo," Finn called over the edge, then turned back to Teagan.

"Cindy and Oscar? Your monkeys?"

"Chimpanzees are apes," Teagan said automatically. "And they don't belong to me—I just work with them. They shouldn't belong to the zoo, either. They should belong to themselves.

That's what I'm working for. That's why it's important that I go to Cornell. So maybe you and I *should* wait until things settle down a bit—"

"Tea." Finn looked grim. "Things are not going to settle. Your relations have come calling."

"You mean the goblins."

"And the Travelers. There's never going to be peace between them. And your family's in the middle of it."

"Are you guys *kissing?*" Aiden shouted.

"Not yet." Finn cocked an eyebrow and lowered his voice so only Teagan could hear. "But I can't wait to get to it."

"'Cause Mamieo said to hurry!"

Finn touched Teagan's face, then turned and jumped, catching the lamppost next to the house with his good hand. She stepped to the roof's edge to watch him swing around it as he dropped. She'd been coming out onto the porch roof since she was little, but her stomach still felt tight if she stood too close to the edge. She would never just throw herself off it like that. Finn landed lightly in the patch of frost-yellowed grass between the sidewalk and the street, then grinned up at her.

Kissing. Teagan pressed her hands into her stomach to stop the trembling, which was threatening to spread to her knees.

"Come on, girl." Finn lifted his arms. "Jump down. You're just the right size for catching."

"Uh-uh." Teagan took a step back. "Not while you have a hurt hand."

"Well, then, could you bring my duct tape down with you?"

"Sure."

Aiden started for the door.

"Finn—" Teagan began, but he had already caught her brother by the collar.

"Not so fast, there," Finn said as Aiden tried to wiggle away.

"I want to know what's happening," Aiden said.

"Thomas is growing feathers." Lennie sounded worried. "Like a bird. That's what."

Lennie couldn't see Lucy and the other the creatures of Mag Mell who were only half present in this creation. But there were some unearthly creatures that were fully present in any of the worlds of the multiverse—angels, Highborn, and Fir Bolg—that even people without second sight could see. And watching a shape shifter transform would give Lennie nightmares.

"I'll take care of it," Finn assured him. "But I'll be needing two brave men to stand guard out here. Do you know where I might find them?"

"We're brave." Aiden stopped wiggling, and tipped his head as if he were listening. "Yep," he said. "There are bad guys coming. We'll fight them!"

Finn glanced up at Teagan, and she shrugged. Aiden had been saving the world from imaginary bad guys daily since they escaped from Mag Mell, sometimes by singing them away, and sometimes defeating them with stick swords and rocks.

"We will?" Lennie looked worried.

"I fought bad guys before," Aiden assured him. "I'll show you how." Lucy had decided the show was over and had settled into his hair again. She always played along with Aiden's imaginary battles.

"All right," Lennie agreed.

Finn looked at Teagan again, and she nodded.

"You two stay right here, then," he said, "until Teagan can walk you across the street to Lennie's house. Got it?"

Finn disappeared onto the porch beneath her, leaving both Aiden and Lennie looking up at her expectantly.

"Jump, Tea-gan," Lennie said. "I can catch you. I don't have a hurt hand."

"Thank you, Lennie," Teagan said. "But I'm going back in through the window. You wait there like Finn said." She wiped her tears on the back of her sleeve. Her eyes were swollen, and her nose felt like a blob. She picked up the roll of tape.

"Aiden. Come to us."

Teagan froze. She knew that voice, and it made her hair stand on end. She stepped as close to the edge of the roof as she dared.

"Lennie!" Aiden said. "The *cat-sídhe* are here!"

"What's a *cat-sídhe*?" Lennie looked around. "Are they the bad guys?"

"Yep," Aiden said. "They're the kind you can't see."

"I hate that kind." Lennie picked up a stick and swung at the air.

Teagan was glad Lennie couldn't see the creatures on the far side of the street. He would have had nightmares for months. At first glance, they looked like large housecats. Dirty, diseased housecats that stood upright. But if you looked closer, you'd notice that their mouths and hands were almost human. Bare skin showed in mangy patches through their filthy fur. The bigger one's ears hung in tatters. Maggot Cat. The last time she'd seen him he'd flicked maggots picked from his rotting flesh at her. The wound on his stomach didn't seem to be open, but even from this distance his bare abdomen still looked swollen. The *cat-sídhe* beside him was younger, and Teagan had seen it before, too. It looked like it had been sleeping in an oil pan. Both of them had hunted Teagan, Aiden, and Finn through the streets of Chicago. The cat goblins were always causing the Irish Travelers trouble and grief.

"Aiden, is Finn already inside?" Teagan asked.

"Ah, ah!" The smaller *cat-sídhe* pointed up at her. "Teagan!"

"Teagan!" Maggot Cat commanded. "Step down."

Her left foot moved a half an inch closer to the roof's edge.

"No!" Teagan said, as much to her own leg as to the goblin.

"Yessssss!" Maggot Cat said.

They can do that, Finn had told her, the first time the goblin creatures had tried to control her body. The *cat-sídhe* could move some people's muscles just for a second—long enough for a car to swerve into a pedestrian if you were driving, or for you to step in front of a train. Long enough to ruin your life. But you could learn to resist them, if you focused.

"Bones," the smaller *cat-sídhe* yowled. "Marr-ow! Marr-ow!"

"I heard something scary," Lennie said. "Like a whisper in my head."

"That's their voices," Aiden explained. "Don't listen." *Cat-sídhe* voices had never had any effect at all on Aiden, but Lennie was a different matter.

"Lennie." Maggot Cat tipped his head, looking at Lennie. "We know your name."

"Shut up!" Aiden said.

Teagan flinched. *Sídhe* creatures had more power to bend you to their will if they knew your name.

Lennie looked around wildly. "Where are they, little guy?"

"Leave him alone," Teagan said.

"Step down now!" Maggot Cat focused on her again. Her right foot moved a fraction of an inch, despite her focus.

"Leave my sister alone!" Aiden yelled, and Lucy came out of his hair like an angry hummingbird.

"Sssprite!" Maggot Cat hissed.

Sprites were *cat-sídhe*'s favorite food—at least in Mag Mell. Lucy zipped toward them. Though Teagan was too far away to see it, she was sure the sprite had pulled her tiny bone knife out of the sheath on her thigh.

"Ah! Dibs!" The smaller *cat-sídhe* leaped into the air, trying to catch her. "Dibs!"

"Leave my Lucy alone, too!" Aiden started after her.

"No!" Lennie caught his collar. "We're not supposed to cross the street without permission, little guy!"

"Hold on to him, Lennie," Teagan called. Lucy was fluttering too close to the *cat-sídhe*'s claws.

She hefted the roll of duct tape. All she needed was a distraction until she could get off the roof. *Cat-sídhe* were not particularly brave. If she threw it hard enough to hit the wall above them, it might do the trick. The sprite could avoid the tape; she was designed for aerial combat.

A minivan blocked her line of sight for a moment, but as soon as it passed, Teagan threw the roll hard, aiming at the brick wall above the *cat-sídhe*. Lucy saw the tape coming and banked to the left, through the path of the tape. Maggot Cat twisted in the air, trying to follow her.

"No!" Teagan gasped as the tape hit him, knocking him head over tail.

"Yes!" Aiden cheered. "You got him!"

Teagan reached the drainpipe before Maggot Cat could catch his breath, grabbed onto the cold metal, and kicked the toes of her tennis shoes into the trumpet vine that wound around it.

"Ah, ah, let go, Teagan," the smaller *cat-sídhe* called.

"Get 'em, Lucy!" Aiden shouted.

Whatever the sprite did stopped the second *cat-sídhe* in mid-yowl. Teagan scrambled halfway down the pipe, then jumped to the sidewalk.

"I'm down, Lucy!" she called. The sprite zipped back to Aiden.

Blood dripped from the smaller creature's arm and shoulder where Lucy's blade had connected. It licked at it, trying to stop the bleeding. Maggot Cat leaned against the brick wall, panting. The duct tape had hit him hard enough to burst the swelling on his stomach. He pressed his hands against it, but pus oozed over his stubby fingers.

"You better run," Aiden said as Lucy settled into his hair, her eyes still flashing. "My sister's going to get you." Maggot Cat flattened his ears and hissed.

"Who is Tea-gan going to get?" Lennie's eyes were wild.

Teagan glanced at her front door. There was no screaming, so she assumed Finn had the situation under control. But she still couldn't send Lennie inside without knowing what was happening in there. She was going to have to take him to his own house—across the street, where the *cat-sídhe* were.

"You need to go play at Lennie's house, Aiden," Teagan said, taking the stick from Lennie.

"But I want to—"

Teagan gave him *the look.*

"Okay."

"Wait. Shake the candy out of your hair. Like you're putting in shampoo." Lucy had peeled M&M's in her nest on Aiden's head. Lennie might believe it was the work of Aiden's own personal tooth fairy, but Mrs. Santini certainly wouldn't.

Tea kept an eye on the *cat-sídhe* while Aiden leaned over and ruffled his hair with both hands. Red, green, and yellow bits of candy shell fell like confetti onto the sidewalk. When it either was gone or had settled to his scalp, Aiden took Lennie's hand, and Teagan walked them across the street, staying between them and the goblin cats, who were edging closer. She waited until the boys were safely inside and the Santinis' door was shut.

"I'm sorry," Teagan said to the *cat-sídhe.* "I was aiming for the wall."

"You missed," the small *cat-sídhe* pointed out.

Maggot Cat flattened his ears and hissed again.

Their voices had less power over her when she wasn't in a situation where one move could be fatal. It was as if fear gave them that tiny bit of control they needed to cause a disaster. If she hadn't already been afraid of the drop, they wouldn't have been able to move her toward the edge of the roof.

"You're sick." Teagan took a step toward them. "I'll help you if you'll let me. I've had a lot of experience with sick or injured"—

she almost said animals—"creatures. If you come with me to the clinic . . ."

"Fear says to bring Aiden," Maggot Cat said. "Bring Aiden to him."

Blood in Aiden's curls, and white bone shards. It was the image Fear Doirich, the Dark Man, had spoken into her mind in Mag Mell. She could see it if she closed her eyes.

"That's not going to happen," Teagan said.

"Keeee-yill." The smaller *cat-sídhe*'s lower jaw started to jitter. Teagan had seen a housecat do the same thing when it made a *ch-ch-ch* sound imitating the call of a baby bird to trick the mother into coming closer. "Keeee-yill, keeee-yill!"

Maggot Cat slashed at him, claws out, and the smaller cat leaped back.

"Bring Aiden to him, and Fear will let you live. He still wants you. *Bring Aiden to him.*"

"I told you, that's not going to happen," Teagan repeated. "And I know he can't come out and get us. There's an angel guarding the way."

"Keee—" The smaller cat began, but clapped his paws over his mouth when Maggot Cat narrowed his eyes.

Teagan started toward the *cat-sídhe,* but the creatures backed away from her, then flattened themselves, seemingly dislocating every joint as they squeezed through a gap barely wider than their skulls in the neighbor's fence.

Teagan glanced at the Santini house. Mrs. Santini had gone to New York to visit a cousin in the Bronx a few years back, and had come away with a healthy respect for rats. There wouldn't be a gap big enough for a mouse to squeeze through in her home, much less a *cat-sídhe.* Aiden and Lennie were watching from the front window.

Stay there, Teagan told Aiden using American Sign Language. She'd had no idea how useful teaching him ASL would turn out to be.

Aiden frowned.

I mean it. She picked up the roll of duct tape, and the foul-smelling smear the *cat-sídhe*'s wound had left on it made her stomach knot.

Her little brother had wanted to kill Fear Doirich and Kyle when they'd had them helpless in Mag Mell.

"They're really bad guys," Aiden had said. "We should smash them with rocks like they were going to smash me."

She'd been the one who'd said no. She'd wanted to get her family out of Mag Mell and home again. And killing Fear Doirich and Kyle had felt . . . wrong. She'd listened to that feeling, because Fear Doirich was bound and gagged.

Yet, not an hour later, she'd fed Ginny Greenteeth to the hellhounds to save her own life. It had been . . . useful.

You can curl up and die of regret and sorrow for what you've done. Or—

She would never do it again. She'd *never* let the Highborn come out the way it had in Mag Mell. Highborn were cold and calculating, born to violence, gifted in war. No matter what she'd inherited from her mother's twisted family, she would choose to be like her dad. John Wylltson was a lover, not a fighter. Teagan took a deep breath, then went back across the street and up the steps to her own front door.

TWO

THE Wylltsons' living room was a landscape of Lego carnage. Aiden and Lennie had pulled the cushions from the couch to build a fort against the wall, and they had spread armies across the floor. Abigail Gagliano was perched on the arm of the cushionless couch, drawing furiously in her sketchbook.

"I thought you were asleep," Teagan said.

"I woke up." Abby flipped the page and motioned with her chin toward Thomas, who was sitting up on a cot in the alcove off the living room. "I can't believe I'm seeing this." Thomas gripped his IV pole with one hand as if he were going to stand up.

"No, no, no." Teagan set the duct tape down on top of the TV and picked her way through armies of dead and dying Lego men to the shape shifter. "I don't think it's a good idea for you to be up just yet. That IV pole doesn't have wheels."

His borrowed pajamas hid the bandages around his chest. He would have looked like a beat poet after a really bad night, if it hadn't been for the black pinfeathers sprouting along the line of his jaw and the skiing-penguin print on the faded pajama shirt.

Teagan's aunt Roisin stood at the foot of the cot wearing Abby's teal merino wool sweater, which was oversize on her, a thin belt, and Teagan's gray leggings and Uggs. Roisin had never experienced cool weather, and she had gone knit-and-boot crazy the moment she saw them.

Grendal, who could have been Maggot Cat's healthy cousin, was draped over Roisin's arms. *"All creatures,"* Mamieo once said, *"from the moment they exist, set about* becoming *through their own free will. Some are becoming more of what they were meant to be, and some becoming less."* Grendal was everything that Maggot Cat should have been—beautiful, sweet, and intensely intelligent in his own strange way. Gold rippled through his orange fur as he shifted in Roisin's embrace, his abalone shell–hued eyes fixed on Thomas. They narrowed as the shape shifter's short dreads flattened into feathers. Grendal jumped from Roisin's arms as the hairbrush she was holding clattered to the floor. He landed on his feet, then hopped up onto the arm of the couch across from Abby, who never looked away from Thomas.

Roisin caught Teagan's eye and started rattling in ancient Irish, pointing at the cot.

"What's she saying?" Abby demanded of Thomas. He just shook his head, then took a ragged breath.

"It's all right, Roisin." Teagan grabbed the IV pole with one hand and put her other hand on the shape shifter's shoulder to keep him from standing. "We'll take care of him."

"Roisin, please!" Thomas's voice rasped. He tried to stand

again, but the pressure on his shoulder was too much for him. Roisin wagged her finger no, no, no, frowning at him.

"What's going on?" Abby asked.

"I don't know," Teagan said. "Where's Finn? Where's Mamieo?"

"Having an argument in the kitchen."

"And my dad?"

"Took a book and went to the basement before any of this started. Where have you been?"

"On the roof." *How long had she been up there before Finn came to find her? Half an hour?*

"T-Tea . . ." Thomas's Adam's apple bobbed, and he tried again. "Teagan. Get Roisin out of here. Don't let her see—"

At that moment, Finn backed into the room from the kitchen, his arms spread wide as he tried to keep a tiny white-haired lady from dodging around him. Mamieo Ida was the image of a sweet Irish granny, except for the butcher knife in her hand. Roisin squealed and put her hand over her mouth.

"What's the knife for, then, Mamieo?" Finn asked.

"A precaution, boyo."

"*Cuimhnichibh air na daoine bho'n d'thainig sibh,*" Finn said.

"What does that mean?" Abby asked.

"'Remember the people you come from.'" Thomas pressed his hand to his chest and coughed.

"So, *now* you're translating?" Abby glared at him. "Why didn't you tell us what your girlfriend was saying?"

"Because that was private," Thomas said.

Finn didn't take his eyes off his grandmother. "We're Fir Bolg, Gabby—"

"It's Abby."

"—created to mend and tend. That's what I'm asking her to remember."

Mamieo grimaced. "I remember well enough, boyo. I remember the goblins that split my Rory open and left him to die in the field like an animal!"

"Your husband was the cursed Mac Cumhaill," Thomas said. "How many goblins did he kill, old woman, before we got him?"

"Not enough, damn you," Mamieo spat. "Haven't your kind hunted my children and my children's children? Don't they hunt them still?"

"Mamieo." Finn stepped closer to her. "Didn't the Almighty himself tell you to tend this creature?"

"The Almighty did tell me to tend the creature." The knife lowered slightly. "But He neglected to mention what I was to do with it when it was mended."

"I'm—sorry." Thomas's voice was softer. "Sorry for your losses. But I—I—!" A sound that was half hiss and half death rattle came from the shape shifter as he started to jerk and fell back onto the cot.

"What's happening?" Mamieo leaned over to look around Finn.

"You've frightened him to death with your big bloody knife," Finn said. "That's what's happened."

Thomas's back arched, his eyes rolled up in his head, and his arms thrashed violently, ripping out his IV.

"Grand mal," Teagan said, pushing the IV pole out of the way. "He's having a seizure." Thomas's back arched again, lifting him off the bed, and he twisted and started . . . shrinking into his pajamas.

"Tea?" Abby leaned forward. "Is that . . . normal?"

"Not in this universe," Teagan said. Matter might turn into energy here, but it didn't just disappear. She supposed the multiverse made some kind of exception for shape shifters, tucking their missing mass into unused nooks and crannies until they needed it again. The shrinking stopped, and a large black bird wiggled out from under the folds of fabric and bandages.

"He's a crow?" Abby said.

"Raven," Teagan corrected. "Four times the size of a crow."

"Ew." Abby wrinkled her nose. "One of those birds that eats roadkill?"

"See?" Finn said soothingly to Mamieo. "It's like I told you. He's a wee birdie." The raven's beak snapped in outrage, and its beady eyes blinked fast.

"Highborn, Mac Cumhaill," Thomas croaked. "I'm a Highborn!" His head tipped, and he pecked at a shiny button on the pajama top. Then he seemed to realize what he was doing, shook himself, hopped to the edge of the cot, and spread his wings.

"I have destroyed armies. Toppled kings!"

"Did you peck them to death, then?"

Roisin looked from Finn to Thomas.

"Bréagadóir!" She snatched the hairbrush from the floor and flung it at the bird, who lifted into the air to avoid being hit.

"Roisin!" he called, but she turned and ran past Mamieo for the stairs. "Roisin, Roisin, Roisin!"

"Don't even think of following the child," Mamieo said,

brandishing her knife. Thomas did a circuit of the room, knocking over a lamp before he settled on the cot again.

"What was that all about?" Abby asked. "What did Roisin say?"

"She called the bird a liar." Mamieo let the knife drop to her side. "What did you lie about, goblin?"

"He told her he turned into something sexy. Like a wolf," Abby guessed.

Thomas turned to Abby, his beak gaping. "How did you know that?" he croaked. *"What are you?"*

"A female," Abby said. "Which means I got instincts." She pulled out her phone. "And I'm talking to a freaking bird. Please say I can tweet this, Tea."

"No, of course not."

"But—"

The door burst open.

"Take cover!" Aiden shouted as he jumped in, slamming it behind him. He dove for his cushion fort, Lucy zipping after him.

"What's after you, pratie?" Mamieo asked.

"The *cat-sídhe.*" Teagan started for the door.

"Cat-sídhe?" Finn said. "There are *cat-sídhe* outside?"

"No!" Aiden shouted. "Not *cat-sídhe.* It's the Skinner! She's coming! I saw her!"

Teagan turned to look out the window. The social worker had somehow managed to find parking just two houses down. She got out of her car, hopped on one foot, and pulled a crutch out of the back seat.

Mamieo crossed herself.

"May those that love us, love us. And those that don't love us, may the Almighty turn their hearts. And if He doesn't turn their hearts, may he turn their ankles, so we'll know them by their limping."

"She's already limping, as you can plainly see," Finn said.

"And doesn't that prove the Almighty was thinking to warn us?"

Ms. Skinner hobbled up the street and stopped in front of the window. She stretched her lips into a smile.

"She knows we can see her, right?" Finn asked.

"The light's behind her," Teagan pointed out. "All she sees is her own reflection."

"Face check," Abby decided as Ms. Skinner stretched her lips again, then puckered. She dug a lipstick out of her purse and applied it. "Uh-huh. Now the hair." As if on cue, the social worker rearranged her ginger bangs, fluffed them, then twisted a strand around her finger to make it curl. "That woman's man-hunting. Hide your dad, Tea."

"Don't let her get Dad!" Aiden shouted from his fort.

"Nobody is getting Dad," Teagan assured him.

"It's mesmerizing." Finn tipped his head sideways as Ms. Skinner practiced a pout, then wiped a tiny bit of lipstick from the corner of her mouth with her pinkie finger. "Like one of those snakes."

Even Thomas was frozen, watching as she fixed her smile in place, then headed for the steps. Teagan shook herself.

"She's coming in. Here!" She gathered the IV tubing, wrapped it around the pole, and shoved the whole thing toward

Abby as the doorbell rang. "Take this into the kitchen." She pulled the covers up over the adult-size pajamas and bandages on the bed. There was nothing she could do about the Legos lying everywhere. Maybe they would make it look as if one of Aiden's little friends was spending the night.

"Who is this Skinner?" Thomas croaked.

Teagan winced. A little friend with a talking raven. She sat down on the cot and wrapped her arms around the bird, holding its wings to its side so it couldn't flap, strut, or posture.

"Please don't talk while Ms. Skinner's here," she said as Mamieo started to open the door. "Just be still."

Finn pushed the door shut with one hand and took the butcher knife from Mamieo with the other. He tossed it toward the overstuffed chair by the door to the kitchen. The knife arced lazily and landed on the seat just as Abby stepped back into the room.

"Gabby," Finn said, "could you take that back to the kitchen?" Abby snatched it up.

"I told you. It's Abby, Dumpster boy." She stomped back into the kitchen, and Mamieo pulled the door open.

"Ms. Skinner," Mamieo said. "This is . . . unexpected."

"I know it's Saturday," Ms. Skinner said, her window-smile still perfect. "But I'm here with good news. Is Mr. Wylltson home?" She craned her neck to see around Finn.

"I'm afraid John Paul's down with a migraine," Mamieo said. "We can't be disturbing the man. What's happened to your foot?"

"I tripped over a cat."

"You wouldn't be part Irish Traveler, would you?" Finn asked. "On your *máthair*'s side, perhaps?"

"Of course not," Ms. Skinner said, as if Finn had accused her of having a particularly despicable disease. She was taking in everything—the Legos, the crumbs where the couch cushions should have been—as if she were inventorying the room for an upcoming garage sale. Her eyes settled on Mamieo for a moment. "You know Aiden's teacher threatened to quit unless he got counseling—"

Teagan hadn't known it, but Mamieo nodded as if it were not breaking news.

"—or was moved out of her classroom. His behavior is apparently . . . contagious."

"Which behavior, exactly?" Mamieo asked.

"His habit of . . . *committing social commentary*"—she emphasized the words as if she were speaking some code that Aiden wouldn't understand—"through song."

Aiden might have a five-year-old's vocabulary, but he was very good at context. He started singing softly beneath the cushions of his fort. Teagan bit her lip to keep from laughing. The song was "Cruella De Vil," from Disney's *101 Dalmatians.*

"Aiden," Ms. Skinner said. "I can hear you."

Aiden sang louder.

Ms. Skinner frowned. "That's not a nice song," she said loudly. "I hope it's not about anyone we know."

"I'm thinking it is," Finn said. "In fact, I'm almost certain of it." Mamieo took his arm and pulled him away.

Aiden was starting the second verse.

"Stop it!" Ms. Skinner demanded.

Aiden's voice never faltered, but he did sing more softly. Too softly to make out the words.

"Now, now," Mamieo said as the social worker studied Aiden's hiding place. "Did Aiden's teacher mention that I'd be volunteering in the classroom, Ms. Skinner? I've done the paperwork and I'll be there with the boy Monday morning. I'm sure he will behave himself. You could have kept your Saturday for yourself."

Ms. Skinner finished her mental inventory of the cushion fort, turned to the alcove, and took a quick step back.

"What is that crow doing in here?"

Teagan saw Thomas's beak start to open, and gently pinched it shut with two fingers.

"Raven, actually," she said as Thomas clawed and tried to flap.

"The kind that eats dead stuff." Abby had come back from the kitchen.

Ms. Skinner's eyes narrowed. "And you are . . . ?"

"The maid, apparently." Abby shot a sharp look at Finn. "You need anything else taken to the kitchen? 'Cause I'm right here, so you could just throw it at me."

"Why is Gabby your business, Skinner?" Finn folded his arms.

"Because she's here. It's my job to know everything pertaining to the environment of a child in my care."

Aiden's words became audible again. Ms. Skinner frowned in his direction.

"You remember my friend Abigail Gagliano, Ms. Skinner," Teagan said. "You met her once when Mom—"

"Oh, that's right," Ms. Skinner interrupted. "I met her just before your mother collapsed." Aiden's singing stopped abruptly, and the slightest upward curl appeared at the corners of Ms. Skinner's freshly painted lips.

Teagan almost gasped. The woman *was* evil. Aiden had told them that when he thought about his mom falling down, the words got all tangled up inside him and wouldn't come out. Teagan, Mr. Wylltson, and the school counselor were the only ones who should have known about it. But apparently, Ms. Skinner did, too.

"Now, about that raven?" she demanded.

"Urban rescue," Abby said before Tea could open her mouth. "That bird had totally been tortured when Tea found it."

"It looks perfectly healthy to me," Ms. Skinner said. "In any event, I'm sure dragging in dirty, diseased animals from the gutters"—she looked pointedly at Finn—"is unwise in a house with a small child. You have an exotic animal permit, I assume?"

"I'm covered by my work at the zoo." Teagan struggled to keep her arms around Thomas's feathered form. He was not happy.

"You were going to give us a message for John?" Finn stepped toward Ms. Skinner. "On your way out?"

Ms. Skinner backed away from him, color creeping into her face.

"I sacrificed my Saturday to find someone who could take Aiden on short notice." She pulled a business card from her pocket. "Ms. Giordano is the only therapist in this town who can work him in."

"And it took you all day to find her?" Finn took the card, even though she tried to hand it to Mamieo.

"She was last on my list. Giordano will take anyone. She does dance therapy for emotionally disturbed—"

"Sounds promising." Finn tucked the card in his pocket. "I'm sure dancing around with the last on your list will do the boyo a world of good. Will he be needing a tutu, then?"

"Please make sure Mr. Wylltson gets that card." She spoke past Finn to Mamieo as he shooed her toward the door.

"I'll make sure."

"She'll be here on Monday at three."

"Here?" Mamieo asked.

"Ms. Giordano doesn't maintain an office," she said as she went out the door. Finn shut it behind her. Aiden came out of his fort.

"I'm a prince. Not a princess." Aiden's words had come untangled the moment Ms. Skinner left. "I don't want to wear a tutu."

"Of course not, boyo," Finn said. "I shouldn't have said it, but the Skinner sets my teeth on edge, and that's the truth."

"Mine, too," Aiden agreed. "I'm going to set a trap to catch her if she comes for Dad. Can I go back to Lennie's house? I need his help."

"No," Mamieo said. "Your dinner is almost ready. You should check on Roisin, Tea. The girl has had a shock. And let your da know we'll be eating soon.

"And you." She pointed at the raven. "Get yourself sorted out. I won't have a bird hopping about the house, and I won't be holding conversations with one, either. You're safe until you've had a discussion with Mr. Wylltson. This home is his, and he'll be deciding whether you stay or go."

Thomas fluffed his feathers. The transformation was faster this time, much faster. Wherever the multiverse had tucked the extra mass, it was all back and, as Ms. Skinner had observed, perfectly healthy. All over.

"I need to speak to Roisin," he said.

Finn rubbed his jaw. "Then I suggest you get off my girl's lap. And put some clothes on, man. You're indecent."

THREE

TEAGAN could feel the heat in her face, even though Thomas had jumped up and covered himself with a sheet. Abby was snorting.

"Lay off, Gabby," Finn said. "The man couldn't help it, could he? I expect he'll be wanting something other than Mr. Wylltson's pajamas."

"Please." Thomas grimaced at the faded penguins.

"You could bring my kit, Tea, after you've seen to Roisin. Thomas can have my spare clothes until he gets something better."

"I'll help," Aiden said quickly.

"All right," Finn said. "But no digging through it. Just bring it to me."

Aiden crossed his heart.

Thomas put his head in his hands. "Please tell Roisin I need to talk to her."

"How can we do that?" Abby asked. "She can't understand English."

"Grendal can translate if he wants to."

"The creature has the gift of tongues?" Mamieo asked.

"They pick up language very quickly," Thomas said. "That's what makes the *cat-sídhe* such excellent spies. Please tell him I'm sorry. Ask him to tell Roisin that we need to talk."

"You'll be talking to me and John Wylltson first," Mamieo said, but she didn't sound murderous. "We're the nearest things she has to parents, and that girl is too young to be thinking about you."

"Plus, you told her you turned into a sexy wolf," Abby said.

"Abigail, you'll be going with Teagan," Mamieo said. "There's a naked man in the room."

"I'm an art student," Abby pointed out. "I see naked guys all the time. Plus, he's wearing a sheet."

Mamieo pointed at the stairs.

"Whatever," Abby said as she retreated. Teagan took Aiden's hand as they followed her.

"You go along, too, Mamieo," Finn said. "I brought the man home. He's my responsibility."

Mamieo nodded. "I'll be in the kitchen, then. With the cutlery."

"I thought I told you to stay at Lennie's house, Aiden," Teagan said as they went up the stairs.

"Lucy knocked something over," he explained. "Lennie's mom thought I did it, so she sent me home."

Teagan made a mental note to ask Mrs. Santini what had been broken, and if they could replace it.

"Where is Lucy?" The sprite wasn't in her brother's hair.

"Hunting," Aiden said. "She's hungry."

Abby was waiting at the top of the steps.

"You can stop laughing anytime, Abby," Teagan said.

"No, no, I can't. Seriously, Tea, you should have seen your face."

"I just wasn't expecting it. He wasn't naked when he transformed from a raven into a man in Mag Mell."

"His clothes had *draíocht* in them," Aiden said.

"That won't wash out?" Abby asked.

"*Draíocht* means magic," Teagan explained. "I don't think it washes out. They were probably made to transform when needed." Magic or not, they had been coated with blood and grime, so Mamieo had burned them.

"Mag Mell is full of *draíocht*," Aiden said wistfully. "I was awesome there."

"That's true," Teagan said. "He was." Dead forests tried to burst into life when Aiden sang in Mag Mell. Crooked paths became straight, sprites danced, and little frog people came out to sing along with him, as if some cosmic Walt Disney had shouted *Cue the cuteness!* Of course, the frog people were carrying spears, and the sprites used their tiny knives on each other.

"You're awesome here." Abby patted his head. "You're our choirboy."

Lucy shot out of the laundry chute beside them, carrying a green M&M.

"Whoa," Abby said. "Floating candy."

"It's just Lucy." Aiden giggled.

"It's like living with polterbeasts, you know?" Abby leaned back as the sprite carried the candy past her face.

"Poltergeists," Teagan corrected.

"Whatever. You can't see them, but they *move* stuff."

"We can see them." Aiden opened his mouth, and the sprite popped the candy in.

"I hid those," Teagan said as Lucy did an aerial roll and dove down the chute again.

"She has to eat them," Aiden explained. "We can't find flies. The only bugs left are spiders and crickets, and Lucy doesn't like spiders."

"I should have thought of that," Teagan said. The sprite had eaten berries and flying insects in Mag Mell, but mid-October wasn't prime fly season in Chicago. "I'll stop by the pet store for mealworms tomorrow."

"Worms?" Aiden made a face.

"Just keep your mouth shut if she tries to share." Teagan knocked softly on her bedroom door, then opened it. The room looked like a dorm since Abby and Roisin had moved in, and smelled like a cross between the girls' locker room, an art gallery, and Christmas. The scents of nail polish, cosmetics, and sweat mingled with the pine and . . . Teagan frowned. Cheeseburgers. Her schoolbooks lay on the desk, along with half-finished applications to Colorado State and University of California, Davis—plans B and C. She'd already sent her application to Cornell. Abby's schoolbooks were tossed on top of the vanity table. Her current project, a painting of the moon rising over the city, leaned against the mirror behind a precarious stack of CDs. Music to paint by, Abby called them.

Roisin was sitting in what looked like a very large pack rat's nest. Grendal had gathered greenery—holly leaves and berries, boughs of juniper and fir trees, and an occasional pinecone—from the neighboring yards, and had arranged them under, over, in, and around the day bed they'd borrowed from the Santinis for Roisin. The girl had one of Mrs. Wylltson's old art pads open on her lap. Sunlight from the window caught her hair, making it glow, and tears sparkled on her dark lashes. Aiden blinked once, then sucked in his breath.

"Don't cry." He made his way through the greenery and took her hand. "Don't cry, Roisin."

"Seriously." Abby grabbed her purse, which was hanging on the back of the door, and followed him. "If I had a face like that, I'd never cry. I've got to get you down to Smash Pad to do some modeling. That face could have a career, you know what I'm saying? We need live models for the Christmas window in a month. You could be our Christmas angel. Or Mary. Here we go." She pulled out a wet wipe, then looked around. "I'm not going to sit on the invisible cat, am I?"

"No," Teagan said. "You're good."

Grendal was on the windowsill, his hands and forehead pressed against the glass. Were the *cat-sídhe* back? Teagan stepped across the room and leaned over to see what he was looking at. Two fat pigeons strutted across the porch roof just outside.

"Thomas said he was sorry," Teagan said quietly to the cat. "He would like you to tell Roisin he needs to speak to her."

Grendal turned his iridescent eyes on Teagan.

"Okay," he said, then spoke briefly to Roisin in ancient Gaelic.

A huge tear tumbled from her nose onto the open watercolor

pad. It splashed into the blue of a pool under twisted trees—Mag Mell trees—making the water lighter where it hit.

"No, no, no." Abby gently pulled the pad away from her with one hand and gave Roisin the wet wipe with the other. "You don't cry on watercolors. It'll make the paint run, see?"

Roisin dropped the wipe, grabbed Abby's hand, and started speaking very quickly. Teagan didn't hear a single word she recognized.

"What did she say?" Teagan asked Grendal, but he had gone back to his bird watching.

"Did he translate?" Abby asked.

"No." Teagan sat down on the edge of her bed.

"That's all right." Abby took the towelette and wiped Roisin's face for her. "When it's a guy problem, we all speak the same language. So your boyfriend's a bird," she said when Rosin's cheeks were tear-free. "It is kind of creepy, but once he changed back, he looked totally Italian."

Aiden had been staring at Roisin the whole time. "Is 'totally Italian' good, Abby?"

"Of course it's good. You've seen Michelangelo's *David*? The guy who posed for that was *totally* Italian."

"They were in Italy," Teagan pointed out. There was a piece of yellow paper sticking out from under Roisin's bed; a cheeseburger wrapper. Grendal couldn't resist dragging the greasy things home, whether he found them in a garbage can or the gutter.

"Where else would they be?" Abby asked as Teagan stepped over the greenery, bent down, and picked up the wrapper.

"Michelangelo was looking for 'beauty and harmony in the male human form,' right?" Abby continued. "Italian guys got extra testosterone, if you know what I mean."

"What's testosterone?" Aiden asked.

"I'll show you a video."

"Abby!" Teagan wadded the wrapper into a ball.

"A really old, clean video. I swear, Tea, I make one little mistake with that Lady Gaga thing, and you're like the Internet police."

"Would you like to talk to Mamieo or Finn, Roisin?" Teagan asked, tossing the wrapper into the garbage pail. Roisin recognized their names at least. She shook her head.

"No *Mac Cumhaill*." Apparently, not only was she mad at Thomas, she wasn't happy with Finn or Mamieo, either. The tears were trembling on her lashes again. Aiden crawled up into her lap and put his arms around her, and Roisin let out a little sob and hugged him tight.

"Well." Abby stood up. "Choirboy's got that under control. Now what's this about you and Finn?"

"Me and Finn?"

"He said you were his girl. And your nose is shiny. What's going on?"

"He said she's his *a ghrá mo chroí*," Aiden said from Roisin's lap.

"Aiden!" Teagan could feel her face turning red. "You couldn't have heard that. I heard the door slam when you and Lennie came out!"

"Nope," Aiden said. "That was Mamieo. I was sitting on

Lennie's shoulders. Then Mamieo said Thomas was growing feathers. She said to get you quick. So Lennie held me up, and I yelled."

Teagan rubbed her temples.

"Why were you sitting on Lennie's shoulders?"

"Because we saw Finn climbing up the drainpipe, and we wanted to know what he was doing."

"Don't we all." Abby sat down on Teagan's bed, pulling Teagan down beside her. "So, spill. Dumpster boy calls you his chopped liver and you fall into his arms?"

"What?"

"Mrs. Le Beau made us eat that gra stuff in French class, remember? It was disgusting."

"That was *pâté de foie gras*," Teagan said. "And I didn't eat any."

"It doesn't mean chopped liver, Abby." Aiden patted Roisin's face. "It means 'love of my heart.' That's what Mamieo said."

"Aiden." Teagan pointed at the door. "Wait for us in the hall."

"But I—" He looked at her and gulped. "Okay. Bye, Roisin." He jumped off her lap and headed for the door.

Roisin looked at Tea, frowned, then collapsed on the bed and pulled her pillow over her head.

"I know, right?" Abby said. "Tea didn't have to give him the scary look."

"I didn't give him a scary look."

"You did."

Roisin wasn't moving.

"I think that's the universal sign for 'leave me alone,'" Abby said. "So let's get the bird man some clothes. And you can tell me more about this chopped-liver business. You kissed, right?"

Teagan felt her face growing warm again.

"Everybody has a first kiss." Abby shrugged. "On a scale of one to ten, firsts usually don't even register. I still want to hear about it, though. Spill."

"They weren't kissing," Aiden called from the hall.

"No kissing?" Abby frowned. "You feel all this electric stuff from him and still no kissing?"

"We'll talk about it later." Teagan turned to Grendal. "If she needs anything, come and get us."

"Thank you," Grendal said. He settled close to Roisin and started purring loudly as they left.

Aiden's room was just down the hall from Teagan's. The Lego carnage downstairs was nothing compared to the chaos there. Medieval armies faced off with working models of catapults and ballistae. His arsenal included one small brass cannon that he was not allowed to fire in the house, and an Aiden-size light saber, which hung over his bed. The glowing blue polycarbonate blade made a perfect night-light—so long as Teagan remembered to replace the double-A batteries.

Finn's mat was the only tidy spot in the room. It was on the floor, halfway between Aiden's bed and the window. His blanket was folded on it, and his kit—the Holy Grail of awesome in Aiden's eyes—hung from a coat hook on the wall.

"I'll carry it," Aiden said reverently as Teagan took it down.

Everything Finn had owned during the years he had lived on

the street was in the battered messenger bag. Aiden put the strap over his shoulder so he could carry it like Finn did.

When they reached the bottom of the stairs, Finn took his kit from Aiden and opened it up.

Thomas was still wrapped in the sheet. The Highborn was standing in front of the hall mirror, turning from side to side, studying his face.

"You never saw a mirror before?" Abby asked.

"Of course I have." Thomas turned away from his reflection.

Finn pulled a tightly rolled pair of jeans and a T-shirt out of the bag and handed them to him.

"There's a bathroom down the hall."

Aiden watched Thomas as he walked away, and then turned to Abby.

"So show me the video, Abby."

"The testosterone?"

"Yeah."

Abby sat down at the computer and brought up YouTube.

"Tea"—Finn had found the duct tape on top of the television, and was holding it gingerly—"There is something gooey—"

"*Cat-sídhe* guts," Aiden said, without looking up.

"*Cat-sídhe?*"

"Two *cat-sídhe* came after you went inside," Aiden explained.

Finn rubbed his chin.

"So your sister attacked them with my duct tape? That's frightening."

"You should see her scary look," Aiden said. "That's really frightening."

"I didn't attack them," Teagan explained. "I was trying to distract them. It probably isn't guts. Just pus." Finn shifted the tape until he held it with just two fingers.

"They were the same *cat-sídhe* we saw in the culvert," Teagan continued. She needed to talk to Finn about what the goblin cats had said, but not in front of Aiden. He was already worried enough about Ms. Skinner.

"The one with the wormies swelling his belly?" Finn looked disgusted.

"It's not so swollen anymore."

"Right. So it's Maggot Cat pus on my duct tape. As soon as Thomas comes out of the restroom I'm going to go wash this in hand sanitizer. Then throw up."

Teagan reached for the duct tape, but he moved it away.

"Don't be touching it, girl. It's disgusting. I'll deal with it."

"I need a sample," Teagan said. "I want to culture it to find out if antibiotics will help them."

"You're not thinking of curing the creatures?" Finn shook his head. "Why would you do it? So they'll be nice and healthy while they cause us trouble and grief?"

"Maybe they cause trouble and grief because they're sick."

"You think it's likely they woke up one morning and said, 'Oi, my stomach aches! I'll just go break an Irish lady's bones, or maybe steal a baby's breath. That'll make it better!'?"

Aiden looked up from the computer. "*Cat-sídhe* steal breath?"

"They do, if they can catch a wee one sleeping all alone. They'll sit on the bairn's chest and suck the sweet breath from it while it sleeps." Aiden cupped his hands over his nose and mouth, and Abby put her arm around him.

"You're scaring him."

"I'm not scared," Aiden said, but he didn't take his hands away.

"I'm telling the boyo the truth. The creatures are evil, that's a fact. And the more he knows about them, the safer he'll be."

"Don't you worry about invisible cats." Abby kept her arm around Aiden. "There's ways of dealing with them."

"What ways?"

"I don't know yet. But we'll deal with it, so don't worry. Here." She pointed at the screen. "This is the video I was talking about. This guy is *totally Italian.*"

Teagan stepped across the room to watch over Abby's shoulder. Finn followed, standing close enough that he could have wrapped his arms around her. *She could feel his heartbeat. Without touching him.*

"Who is it?" Aiden asked through his fingers.

"Rocky Balboa," Abby said. "And this"—she punched the play button—"is testosterone." Aiden's hands fell away from his mouth as the first trumpet notes of "Gonna Fly Now," the *Rocky* theme song, sounded. Abby looked up at Teagan as if to say, *I told you. Clean.*

Aiden and Finn were both fixated on the screen as Sylvester Stallone started his workout.

Teagan felt Finn's breath on her neck, and it made her shiver. She glanced up at him, but his eyes were on the video.

"Just hold the duct tape one more minute," she said, scooting out from between Finn and Abby's chair. His closeness was completely distracting. "I . . . I've got to get something in the kitchen." She stepped into the kitchen and leaned against the wall. There was always a brief moment as she came through the doorway that she expected to see her mom sitting at her easel in the far corner. Teagan bit her lip. The flash was gone quickly this time, but not the longing. Abby was right. She needed to talk to someone about Traveler boys who sizzled, and goblin gods determined to kill her little brother. She needed her mom.

The teakettle was steaming on the stove, and Mamieo had just pulled a pan of potatoes, cheese, cabbage, and leeks from the oven.

"Is the creature decent, then?"

"He's getting that way," Teagan assured her. "Mamieo, there were *cat-sídhe* outside—they said they had a message for me. From Fear Doirich."

"The beasties lie." Mameio looked at the bubbling cheese approvingly. "They want us jumping at every sound, afraid to live our lives. What did they say?"

"They said I was to bring Aiden to him."

"Of course they did. They're just caterwauling as usual. Thinking if they can't control us with their voices, they'll keep us running afraid. It's the nature of the goblin beasties, isn't it? But we'll keep a close eye on the boyo."

Teagan nodded. Mamieo Ida had been dealing with the Otherworld all her life. She'd lost a husband and children to the goblins, and she still had fight in her. Fight, and hope that she could beat them.

"The rumpledethump is ready," the old woman said. "I'll be making the salad, and then it's done. Will you bellow for your da in the basement? Let the man know dinner will be done soon."

"I'll go down and get him," Teagan said. "I just need to get a sample first."

Lucy had somehow managed to pry open the drawer of odds and ends, where Teagan kept empty pill bottles and where she had hidden the M&M's. The sprite was sprawled on top of the bag of candy, her eyes changing colors like a slow-motion kaleidoscope. The shells she'd peeled off the M&M's were all around her.

Her eyes flashed green and blue.

"The wee girl's intoxicated," Mamieo said. "She's been at the chocolate more than is good for her."

"That's not a safe place to sleep," Teagan told the sprite. "You could get shut in the drawer." Lucy waved a lazy wing, and hiccupped.

Teagan scooped her up carefully and moved her to a china teacup. The sprite curled up inside it and wrapped her wings around herself. Teagan set the cup on top of the cupboard, where Lucy would be safe, then went back to the drawer to find a bottle to keep her sample in.

The Rocky Balboa training montage had just ended when she got back to the living room, and Aiden's mouth was hanging open. Even Finn looked impressed.

"It's the music," Finn said. "He's just running about and punching, isn't he?"

"Some people have music over them." Aiden didn't look away from the frozen image of Sylvester Stallone. "Like in the movies. That's how you know what's going to happen. Lennie can't hear it, so I have to tell him." Aiden touched the screen with one finger. "How did Rocky get that way?"

"Garlic," Abby said. "Italian mamas feed their boys garlic. Do I have music, Choirboy?"

"Yep. 'That's Amore,'" Aiden said. "Like Dean Martin sings it."

Abby flushed. "That's totally not my song."

"*Amore.*" Finn's eyebrows lifted. "That's love, isn't it?"

"It is," Teagan said. "I thought you'd given up boys for art school."

"If I had a song, you think it would be one of those moldy-oldies?" Abby said. "That's totally *not* my song. You're hearing Teagan's song, Aiden. She's the one who's gone all goose-liver over a guy."

"It's yours, Abby," Aiden insisted. "Want me to sing it for you?"

"No. And, if that's my song, change it." She tapped his forehead. "You can change channels, right?"

"Maybe," Aiden said uncertainly. "I've never tried to do it by myself before. But—"

Thomas came out of the bathroom in the hall. He wasn't shaped quite like Finn, and as a result the shirt was a little too tight across the shoulders and the jeans a little too short.

"Is he still totally Italian?" Aiden whispered to Abby.

"Yeah," Abby whispered back. "But those clothes don't do anything for him."

Thomas glanced up the stairs. "Is Roisin coming down?"

"Nope." Aiden glared at him. "You made Aunt Roisin cry. If you do it again, *I'll make you stop*."

Thomas looked at Finn, as if he were asking what to do about the puppy attacking his foot.

"The boyo has a point," Finn said.

Thomas turned to Teagan. "If you'll just bring her down here . . ."

"Don't, Tea." Abby folded her arms. "Goblins had her all locked up in that tree in Mag Mell, right? And she never had anyone to talk to but this guy. Who *lied* to her!" Abby rolled her eyes. "I am *so* Team Aiden."

FOUR

TEAGAN took the roll of duct tape to the bathroom and carefully scraped some of the pus into the pill bottle, then washed the rest away with soap and then hand sanitizer. Even if she never cured a *cat-sídhe,* she needed to know what was causing their flesh to rot, in case Grendal caught it. She hoped it was just a common feline bacterium, treatable by antibiotics. She dried the roll and examined it one more time before she left the bathroom.

"All clean." She tossed it to Finn on her way past. "I'll get Dad while you guys wash up." She went through the kitchen, where Mamieo was chopping vegetables for the salad, and pushed open the hidden door to the maid's stairs.

As a child, Teagan had pretended that the secret stairs that ran up and down through the whole house were her own private entrance to Narnia, but now the stairway and basement art gallery reminded her too much of Mag Mell, tucked between the walls of the multiverse, with doors into all the worlds of creation.

Teagan sighed when she spotted three cheeseburger wrappers stuck like a greasy triptych to the wall at the bottom of the steps. She pulled them down, then turned the corner into the wide basement gallery.

Every wall was covered with her mother's art, beautifully hung and lit. Her stomach tightened. There were forms hidden in the paintings, forms she'd never noticed before she walked in Mag Mell. But now she saw the hint of an antler or hoof, the suggestion of a dog's head on a man's shoulders, and her mind filled in the rest.

She'd had to research in other books to find out what the creatures were, because her mother never mentioned them by name.

Phookas. A pack of phookas and naked Highborn, smeared with filth and mad with bloodlust, had hunted them in Mag Mell. She still had the mark of the claws across her back.

"Dad?"

Mr. Wylltson was sitting on the floor under a painting of a little girl dancing in front of a wonderful tree. The face of the green man peered out from the leaves, watching over the child. He didn't look up until Teagan sat down beside him.

"Yggdrasil," Mr. Wylltson said. "A Nordic tree in a Celtic world. I always told your mother that was literary drift."

"It feels like a cathedral inside, like centuries of prayers have seeped into the walls. It's the only place in Mag Mell Fear Doirich can't go. The only place where Mom and Roisin could be safe."

Teagan stacked the cheeseburger wrappers. She folded them in half, then in half again, before she realized that her father was watching her.

"It was bad there?" he asked.

She nodded and pressed the wrappers flat.

"It was really like"—he waved at the creatures all around them—"this?"

"It was."

"In college, when people criticized your mom's art for being too scary for children, she'd quote Chesterton: 'What fairy tales give the child is his first clear idea of the possible defeat of bogey. The baby has known the dragon intimately ever since he had an imagination. What the fairy tale provides for him is a St. George to kill the dragon.' I always thought I'd be her Saint George, no matter what. But when the dragon came, I couldn't even see it." The grief in her father's voice was so raw it crushed Teagan's heart.

"You remembered, Dad." She laid her head on his shoulder. "You remembered that she's dead."

Mr. Wylltson's brain had not been able to register Mag Mell. He'd walked in delirium the whole time he was there, a delirium in which Fear Doirich had stolen his memories of his wife's death, leaving him to live through the grief of losing her all over again. It was when he tried to remember his last days with her that his mind went into what Abby called reboot mode—something was going on inside, but the screen was blank.

"She's dead," he said flatly. "I remembered, Tiger. Not the pictures. Not the real memories. Only that you told me she was dead before I came down here. And I forced myself to believe it."

Teagan hugged him. He hadn't been able to hold the memory even *that* long a day ago. "Please don't call me Tiger, Dad."

"I've always called you Tiger."

"You called me Rosebud, and Mama was your wild Irish

rose, remember? The first time you ever called me Tiger was in Mag Mell."

"It was?"

"You were reciting Blake."

"*Tyger! Tyger! burning bright,*" Mr. Wylltson began,

> "*In the forests of the night,*
> *What immortal hand or eye*
> *Could frame thy fearful symmetry?*
>
> *In what distant deeps or skies*
> *Burnt the fire of thine eyes?*
> *On what wings dare he aspire?*
> *What the hand dare seize the fire? . . .*"

He paused.

"Dad! Did you remember *The Tyger,* or . . ."

"Or." He handed her the book he'd been reading. It was Blake's *Songs of Experience.* "I just read it."

Teagan rubbed the book's embossed cover. Her dad had always been able to remember a poem or song after one reading. He'd told her it wasn't a photographic memory. There were no pictures involved. The words just settled into him and stayed. He had a whole library in his mind. Half a library now. Somehow, even with a *draíocht*-fogged brain, he'd realized what was happening to him in Mag Mell. Fear Doirich was draining memories out of him. He'd fought back—by spilling poetry and children's stories, whole books of Blake, Wordsworth, Kipling, and Dante.

He put his arm around her. "The advantage to losing all the poetry in my brain is that I can read it again, and it's all new. Blake is wonderful. So, my lovely Rosebud, what was all the commotion upstairs?"

"Thomas turned into a raven, then back into his human form. Oh, and Ms. Skinner stopped by. She set up an appointment for Aiden with a dance therapist."

"A dance therapist. I come down here for an hour of peace and quiet, and the world goes crazy."

"It's been crazy for some time now, Dad."

"I guess that's true."

"The therapist will be coming over on Monday."

"Hmmm. Anything else?"

"Mamieo cooked rumpledethump for dinner."

"She made cooked cabbage, and Aiden's still in the house?"

"Yes. Dad, I just told you Thomas turned into a raven, and you didn't even blink."

"I'm a librarian," Mr. Wylltson said. "We practice believing six impossible things before breakfast."

"Like rabbits with pocket watches?"

"Like library funding will be available next year."

"I'm serious."

"All right. I haven't lost my senses, Tea, just some of my memories. I know the Otherworld has moved in around us. I know it broke my mind, and troubles my children. And I *can* keep the fact that it killed my Aileen in my head. Go over it again."

"Dad—"

"Go over it again. If I can force my mind to actually *remember*

Mag Mell instead of just your words, it might help me keep you and Aiden safe. A young man came in the back door—"

"Kyle." Teagan put the book down. "He's a Highborn Sídhe and a bilocate. His soul can walk in this world while his body sleeps in Mag Mell."

"I remember his eyes. They were black from lid to lid, like used motor oil. Finn had his knife out. Kyle tried to grab Aiden, and then . . . my own bed, and the mother of all headaches."

"Kyle grabbed you, instead of Aiden, just as Finn's knife hit him. And then he exploded, and the explosion dragged you into Mag Mell where his body was sleeping."

"Because the knife was made of iron. That fits the old Celtic stories, even if Yggdrasil doesn't. And then Finn's friend Raynor picked us up in his truck, and hellhounds chased us through the streets of Chicago, until Finn and Raynor killed them. While I was sleeping. How could I have slept through my children being chased by hellhounds?"

"You were in pretty bad shape," Teagan said. "You slept for three days. So, did you remember anything this time?"

Mr. Wylltson sighed. "Nothing. It's like staring into total darkness, searching for the tiniest bit of light."

"Do you want me to come home early on Monday?" Teagan asked. "I could be here when the therapist arrives."

"Tea." Mr. Wylltson stood up and pulled her to her feet. "I may have holes in my head, but I'm still your dad. I can handle Ms. Skinner and any number of dance therapists. At the same time. Did you say Mamieo made dinner?"

"It should be ready."

Mr. Wylltson took her arm as they started to walk. His body

was still working its way back from the damage that had been done in Mag Mell, too.

Teagan pretended that the slow pace at which they climbed the stairs was normal. Her dad stopped once, halfway up, and neither said anything while they waited.

"The point is," Finn was saying as they finally came up into the kitchen, "if I'd have been throwing it at you, it would have stuck, wouldn't it? Like that." He pointed to his knife, which was sticking hilt-deep in a large box of oatmeal on the counter. The Quaker gentleman on the label looked mildly surprised. Mamieo, Thomas, and Aiden looked impressed. Abby didn't.

"I assume this was a knife-throwing demonstration?" Mr. Wylltson asked.

"It was," Finn agreed. "Gabby thinks I flung a knife at her. Tossed the thing onto a chair, didn't I? It's aggravating to be accused of—"

"Poor aim?" Mr. Wylltson pulled the knife from the box, and a trickle of dried oats leaked out of the hole it left. "I can see how it could cause aggravation. Abigail, Finn is very good with a knife. Finn"—he handed the knife back—"we generally don't throw or toss knives in the house."

"Aren't you going to tell him to put it away in his kit?" Aiden asked.

"No," Mr. Wylltson said. "Finn knows when to use a knife. But *you* don't play with knives at all, son. And Thomas, it's good to have you eating with us at last." His eyes went to the chair Aileen Wylltson should be sitting in, and Teagan saw them cloud with confusion and then pain. But he remembered. He'd remembered again without being told. "Shall we sit for grace?"

Roisin's seat was still empty, and Grendal wasn't in the corner where he usually curled up, but no one commented on it as Mamieo served the food.

Abby and Finn were glaring at each other; Mamieo was watching Thomas as if she were waiting for one wrong move. Aiden rested his elbows on the table, his head in his hands, and stared at the lump of cabbage and potatoes on his plate.

Teagan started to pull out her chair, but Finn stepped forward quickly and pulled it out for her. She saw her dad's eyes rest on Finn for a moment before he sat down himself.

"Elbows off the table, son," he said as soon as everyone was settled. "And bow your head for the blessing."

Thomas looked uncomfortable as Mr. Wylltson started speaking:

"May the King who kindled the stars
kindle in our hearts
a flame of love for our neighbors,
for our foes, for our friends,
for our kindred all.
For the brave,
for the knave,
for the thrall.
Without malice,
without jealousy,
without envy,
without fear,
or terror of anyone under the sun."

Aiden made a gagging noise in the back of his throat.

"Aiden Wylltson!" Mr. Wylltson said. "We do not gag at grace."

"I was gagging at the cabbage," Aiden replied. "Does kindle mean burn up? Because I *wish* someone would burn it up."

Abby got up, went to the cabinet, and took out a little jar. She set it in front of Aiden, and hummed the first few notes of "Gonna Fly Now."

"Is that—" Teagan began.

"Garlic," Abby finished.

Aiden glanced at Thomas, took the lid off, and poured it on his rumpledethump.

"Son," Mr. Wylltson said. "Are you sure you want that much?"

"Uh-huh," Aiden said. "Can I use a table knife?"

"If you'll eat."

Aiden cut a piece of cabbage with his table knife and lifted it to his mouth. He grimaced as he chewed, and tears came to his eyes. He put down his fork and grabbed his milk.

"Why did you put that much garlic on your food?" Mr. Wylltson asked when Aiden had set the glass back down.

Aiden wiped his milk mustache and then pointed at Thomas.

"He's not a good guy. I need testosterone in case I have to fight him."

Mr. Wylltson blinked. "There will be no fighting, and we'll talk about . . . testosterone later." He turned to Thomas. "My son claims that you are not a good guy?"

Aiden raised his hand as if he were at school, but didn't wait to be called on. "He asked Fear Doirich to plant Eógan in Mag Mell so he couldn't get away. Eógan grew *roots,* Dad. That was *bad.*"

"Lower your hand and let Thomas talk now, son," Mr. Wylltson said.

"He's right." Thomas put down his fork. "I wouldn't know how to be a good guy. Asking Fear to root Eógan is the least of it. But I mean no harm to anyone in this house. I'll swear that on what's left of my soul, if you'd like. I am asking you to let me keep Roisin safe."

"Just keep her safe?" Mr. Wylltson asked. "Because it seemed to me there was some understanding between you in Mag Mell."

"I promised to love her as long as my heart beat, and she promised to wed me and no other. I'll release Roisin from her promise if she asks. There's a chance for her to live in this world like Aileen did."

"You knew my mom?" Aiden frowned.

"Of course. Everyone knew the daughters of Maeve and Amergin the Milesian bard. They were Queen Mab's nieces, after all, and the daughters of the man who defeated Fear Doirich with song. I never saw much of Amergin in Aileen, though. She was more Highborn than Milesian. If I hadn't known she was mixed blood, I'd have said she was Highborn to the core."

"What exactly do the Highborn do?" Teagan asked. "Other than bilocating into this world?"

"Only a few can bilocate," Thomas said. "Those of Mab's family. But Aileen was not a bilocate. She was gifted in strategy.

The various factions at court play strategy games, vying for power. Aileen was very good at that, even as a child."

Aiden pointed his fork at Thomas. "My mom didn't play goblin games."

"Saying Aileen was gifted in strategy is a compliment. She was brilliant at twelve. She might have grown up to rival Mab, if she'd stayed. Highborn also party—blood sports, such as hunting or phooka baiting, and feasts. Dances and seductions as well, of course. Most go slumming from time to time, stepping into this world in the flesh to cause chaos and carnage."

"My mom never did that, either," Aiden said.

"Didn't she? Even though she was a child, everyone knew Fear Doirich had plans for her. Mab had plans as well, of course." He looked around the table. "Apparently Aileen had plans of her own. She stepped out of Mag Mell to achieve them."

Something slammed against the window, and they all jumped.

"Just a bird," Teagan said. "They do it all the time."

She'd put up stickers on the glass to keep them from flying into it, but it didn't seem to help, especially during the fall migration. Sometimes the birds hit the window with enough force to break their necks, but most of them were only dazed, and got up to fly away a few moments later. *But this one wouldn't be so lucky,* she thought. *Not if the* cat-sídhe *were waiting outside to pick it up and squeeze the life out of it.*

"I'll just go check on it." Teagan picked up a dishtowel on her way out the door. If it wasn't dead, she could bring it in until it could fly again. Outside, she saw movement under the bushes, and pulled them aside. It wasn't a bird. It looked like a baby aye-aye—the same patches of long hair, thin arms and legs, the same long-fingered hands, bulging red eyes. Only this aye-aye had leathery wings. It was dragging its wing tips on the ground as it staggered in circles, both hands to its head. It had to be a creature from Mag Mell. No animal in this creation had arms, legs, *and* wings.

"What is it, then?" Finn had followed her out, with Thomas and Aiden right behind him.

"That's a swat-bat," Thomas said. "They don't bite. Unless you're a"—he hesitated, as if searching for the word—"bug. I guess they would be considered bugs."

The creature took its little hands off of its head and blinked up at Teagan. *A mix between an aye-aye and one of the evil monkeys from* The Wizard of Oz, she decided.

"It's hideous," Finn said. "I'm glad they don't come bigger."

"Oh, they do. There are much larger varieties," Thomas said. "We don't swat those, of course. They're vicious."

"Of course they are," Teagan muttered as she moved to keep the swat-bat from waddling away. The monkeys of Oz had flown through her nightmares for years after she'd read the book.

"Flying goblins?" Finn shook his head. "I've never heard of such a thing."

"They're not goblins," Thomas said. "None of them followed Fear Doirich. They are just animals, and rather stupid."

Teagan was glad to hear that. The thought of Fear Doirich controlling flights of intelligent, winged bat-monkeys was horrifying. She knelt down to get a closer look.

"Tea will take care of you," Aiden told it. "She likes ugly things."

The creature stopped staggering and turned toward the sound of Aiden's voice, squeaking excitedly. It made a dash for him, but Teagan wrapped the towel around it before it could reach him.

"Why do you call them swat-bats?" Teagan asked as she made sure it was secure.

"It's a game," Thomas said. "When you hit them with a bat, they . . ." He looked from Teagan to Finn. "You don't want to know."

"You're a really, really bad guy," Aiden said.

The swat-bat's ugly little face turned toward the sound of Aiden's voice again, and Teagan could have sworn it smiled. A wide, toothy smile that was nothing at all like an aye-aye's. Mamieo, Mr. Wylltson, and Abby were watching from the window. Lucy was plastered against the glass, eyes flashing red and orange.

"More invisible creatures?" Mr. Wylltson asked when they came back in.

"A little batlike thing escaped from Mag Mell," Teagan said, shooing Lucy away. "I'll take it back to the park after dinner."

"There must be some technology that would let me see them," Mr. Wylltson said.

"It's not much to look at," Mamieo assured him. "Like a wee monkey." Teagan put the swat-bat in a laundry basket with a towel over the top, and Lucy stationed herself beside it.

"So," Abby said when they were seated again. "How do the Highborn cause chaos?"

"We're catalysts."

Abby passed him a basket of soda bread. "You chase cattle? What, like cowboys?"

"A catalyst is a change agent," Teagan said. "It's a chemistry term. A chemical reaction requires a certain minimum amount of energy, called activation energy—" Teagan stopped when she realized Thomas was staring at her.

"She gets it from her da," Finn said. "The man's a librarian."

"That explains the smell," Thomas said.

Mr. Wylltson sniffed. "I smell?"

"Like books or old magic. Sometimes it's hard to tell them apart. In this case . . . I'd swear you smell of both. I wonder if that's why Aileen chose you."

"Of course not," Mr. Wylltson said. "It was my looks."

Everyone focused on their plates.

"What?" Mr. Wylltson looked around the table. "I'll have you all know Aileen liked tall, thin redheads!"

"So, what have *you* changed?" Abby asked Thomas.

"Kingdoms." He shrugged. "Worlds. I've destroyed armies and toppled kings."

"You said that before," Aiden informed him. "When you were a *wee birdie*."

Abby snorted, but Thomas went on, ignoring them both.

"When my kind of Highborn step into this creation, we *tune* the gifts of those around us. Inspire them to greatness. They do their finest work because we are near."

"Great mischief and mayhem," Mamieo said. "What was your specialty? War? Murder?"

"Poetry and song."

Finn set his milk down.

"The poets and singers you inspired destroyed armies and toppled kings?"

"Sometimes," Thomas said. "Other times, they simply sowed despair."

"*Lhiannon-sídhe.*" Mamieo slapped the table. "You're a damn *lhiannon-sídhe*!"

"I am. And very likely damned for the things I've done."

"What's a *lhiannon-sídhe?*" Teagan asked.

"A Celtic muse," Mr. Wylltson explained. "But Yeats said *lhiannon-sídhe* were women."

"He was an Irish poet?" Finn asked.

"He was. William Butler Yeats wrote that most Gaelic poets have had a *lhiannon-sídhe* who inspired them. That's why they die young. The *sídhe* suck their blood in payment for inspiration. I'm sure he said they were women."

"Sucking blood is optional," Thomas said. "Our presence ignites talent. We use our special skills to draw the art out, make it darker and painful. It's a game."

"Called *sídhe*-haunting," Mamieo said. "It's a terrible thing the *lhiannon-sídhe* do."

"Who have you haunted?" Mr. Wylltson asked. "Personally, I mean."

Thomas pursed his lips, then quoted:

"And his eyes have all the seeming of a demon's that is dreaming,
And the lamp-light o'er him streaming throws his shadow on the floor—"

Thomas hesitated, and Mr. Wylltson took over:

"And my soul from out that shadow that lies floating on the floor
Shall be lifted—nevermore!"

"What's that?" Abby asked.

"The last stanza of 'The Raven' by Edgar Allan Poe," Mr. Wylltson said.

"You should know what I have been, if you're going to let me sit at your table," Thomas said. "We killed everyone whom Edgar loved. His mother when he was two. His young wife. She was singing to him when she started coughing up blood. Did you know that? Edgar loved her voice. So we took it. Then we took her. But there was something in Edgar. Hope. Nothing we did could crush that last spark of hope. No matter how many people he lost, he always tried to love again."

"Poe died an alcoholic," Mr. Wylltson said. "That doesn't sound hopeful."

"They found him unconscious outside a saloon," Thomas agreed. "But he hadn't been drinking. Edgar died of rabies. It wasn't even our doing. A rabid bat bit him while he was visiting a cemetery. How ironic is that?"

"Why didn't you just kill the man," Finn said, "and have done with it?"

"Death is not the point of the game," Thomas said. "It's seeing how far you can push a creative person before they go mad."

"So you tortured Irish poets," Teagan said. "Like Jim Morrison."

"You've been talking to Raynor, I see. Morrison wasn't mine, but yes, he was *sídhe*-haunted."

"Raynor? The mechanic guy who gave you guys a ride when you came out of Mag Mell?" Abby sat up straighter. "The one whose truck my cousins gave a makeover? What would he know about it?"

"More than any other *aingeal* in creation."

All movement at the table stopped. Mamieo was staring at Thomas as if he had just grown horns.

"Finn?" the old lady asked at last. "Is this true? Raynor—the man who gave you a ride in his pickup truck, the one who brought Thomas to this doorstep—is an *aingeal*?"

"He is, Mamieo," Finn said. "He asked us not to tell anyone."

Thomas shrugged. "I don't know why he'd be bashful about it. He's been the guardian of Irish saints since before there was an Ireland."

"What is he doing in Chicago?" Mr. Wylltson asked.

"I just told you—he's a guardian angel to Irish saints," Thomas said. "The man he's guarding is sitting right beside me. I wouldn't be alive today if anyone else had carried me out of Mag Mell. Raynor trusts Finn."

FIVE

"WAIT," Abby said, as if Thomas's words were still sinking in. "The mechanic's an angel! I knew it, right? I drew him in my pad during my angel phase. I'm totally psychic. But"—she pointed her fork at Finn—"*he's* a *saint?*"

"No, I'm not." Finn shook his head. "No."

"Of course he is," Mamieo said at almost the same moment. They glared at each other.

"Thomas. You were saying?" Mr. Wylltson asked. "About us letting you sit at our table?"

"I have no right to be here." Thomas looked at Mamieo when he said it. "But I'm asking you to let me stay."

Mamieo sniffed.

"You said, 'We killed everyone Edgar loved,'" Mr. Wylltson said. "Did you do it yourself?"

"No. I was losing my stomach for it. I left it to the shadows. But . . . I can't pretend there is no blood on my hands. I've killed many others." Everyone turned to Mr. Wylltson, waiting. He took a deep breath.

"He who is not against us is for us."

"Is that another quote?" Abby asked.

"From the Good Book, Abigail." Mamieo looked disapproving. "Though I can't see how it applies, considering the company."

"No? How about '*The enemy of my enemy is my friend*'? That's a Chinese proverb, I believe." Mr. Wylltson picked up the basket of bread. "Aileen has—"

"Had," Teagan said softly, and saw her father wince.

". . . had very strict rules about the hospitality of our home. If she were going to throw someone out, she'd take him by the ear and throw him out right away. Not invite him to our table to share a meal. I believe she learned that from you, Ida." He offered the basket to Thomas. "Bread?"

Thomas looked relieved. "Thank you."

"Rats," Aiden said.

"Eat your garlic, son." Mr. Wylltson took the breadbasket back from Thomas.

"I will be useful to your household in any way I can, John Wylltson," Thomas said. "In any way that does not break my promise to Roisin."

"We'll discuss Roisin later."

"Can we talk about the saint stuff?" Abby asked. "Because"—she pointed at Finn—"there's no way he's a saint. There's rules, right? You have to be dead, for one. And celibate."

"Fir Bolg do saints a bit differently, dearie," Mamieo said.

"I'm no saint," Finn insisted.

Teagan stood up. "May I be excused? I need to take the swatbat to the park and have a talk with Raynor."

"I'll come with you," Finn said quickly.

Mr. Wylltson glanced at Finn, his eyebrows rising slightly.

"Me, too." Aiden jumped up.

"Sit down and finish your cabbage, son," Mr. Wylltson said, still looking at Finn.

"But I need to go," Aiden said. "I need to take care of Teagan!"

"I'll watch over her," Finn assured him.

Aiden shook his head. "You can't sing. What if the really bad guys come? What if *he* comes out of Mag Mell?"

"How about this?" Teagan leaned against the back of her chair. "You can sing 'Pádraig's Shield' over me before I go."

Aiden looked at his dad. "Can I sing at the table?"

"Just this once," Mr. Wylltson said. "If you promise to eat your cabbage when you're done."

Aiden looked at the pile on his plate.

"I have to," he said grimly. "Because it's *important.* But 'Pádraig's Shield' isn't the right one." He closed his eyes and tipped his head as if he were listening hard, then started humming, too softly for Teagan to make out the tune. He frowned, smacked the palm of his hand into his forehead, and started again. This time he sang loudly enough that everyone could hear:

> *"Better be gone.*
> *It's half past 'leven now.*
> *Get on the deck.*
> *You better get on.*
> *It's half past 'leven now."*

Goose bumps rose on Teagan's arms. She wanted to tell him to stop, but the fabric of reality was twisting around her, and all she could do was grip the chair and hold on. Aiden hadn't left his magic behind in Mag Mell. Not all of it. The swat-bat squeaked excitedly.

"Fairly well, we can tell
nothing but moving will do.
And it will be all right . . ."

The swat-bat bashed against the side of the basket, squeaking so loudly that Aiden stopped singing, but still Teagan couldn't move.

"Shhh," Aiden told the bat. "This is the most important part.

"Hey, hey, hey, the night is waiting for you.
Take a picture of the silver moon.
Oh, oh, oh, she will be shining for you
on your journey home.

Better be gone,
so find your pocket watch
and all of your hope now.
The hour is long.
Before I try to say too much,
fair thee well 'cause we can tell
nothing but courage will do.
And it will be all right.

Set your sails upon
the mighty winds of May."

There was a vibration in the air around her, almost as if she were feeling thunder. Something had changed. Aiden's songs had never had power in this world before.

"Set your sails upon the hope
of June.
Set your sails upon the air
of warm July.
Set your course for Heaven's shore."

"Aiden," Teagan asked when the air went still, "did you just . . . change the channel?"

"Yep." Aiden looked very pleased with himself. Thomas dropped his eyes to the tabletop, smiling slightly.

"Change it back."

"Nope. *Now* it will be all right."

"What's this about changing channels?" Mr. Wylltson asked.

"Like with the radio, Dad," Aiden explained. "I didn't like the song I heard, so I changed it to one that fits."

"Fits?" Mr. Wylltson asked. "Fits with what?"

"With the *cantus firmus*," Aiden said.

Mr. Wylltson smiled. "Where on earth did you hear that term?"

"Father Gordon said it. When we were practicing special songs for Mass. Father said the *cantus firmus* is the oldest song, and all the new songs had to fit with it." Aiden shook his head. "The song over Teagan didn't fit. It was *wrong*."

Thomas rocked back in his chair. "This *cantus firmus* you're hearing," he began. "Is it the one the Dark Man calls the Song of Creation?"

Aiden frowned. "That bad guy can't sing it. He's worse than an E.I."

"Worse than a what?" Thomas looked confused.

"An Elvis Impersonator," Teagan explained. "They just can't sing like the King."

Aiden looked around as if a rhinestone-studded fat man might jump through the door. "Don't talk about them," he whispered.

"It's all right, Choirboy," Abby said. "If an E.I. gets in here, I'll deal with him."

"Are you sure?"

"Positive," Abby said. "So, what song were you hearing before you changed the channel? Was it 'That's Amore' again?"

"No, Abby," Aiden said. "That's *your* song. Teagan's song was 'Bad Moon Rising.'"

"Creedence Clearwater Revival?" Mr. Wylltson nodded thoughtfully. "Well, I like the one you chose for her better, son. I've never heard it before."

"Of course not. Future of Forestry's not a moldy-oldie band." Abby blushed. "Did I say that out loud? 'Cause I meant, that's one of my painting songs. 'Set Your Sails.'"

"My music is not *moldy*, Abigail. It's *classic*."

Teagan left them arguing and went to get her jacket from the coat closet, the CCR song playing in her brain. If there *was* a bad moon on the rise, she certainly hoped Aiden's song had changed it. Because she had to go to the park, where the maw of Mag

Mell gaped, and any number of creatures from that world would be happy to take her life.

When she went back into the kitchen for the swat-bat, Aiden was choking down his cabbage as promised.

The creature had recovered enough to slip away from Teagan as soon as she lifted the towel, and it headed straight for Aiden. Finn snatched it out of the air before even Lucy could catch it.

"Careful, careful." Teagan took it from him and swaddled it like a tiny ugly baby so it couldn't flap or wiggle. "We'll be back in a little while," she said, tucking it under her arm.

Mr. Wylltson followed them to the front door. As soon as she opened it, she was glad she had the jacket. The October wind had turned sharp, but there was a delicious scent of burning leaves in the air.

"I'll walk you down the steps," Mr. Wylltson said. He pulled the door shut behind him, then shoved his hands in his jean pockets. "Do you remember that talk we had when you visited last spring, Finn?"

"I do." Color rose in Finn's face. "I'll be needing to speak to you about your daughter, John."

Mr. Wylltson pursed his lips.

"You just insisted that you're no saint, and you want to speak to me about my daughter."

"I do," Finn said.

"I see. Well, nothing has changed."

"Dad," Teagan said. "I want to go out with Finn."

Mr. Wylltson looked surprised.

"Well. Something has changed." He looked from her to Finn. "So, just dating?"

"I intend a good deal more than that," Finn said. Mr. Wylltson's eyebrows lifted again, and Finn flushed completely red.

"I mean to say I'm a marrying man."

"Tea's seventeen," Mr. Wylltson said flatly. "And you are . . . ?"

"I know what you're thinking." Finn took Teagan's hand. "And you're right. I'm eighteen years old. But I'm the man who can keep her alive when the goblins come hunting."

"Her own Saint George." The grief was back in Mr. Wylltson's voice. "And one who can see things I cannot see. I'm not sure I'm ready for this."

"You lost me with the Saint George," Finn said. "But I am the man for your daughter, if she'll have me."

"Tea?"

"I haven't said I'd have him yet. Exactly."

"Ah. We'll discuss it when you get back, Mr. Mac Cumhaill. I'd like some time to think this over. Give the angel my regards. I don't suppose he could come to the house?"

"He's guarding the gateway to Mag Mell," Teagan said. "Keeping the shadows in."

"Shadows?"

"Like the one that killed Mom."

Teagan saw the new, raw grief pass over his face again. "Killed your mom. That's right. Of course. Tell him I'd like a long talk with him as soon as I can walk that far."

"I will, Dad."

He went back up the steps and into the house.

SIX

FINN hadn't released her hand, and more than electricity hummed through her at his touch. She felt . . . *safe* wasn't the word for it. *Protected* wasn't quite it, either. *Loved*. She felt completely loved.

"Your da's a scary man," he said as they started to walk.

"You've faced hellhounds, and you think my dad's scary?"

"I do. I thought my knees would buckle, and that's the truth." Finn jumped as the door slammed behind them. Abby was pulling on a sweater as she ran after them.

"Dear God," Finn said, looking heavenward. "What have I ever done to deserve this?"

"Sorry I'm late, Tea," Abby said as she caught up. "I was talking to your dad."

"Gabby." Finn pulled Teagan a little closer. "We were hoping to be alone."

"Really?" Abby zipped up her sweater. "'Cause I've dated guys who weren't saints. I know what they do when they get you alone."

"I'm never going to live that down, am I?"

"Probably not," Teagan said. "Let her come. She's got a thing about angels."

"And werewolves," Abby agreed. "Those are really sexy. I read this novel about a lost angel, and—"

Teagan thought she caught a movement out of the corner of her eye, something too large to be a *cat-sídhe,* but when she turned to look, the street was empty.

"—vampires." Abby was still ticking off her paranormal crushes. "But not the sparkly kind. I like them with teeth."

"I'll keep it in mind," Finn said. "And if I ever meet one with teeth, I'll send it right over."

A very realistic plastic garden zombie was crawling out of a newly dug grave in the neighbors' yard. Abby nodded toward it.

"But not those guys. I've never seen the appeal. I'd always be wondering which part was going to fall off next, you know?"

Teagan could see the tops of the park's trees as soon as they turned the corner, their blaze of autumn color just past its peak. The wind seemed to shift, and instead of ice and burnt leaves, it smelled of wild jasmine.

The mighty winds of May. There was no way she was ever setting her sails for Mag Mell again, no matter how sweet it smelled.

Tea moved closer to Finn, and he squeezed her hand. But the swat-bat tried to wiggle free as they reached the library, and she had to let go of Finn entirely to settle it.

The tall brick building almost hid the park behind it from the street. They went up the walk and through the wide gate. Teagan had played here almost every day of her life when she was small. Everything was exactly the same as it had always been—the wide, well-tended lawn where her mother painted and her father held book events in the summer; Aiden's secret house hidden behind the trumpet vines that covered the rusted gate; and the ramble of old trees, shrubs, and pathways that took over when the lawn ended. The old trees Aileen Wylltson had loved. The ones she'd painted into her books, and the ones that had opened a doorway to Mag Mell after her ashes were scattered among them. Teagan had nearly died here at the gateway twice, which was as many times as she'd walked in Mag Mell.

Raynor Schein was sitting at a cement picnic table on the library lawn, studying something on the tabletop. His blue jeans and work shirt were beginning to show signs that he'd been living in the park, but his hair was pulled into a neat ponytail.

"So that's really an angel?" Abby asked. "What's he doing?"

"It looks like he's found an engine," Teagan said.

"He's mechanical minded," Finn explained. "He told us all about rebuilding Brynhild."

"He refurbished that truck himself?" Abby sounded impressed. "My cousins say it's perfect."

"He *is* an *aingeal*," Finn pointed out. Raynor looked up at them through his round John Lennon glasses as they approached.

"Oh, good, you caught it," he said when Teagan held out the swat-bat. "I've had the hardest time keeping them in today—" He suddenly realized that Abby was with them, and shut his mouth.

"Don't mind me." Abby lowered her voice. "I know your secret."

Raynor frowned at Teagan.

"I didn't say a word," Teagan assured him.

Finn nodded. "It was Thomas. He told everyone."

"Of course he did."

Abby squinted. "So, where are the wings? Are they in stealth mode?"

"What wings?"

"Sandro Botticelli? Leonardo da Vinci? Raphael? They all painted angels with wings. In the movies they *unfurl*." She looked at Raynor expectantly.

"Sorry to disappoint," Raynor said.

"So, I guess they do angels different in Ireland as well?"

"As well as . . . ?"

"I don't want to talk about it," Finn said.

"No shadows have come out?" Teagan asked, changing the subject. Raynor glanced at the gathering darkness under the trees.

"They come every night. When they see me, they go back. But I've been shooing an endless number of small creatures back in all day Lots of these—"

"Thomas called them swat-bats," Teagan said, handing it to him.

"That sounds . . . unpleasant. Just like Thomas. I think this is the only one that got away." They watched as he walked to the trees.

"Where's he going?" Abby asked.

"The door to Mag Mell is under the willow tree," Teagan said. "Can you see the shimmer?"

"No," Abby said. "Just the towel." Raynor unwrapped the swat-bat and tossed it into Mag Mell. It popped out again ten seconds later, but he flapped the towel at it, shooing it back in. "If I walked under that tree, would I get into Mag Mell?"

"No," Finn said. "Only three peoples—of those you can see, anyway—can walk in Mag Mell, Gabby: the Aingeal, like Raynor; the Highborn, like Teagan; and the Fir Bolg, like me."

Abby folded her arms. "So, what are Italians? Chopped liver?"

Raynor was shaking his head as he came back to the park bench. "There've been sprites and woolly squirrelephants—"

"Woolly squirrelephants?" Finn asked.

"I made that name up." Raynor sounded very pleased with himself. "They're little shaggy elephants that climb trees."

"We saw them in Mag Mell," Teagan said. "They seemed shy."

"Something is causing them to come out. Larger creatures have been peeking out as well. I've never seen this happen before."

His gaze went to Teagan's face. Their eyes met for a moment, and Teagan looked away. She hated the way Raynor looked at her since she'd come back from Mag Mell. As if she were tainted.

"I've sent for a friend who can help. He may be able to have a chat with the trees and find out what's going on."

"Another *aingeal*?" Finn asked.

"Joe's not an *aingeal*. He's—"

"Wait, wait, wait!" Abby shook her head. "If you're really an angel, and the bad guy is in there, why don't you just go in and get him?"

"Love to. But Fear Doirich heard the Song of Creation and he can twist it. He's used it to lock Mag Mell up tight. He can come to me, but I can't go to him."

"What would you do if he did come out?" Abby asked.

"My job," Raynor said simply.

"So . . . you could take on all those shadow things Tea talks about? The ones that killed her mother?"

"Yes," Raynor said. "I will stop the shadows."

"What's all this?" Finn asked, picking up a piece of machinery off the table.

"A little piece of heaven," Raynor said. "Take a peek in Aiden's secret house."

They followed him across the lawn. Dry leaves and seedpods rattled as Teagan pulled the vines back. The secret house was almost full of parts—something that looked like the rusted bones of an ancient motorbike, two spoke wheels, and other objects that were totally unfamiliar to Teagan.

"Heaven's a junkyard?" Abby asked.

"That's not junk," Raynor said. "It's a 1930 Indian Four. One of the most beautiful machines ever created. I've got a picture right here." He pulled a folded magazine page from his pocket.

"How did you get the thing?" Finn asked.

"Providence," Raynor said happily. "It was in the back of a truck headed to a recycling center. The woman just happened to stop at the library."

Abby took the magazine page from him. "Providence, like God sending you stuff? Why didn't he just send you one that looked like this?"

"Because this one needs me," Raynor said. "The woman who was going to recycle the parts said her father had rebuilt the engine years ago. After he died, it just sat in the garage. I'm going to have to take it apart, make sure he did the job right. Even if he did, after so many years I'll still have to lubricate everything. I'll need a socket set and some white gas. All I've had to work with was what was in my pockets when I got here."

Teagan looked at the array of crescent wrenches and screwdrivers on the bench.

"These won't do?"

"Of course they won't. You need the right tools for the job. I'm going to be needing lots of parts as well."

"Do you have a list?" Teagan asked.

"Funny you should mention that." Raynor pulled another piece of paper from his pocket. "The first column is tools. The second column is parts for the bike."

Teagan took the folded paper. "I'll see what I can do." She paused. "There were two *cat-sídhe* at my house today. One of them said, 'Fear Doirich says to bring Aiden.' The Dark Man wants to kill my brother, Raynor."

"I know." Raynor picked up an engine part and squinted at it. "That's why I'm here. I have a feeling Fear Doirich wants to kill Aiden worse than he's wanted anything for centuries. Maybe even enough to risk stepping out of Mag Mell. And if he does . . . just one step . . . he's mine."

"Why would he want to hurt my Choirboy?" Abby asked.

"Aiden's the grandson of the bard who helped chase the *sídhe* into Mag Mell. He has his grandfather's gift in him. And more than a little bit of Myrddin's as well."

"Who?" Abby asked.

"Myrddin Wyllt," Teagan said. "The real Merlin the Magician. He was a Welsh bard. Dad's side of the family."

"That makes Aiden quite unique," Raynor said.

"So, Choirboy's like the Chosen One in a movie? He's got some kind of *destiny?*"

"There's no such thing as 'destiny,' Abigail. Just becoming. Choosing to become what you were created to be, or choosing to walk away from it. And since all the creatures around you are becoming at the same time, it gets very complicated. Aiden has choices to make, like any other creature. Speaking of choices"—Raynor glanced at the tree line—"you'd better head home."

"Why?" Abby said. "Aren't all the goblins locked up in the park?"

"There were creatures who wandered into Chicago before I moved into the park. They are still here, and all goblins grow stronger in the dark."

"So what happens when you fall asleep?" Abby asked. "Do the shadows get out?"

"*Aingeal* don't sleep."

"Right," Abby said. "They build motorbikes."

"Raynor's right." Finn took Teagan's arm. "We should be going."

"Night-night," Raynor said. "Say your prayers, and don't forget the list!" Teagan patted her pocket. "And Finn, watch Thomas."

"I'll do it."

They were just at the park gate when a gust of wind picked up a handful of dead leaves and swirled them around Teagan. Finn stopped and tipped his head, listening.

"Did you hear that?"

"I heard the wind," Teagan said.

"Maybe so. Maybe that was it."

"Could you walk a little faster?" Abby looked back at them and rubbed her arms. "It's cold out here. This sweater isn't warm enough."

When they reached the front door of the Wylltson house, Abby went through first. Finn caught Teagan's elbow with his good hand and pulled the door shut behind Abby with two fingers of the other.

"I wish you'd told me what the *cat-sídhe* said before we went to see Raynor. We're in this fight together, and you've got to trust me, girl. It's the only way I can stand between you and whatever comes."

Something was tapping on the door, but Teagan ignored it. She felt it again, standing this close to Finn, inside his electric shadow. Loved. She wanted Finn to feel it too, and she wanted to *know* he felt it.

"Do you remember you once told me that the Mac Cumhaill never dies old and gray?" she asked, leaning a little closer.

Finn's breathing went ragged. "I do."

"Maybe *I'll* stand between *you* and whatever comes, Finn Mac Cumhaill."

"You plan on attacking it with duct tape, girl?"

"The most useful stuff in the world." Teagan reached up and cupped her hand just close enough to his face that the electricity danced between them. Finn sucked in his breath.

"So, you do feel it too," Teagan teased. "That's good."

"Tea." He caught her hand and pressed his lips into her palm, and lightning shot through her. He released her hand and pulled her close.

It took her half a second to realize the heartbeat she felt pounding through her was Finn's and not her own.

"I've never been so afraid in my life." He was trembling. "I've had nothing of my own. I'm so afraid that they'll take you. That something's going to take you."

"We beat them," Teagan said. "We went to Mag Mell and beat them."

Finn shook his head.

"Talk in daylight," he said. "When we're sure there are no creatures about. Mamieo will be looking after the boyo, but I'm thinking of getting a job at your school. You need someone watching over you."

The door rattled back and forth.

"Finn?" Teagan whispered.

"Hmmm?"

"Are you holding the door shut?"

"I am."

"Abby's going to break it down."

"Might as well face him, then."

"Him?"

"Your da." Finn sighed and let go of the knob, and the door flew open.

"What's wrong with your brains?" Abby asked. "Never mind. I can see what's wrong. Get inside."

PART II: ITALIANO

SEVEN

MR. Wylltson was standing behind Abby in the foyer as they entered, wearing a pale pink ruffled apron. He had soapsuds up to his elbows and a serious look on his face.

Roisin and Grendal had come downstairs and were sitting beside Aiden, but neither of them looked up. They were staring at *Lady and the Tramp* on the television screen. Thomas was leaning against the kitchen door, staring at Roisin.

"We'll have that talk now, Mr. Mac Cumhaill." Mr. Wylltson wiped his hands on his apron, untied it, and tossed it to Teagan. "You can help Mamieo finish cleaning the kitchen."

Finn glanced at the front door as if considering bolting through it, then shook himself and followed Mr. Wylltson up the stairs.

"What's going on?" Abby asked.

"Dad wants to talk to Finn."

"About . . . ?"

"Me," Teagan said. She caught Abby's shirttail as Abby started for the stairs. "Where are you going?"

"To listen at the door."

"No, you're not," Teagan said. "You're going to help with the dishes."

When Teagan managed to drag Abby into the kitchen, they found Mamieo leaning against the sink.

"Are you all right?" Teagan asked.

"I'm fine. But I could use one of my wee pills, dearie. They're on the table by my bed."

"Pills?" Abby asked.

"Nitroglycerin," Teagan explained. "For her heart. I'll get it."

Teagan pushed open the door to the maid's stairs and ran up the two flights to the attic. Mr. Wylltson had tried to give Mamieo his room on the second floor, but Mamieo insisted she needed the exercise. The top door in the stairwell opened into the cheerful yellow attic room with sloped, polished wood ceilings. It was directly over Teagan's bedroom, but only half the size, and its single window looked out over the backyard. Everything in the room was three-quarter size, from the antique bed to the rocking chair. Since Mamieo was less than three-quarters the size of an average person herself, the room and furniture were a perfect fit.

Teagan crossed the floor in two steps and sorted through the various pill bottles on the bedside table. When she found the nitroglycerin, she checked the label twice, shook it to make sure there were actually pills inside, then ran back down the stairs.

"Cuimhnichibh air na daoine bho'n d'thainig sibh," Mamieo was saying when Teagan got back. "Remember the people you come from. And didn't I forget it?"

"Why are you still doing the dishes, Mamieo?" Teagan opened the pill bottle, shook one out, and handed it to the old lady. "You should be sitting down."

"I told her," Abby said.

"I'll be still and cold soon enough," Mamieo said, taking the pill from Teagan and popping it in her mouth. "Until then, I'll keep working, thank you."

"Even Choirboy says Thomas is a bad guy," Abby pointed out, apparently continuing a discussion they'd been having while Teagan was upstairs. "And he *did* lie to Roisin."

"I've no doubt of it," Mamieo agreed. "But I should have considered not only what he's been, but what he's becoming, shouldn't I? And what part I have in that. Now I find out it was an *aingeal* that brought him to my doorstep! What would this Raynor have thought if I'd clipped the creature's wings, or worse?"

He'd have probably been all for it, Teagan thought as she put an arm around Mamieo. "Before he brought Thomas here, Raynor said that your heart is closer to the Creator than your head. And that your heart would straighten out your head."

"The *aingeal* said that?" Mamieo lifted her apron and pressed her face into it, wiping away tears. "Maybe I'll lie down a bit now. If you girls will put these all away, I have some complaining to do to the Almighty."

"About Thomas?" Abby asked.

"About springing an *aingeal* on a good Christian woman without warning. It's unsettling."

Teagan waited until she was sure Mamieo was up the stairs before she let herself smile.

"You think she's really complaining to God about angels?" Abby asked.

"Oh, yes." Teagan took down the china cup she'd put Lucy in and checked on the sprite. Lucy flashed her eyes green and blue, stretched, and flew off to find Aiden. Teagan washed the cup and gave it to Abby to put away with the rest.

"Bella Notte" was playing through the Xbox speaker system when they stepped back into the living room. Lady and Tramp were sharing a plate of spaghetti.

"God, I love this part," Abby said. "It's so romantic."

Teagan sat down at the computer and opened her Facebook page. Her "relationship status" read, "Teagan Wylltson is in a relationship with . . . *Grzimek's Animal Life Encyclopedia. It's complicated.*"

Well, this was it. If Finn could talk to her dad, she could do this. She deleted the old status and started again. "Teagan Wylltson is in a relationship with *Finn Mac Cumhaill.*"

"This is going to cause trouble," Abby said. "You understand that, right?"

A chat window popped up. It was Agnes, the vet tech who worked with her at the zoo.

OMG. You've dumped Grzimek's for a guy? Who are you, and what have you done with Teagan?

"See?" Abby said. "I told you. You're Teagan Wylltson. People have expectations."

I'll bring him by so you can meet him, Teagan typed.

Did you get the msg from Dr. Max?

No.

Gotta go. See you Monday.

Not scheduled for Monday.

Call Dr. Max. See you Monday!

Teagan turned away from the computer and dialed his number on her cell phone.

"Teagan," Dr. Max said. "I'm glad you called back. Did you listen to my message?"

"Not yet. Agnes told me to call."

"I see. We have a group of politicians coming in. They are researching primate issues for a congressional committee, and one of them—a very important woman—is from Texas."

Teagan was suddenly completely focused. One of the last research labs to use invasive techniques on primates was just outside of San Antonio, Texas—and politicians held their purse strings. If this woman could persuade them to drop funding for the Texas lab, two dozen chimpanzees could be released from the tiny metal boxes they'd lived in their whole lives—boxes just large enough for them to lie down, stand up, and turn around—and sent to a sanctuary.

"This could be a turning point, Tea. They need to see Cindy and Oscar at their best," Dr. Max said. "I was hoping you could come in."

"What time?" Teagan asked.

"Nine thirty."

She'd miss half a day of school, but she could ask Molly to take notes in her morning classes.

"I'll be there. See you Monday." Teagan hung up.

She turned back to the computer to e-mail Molly about taking notes, then checked Craigslist for motorbike parts. Not surprisingly, there was nothing for a 1930 Indian.

"I'll call the Turtles," Abby said. "Leonardo owes the angel." Abby was related to half of Chicago, but she was closest to her cousins Leo, Angel, Donnie, and Rafe.

"You'll remember not to mention that he's an angel, right?"

"You're asking an Italian if she can keep a secret? Did I ever tell you I know where Jimmy Hoffa's buried?"

"No."

"See? I can keep secrets. Is your grandmother still forcing us to go to church tomorrow?"

"The soloist has strep," Teagan said. Aiden was Father Gordon's emergency plan whenever a soloist dropped out. He didn't need to practice. If he heard a song once, he would have it forever, in perfect pitch.

"Then I'll tell them to meet me at church tomorrow."

"The Turtles don't go to church."

"I'm not going to suffer alone," Abby said. "They'll be there."

"Hey, doesn't one of your relatives work at the school?" Teagan asked. "Finn was saying he'd like to get a job there."

"At our school? What, like mopping floors? I'll ask Leo about it."

Teagan left Abby at the computer. She checked on Aiden and Lucy before she headed upstairs. She didn't have to worry about tucking in Aiden anymore. Mr. Wylltson had started putting him to bed again, singing the monsters away just like he used to.

When she reached her room, she set up a lap desk at the head of her bed by the light and settled into the admission essay for Colorado State. She worked on it for an hour before Abby came into the room.

"Are you busy?" Abby asked.

"Mm-hmm," Teagan said. "Why?"

"Because I think Choirboy got us mixed up. I painted a picture of the moon, and you get a song about it. You're in love, and *I* get a song about it."

"There's a moon in 'Amore,'" Teagan said without looking up. "It hits your eye like a pizza pie, remember?"

"You think my moon looks like a pizza?"

"No," Teagan said. "It's a wonderful moon."

Abby settled on the bed with one of Teagan's mom's art pads. She was quiet for all of three minutes.

"What was with your mom and the birds?" she asked. "They're in all of her sketchbooks."

Teagan put down her pen. "They're kingfishers. From a poem called 'As Kingfishers Catch Fire' by Gerard Manley Hopkins. Dad read it to her when they were first dating." Teagan took the pad from Abby and flipped through the pages. "See?"

Her mom's calligraphy curled lovingly around the poet's words, illuminating them with flourishes like wings. She read aloud,

> "*As kingfishers catch fire, dragonflies dráw fláme;*
> *As tumbled over rim in roundy wells*
> *Stones ring; like each tucked string tells, each hung bell's*
> *Bow swung finds tongue to fling out broad its name;*
> *Each mortal thing does one thing and the same:*
> *Deals out that being indoors each one dwells;*
> *Selves—goes itself;* myself *it speaks and spells,*
> *Crying* Whát I do is me: for that I came."

"Your parents were perfect for each other." Abby sighed. "They were both into moldy books and art and songs." She traced the kingfisher, the tip of her finger almost touching the paper, as if she were memorizing the lines. "So, what happens if you fall for someone, and they're really different?"

"Like me and Finn?" Teagan asked.

"Sure." Abby's finger missed the curve of the wingtip, and she frowned.

"You're *not* talking about me and Finn."

Abby shut the sketchpad.

"Maybe I'm talking about Roisin and Thomas. He's got to be, what? A billion years old? She's never done anything, Tea. Not even gone to school. How's that supposed to work out?"

Teagan stood up. "You're changing the subject."

Roisin and Grendal came through the door before Abby could answer. Roisin went straight to the closet and started looking through Abby's clothes.

"Looking for something to wear to church tomorrow?" Abby stood up as Roisin pulled out a cable-knit sweater, a skirt, and a blouse. "I seriously have to get you down to Smash Pad. You know what a boutique is? No? Well, you're going to go crazy." Abby went to stand beside her. "Let's see. We'll be walking, and it will be chilly, so you want to layer, right? Let's go with chocolate brown." She held up a shell top, and Roisin shook her head no.

"Trust me," Abby said. "With that hair and those eyes, warm tones and maybe a scarf to make your eyes pop. Let's just try it . . ."

For the next hour Grendal curled up on the foot of the bed and Teagan worked on her essay while Abby dressed and accessorized Roisin like a live window display model, mixing and matching Teagan's clothing and her own.

When Abby was finished, Roisin smiled and gave her a kiss.

"I think that means she likes it," Teagan said.

"What's not to like? She's beautiful and I'm brilliant." Abby walked over to the dresser, pulled open Teagan's top drawer, and started rummaging through it.

"What are you looking for?" Teagan asked. "She's perfect."

"Found it." Abby held up Teagan's crucifix triumphantly. "And it's not for her. It's for me. I'm sleeping with it." She went over and touched the window latch, making sure it was locked.

"What are you doing?"

"I'm not just a fashion goddess, Tea. You heard what the angel said about goblins in the dark. If Finn can climb that drainpipe, other things can, too. I got a responsibility to the universe—to keep you safe. The goblins just figured out that you're special, right? But I've always known it." She held up the crucifix. "If they want you, they're gonna have to deal with a Gagliano first."

Roisin and Grendal both looked impressed.

"Abby—" Teagan began, but someone knocked on the bedroom door. It opened a crack.

"May I come in?" Mr. Wylltson asked.

"Yes," Teagan said.

Mr. Wylltson stepped through the door, and hesitated when he saw Abby.

"Conducting an exorcism, Abigail?"

"Depends," Abby said. "Did you cast Finn out? It would save me the trouble."

"No. We talked like civilized men, and came to an understanding."

Abby lowered the crucifix. "What understanding?"

"That we would talk again. Finn reminded me of a certain prayer that your mother spoke over you every night, Tea. I thought maybe we could pray it together. Will you join us, Abigail?"

"No, I'm good," Abby said.

"Roisin?" Roisin shook her head and picked up a pair of Abby's ankle boots.

"You know what would go great with those?" Abby asked. "I'll show you—"

"Maybe we should just step into the hall," Teagan said. They stepped out and Mr. Wylltson pulled the door shut behind them. He put his hand on Teagan's head and spoke her mother's prayer over her like a blessing:

"I do not ask for a path with no trouble or regret. I ask instead for a friend who'll walk with me down any path.

"I do not ask never to feel pain," his voice caught, and he cleared his throat. *"I ask instead for courage, even when hope can scarce shine through.*

"And one more thing I ask: That in every hour of joy or pain, I feel the Creator close by my side. This is my truest prayer for myself and for all I love, now and forever."

"Amen," Teagan whispered.

"Tea," he said, taking his hand away. "I know you think you love Finn. And he thinks he loves you. But love is something that grows. You've really only known each other for a few weeks. He's a fine young man, and very serious about this. But walk together a little longer before you decide about something like marriage. A lifetime is a long time to be together."

"What if it's not?"

"Ah." Mr. Wylltson was quiet for a long moment. "You have to live each day as if you are creating the future, Tea. As if what you do will last. Because it will. Somehow, it will. You and Aiden were your mother's finest work."

"Dad . . ." Teagan buried her face in his shirt.

"It hurts." Mr. Wylltson rubbed her back. "If we never loved, then maybe we would never feel pain. Love anyway. It's worth it. But let it grow *slowly*. Intentionally. And keep in mind that all you have to do is say the word, and I will throw that young man out the door."

Teagan hugged him hard.

"Now I have to go sing your brother to sleep. He needs to learn *Panis Angelicus* for tomorrow."

"Good night, Dad."

Abby didn't even ask what they had talked about until Roisin and Grendal had gone to bed.

"So," she said after Tea turned out the light and crawled under the covers, "what did they talk about? Jobs? Education? Finances? How Finn's going to support you?"

"No. I think they talked about Mom." Teagan felt a little strange speaking about it with Grendal and Roisin listening in the dark. Roisin couldn't understand a word, but the cat could.

Abby was quiet for a few moments, and then she rolled over to face Teagan.

"Tea. Can you feel Finn's sparkles through the wall?"

"Sparks," Teagan said. "No. But I can feel them all the way across a room."

"That's some creepy superpower."

"I don't think it's a superpower," Teagan said. "I think it's a completely natural thing called electroreception. Some animals can do it. They sense the electric impulses bodies use to move."

"Which animals do this electrocution thing?"

"Electroreception," Teagan corrected. "Monotremes and members of the subclass Elasmobranchii."

"Oh, good. You're back to normal again. So, what are we talking about, exactly?"

"Platypuses and sharks. Sharks actually use electroreception most heavily during the final stages of their attack."

"Yeah. Like shark attacks are totally natural in dating situations, Tea. Hormones are hard enough to deal with. Now you've got feeding frenzies?"

Grendal started purring, and Roisin yawned loudly and started humming to herself.

"That's not what I meant," Teagan said. "Did you ever touch something that was dead?"

"My Chinese fighting fish. After the goblins got into my apartment and stuck them to the ceiling with toothpicks."

"And they felt different, right?"

"Like . . . dried anchovies. It had been a couple of days." Abby was quiet for a moment.

"I'm sorry," Teagan said. "When I touch an animal that has just died, it feels wrong. There's no *spark* in it. I've always felt that spark in creatures. It's just that the *spark* in Finn is a lot stronger. Like he's more alive, and when we're close, our sparks get . . . stronger." *And all tangled together in a really good way.*

"So you guys were, what? Sparking each other on the porch?"

"It was amazing." Teagan paused. "I'm sorry about your fish, Abby. I don't think I ever remembered to say that."

"Shut up. You're the only person I know who can love someone else's stupid fish. That's why I worry about you thinking you love Finn. Everything sparks at you, right? You're, like, in love with the whole world. Especially the ugly little things like fish."

"Not in the same way. And your fish weren't stupid," Teagan said. "They used to wiggle when you came home. They were glad to see you."

"You're really serious about Finn? It's the big L for sure? 'Cause you've never done this before, and you could be mistaken."

"I'm not mistaken. I just don't know what to do about it. I would appreciate it if you'd just be nice to him."

"All right. I guess I can be friendly until you figure it out. What does he like to talk about? Goblins, right? I'll try talking to him."

"Good."

Abby was quiet so long this time Teagan thought she'd fallen asleep.

"I've been thinking, Tea. You should convert."

"Convert?"

"To Italian. Our angels have wings. Our saints stay in church where they belong. If the goblins haunted one of us like Thomas was talking about, the Family would take care of it. You know what I'm saying?"

"And your guys have extra testosterone. Like Stallone."

"I like a little Rambo in a guy," Abby admitted. "Plus, the food is better."

"Abby? You always make jokes when you're worried about something. What's really going on?"

"What do you mean?"

"The crucifix? The window?"

"When we were leaving the park, I heard it."

"Heard what?"

"Something called your name, Tea."

"It was the wind."

"No, it wasn't. You know how I used to work at Uncle Rob's funeral home before I got the job at Smash Pad?"

"Yeah . . ."

"I wouldn't touch the bodies, but sometimes when Uncle Rob moved them, the air trapped inside would come out. Like the corpse was trying to say something, but the lips wouldn't move, you know? That's what it sounded like."

"Okay," Teagan said. "I'm officially having nightmares. And Italians are more disturbed than the Irish have ever been."

"Whatever," Abby said. "You know what you do when *you're* worried about something? You talk like an encyclopediac."

"Do you mean like an encyclopedia or an almanac?"

"I mean like somebody who's read too many of both of them. You're not as sure about this Finn thing as you're pretending to be. He's your first boyfriend, and you don't know what the heck is going on. Your dad told you to slow down, didn't he?"

"So, how long should I know him before I get serious?" Teagan asked, instead of answering.

"Four years," Abby said without hesitation.

Grendal was still purring, but Roisin was snoring softly.

"Four years? Did you hear that on the Oprah channel?"

"No. Something this important might take that long to figure out, you know what I'm saying?" Abby yawned. "And I was serious about converting. I'm pretty sure God is Italian. That's why the *real* saints listen when *we* ask for help."

EIGHT

"SO," Teagan said, picking up a fast-food bag someone had left on the sidewalk, "what *did* you and Dad talk about last night?"

"The man gave me some things to think about," Finn said.

"Uh-huh."

She was glad of the six-block walk to St. Drogo's this morning, even if it did give Grendal a chance to scout for promising garbage cans. If she didn't burn off some energy, she'd never be able to sit through the Mass Mamieo insisted they attend. She was practically bouncing from the electric mix of Finn walking next to her and the thought of Monday at the zoo. Plus, there was no way to speak to Finn alone in the house. "Is that why you're not holding my hand?"

"That, and the fact that Crabby keeps giving me the stink-eye."

Mamieo, Aiden, Lennie, Abby, Roisin, and Grendal were all walking ahead of them. Lennie had given up his seat in Mrs. Santini's tiny Geo Metro so that Mr. Wylltson could have a ride.

Mamieo, wearing her Sunday best and a little lace cap on top of her white puff of hair, was waging a running battle with Lucy, who kept trying to settle into Aiden's slicked-down curls.

Abby turned as if she had heard her name mentioned, and looked at Finn.

"See? She did it again!"

"That's not the stink-eye," Teagan told him. "She's dressing you in her mind."

"That's disgusting!"

Teagan laughed. "Dressing. Not *un*dressing. It's what Abby does. Makes people look good."

"I already look good."

At the moment, Finn's Sunday best was jeans, well-worn lace-up boots, and a faded blue shirt. Abby had scolded him until he'd pointed out that he had no other clothes. He'd given his second set to Thomas, and Mr. Wylltson's wouldn't fit him. Then he'd tied a bandanna on gypsy-style to annoy her.

But he's right, Teagan decided. He still looked good.

"Maybe we should ask her to take you shopping," she said. "That's how Abby makes friends."

"I don't want to be friends."

Finn stopped and pointed. Maggot Cat was perched on a windowsill above them, just out of reach. He'd wrapped a dirty rag around his belly, making him look like a furry leper. Teagan wasn't sure whether it was because Finn was standing close beside her or because Maggot Cat looked sicker, but seeing him didn't make her hair stand on end today.

"What are you doing?" Finn asked the *cat-sídhe.*

"Watching."

"Come down here," Finn told him. "I'll give you something to watch."

Maggot Cat gripped the windowsill with one hand, leaned forward, and projectile vomited. Finn jumped back, and the foul mess hit the pavement at his feet.

"Oh, that's pleasant. If I had something to throw, I'd knock him down from there."

"Or break the window," Teagan said.

"There's that."

They stepped around the green-brown puddle and continued down the walk.

Teagan looked back over her shoulder.

"Why aren't there more of them? Even yesterday, he had little Ugly with him."

"The hordes are probably out harassing the homeless," Finn said. "They know we're not leaving town, so one keeping an eye on us will do."

Teagan looked back again one more time before they turned the corner. Maggot Cat was still perched like a pigeon on the windowsill.

"We'd best catch up before Gabby comes back to get us," Finn said. "I'm not going shopping with her. I'm not that keen on being friends."

"You guys have a lot in common."

"Like?"

"Abby isn't happy about going to Mass, either. She's been avoiding it for years." Teagan dropped the trash she'd picked up into the can outside Berti's Bagels. "But enough about Abby. I want to talk about you. And why you're not holding my hand. If it's because of something my dad said—"

"Tea." He took her elbow as they prepared to cross the street.

His touch completely derailed her train of thought.

"Now." He grinned down at her, and that *definitely* muddled her mind. "What was it you were saying to Mamieo at breakfast? Something about monkeys living in boxes? Gabby was yapping so loud I couldn't hear you. Chimps, maybe?"

"I told you, chimps are apes, not monkeys. I was saying to Mamieo that the United States is the only developed country in the world that still allows invasive research on chimpanzees."

"Hmm." He released her arm as soon as they were on the sidewalk again, and shoved his hands in his pockets. "What's *invasive* research?"

"Any research that causes death, bodily injury, pain, distress, fear, or trauma is invasive."

"It's another word for torture, then."

"Exactly," Teagan said. "Chimpanzees are smart and very social. They have friends and play games. They can learn sign language and even make up their own new words and phrases. But most research chimps are locked in cages all alone. They can live for fifty years that way in a lab. They rarely come out of the cages except for medical procedures."

"And you can stop this?"

"I can help stop it. I want you to come to the zoo with me tomorrow and meet the two chimps I'm working with."

"Cindy and . . ."

"Oscar. Cindy loves Oscar. But technically he's government property, controlled by the National Institutes of Health, and on loan to Dr. Max. The NIH could take Oscar back at any time, and use him for medical research."

"That doesn't seem right."

"It isn't."

"And that's why you work at the zoo, then?"

"Cindy and Oscar are very important to me," Teagan said. "But it's the clinic I love best. Dr. Max allows me to have time and supplies for my urban rescue. I love making animals well again. Now, what did you and Dad talk about?"

"Well, we . . . would you look at that? There's the man himself!"

Mrs. Santini's green Metro was in one of the handicapped parking spaces right in front of St. Drogo's, and Mr. Wylltson was waiting for them on the steps.

Teagan punched Finn's arm. "We are talking about this after church."

Finn opened his eyes wide. "About what, girl?"

"You *diverted* me on purpose!" She'd seen a mentalist named Derren Brown do something very similar—touching someone to plant a memory or make them forget something they had just been talking about.

"Did I?" Finn grinned. "You're cute when you're diverted."

"Where'd you learn to do that?"

"You pick up things on the street," Finn said. "Even grifters and confidence men know a thing or two worth learning."

Teagan wanted to ask him more about it, but they'd caught up with Mamieo and Aiden.

"Can Lucy go in with us?" Aiden had stopped beside the smiling statue of Saint Drogo the gardener leaning on his hoe. Roisin—who apparently had no worries about taking Grendal in with her—and Abby were already at the church door waiting for them.

"Of course she can," Mamieo said. "Isn't this just a wee room in the Almighty's vasty creation? Even that heathen Highborn could come if he wanted to."

Thomas had flatly refused to come with them. They'd left him at home hunting through Mr. Wylltson's books.

"By that reasoning, my library is just another room in the Almighty's 'vasty' creation," Mr. Wylltson commented.

"It is," Mamieo agreed. "But the company's not as good, is it? We're gathered together here. That's what makes the difference. And he'll miss hearing the pratie sing."

"You're *sure* she can go in, Mamieo?" Aiden was still looking worried. Lucy didn't look happy, either. Teagan was sure the sprite knew that this building had something to do with the fact that every trace of her nest had been combed out of Aiden's hair. "God won't *squish* her?"

"What kind of a Creator would squish his own creatures? Didn't I tell you that it was in a church that I first met the Green Man? Standing in his great green altogether, studying his own face carved in a column."

"The Green Man?" Mr. Wylltson asked.

"Him that grabbed the corner of the night and ripped a hole

into Mag Mell so Mamieo could step in to save Aunt Aileen," Finn said.

"I haven't heard that part of the story." Mr. Wylltson opened the door for Mamieo.

Aiden was still hesitating. Teagan put her hand on his shoulder.

"Remember what Raynor told us about Drogo? He was a Highborn like our grandmother. That's how he could be at Mass and work in the garden at the same time."

"Because he was *sleeping* in church," Aiden said.

Teagan hadn't planned on mentioning that.

"But God didn't squish him." Aiden nodded. "It's okay, Lucy. We're going in." The sprite managed to zip past Mamieo and settled onto Aiden's head, grabbing handfuls of hair so no one would try to pull her out.

Mamieo sighed and spoke to Roisin in old Irish.

The girl shook her head. "Teagan," she said.

"Teagan what?" Aiden asked.

"I told her there'd be a bit of kneeling, bowing heads, and such out of respect for the Almighty," Mamieo said, "and I'd be happy to show her what to do. But . . ."

"Teagan," Roisin insisted, taking Teagan's hand.

"All right," Teagan said. "I'll show you."

Abby and Finn were glaring at each other just outside the door. Abby turned and marched through, but Finn hesitated. He glanced at Teagan, then pulled off his bandanna before he went inside.

Teagan dipped her fingers in the laver and crossed herself,

then waited for Roisin to do the same before she led her into the nave.

The moment they stepped into the sanctuary, Lucy shot out of Aiden's hair. Teagan was sure that if sprites could gasp, she would have. The tiny girl hung in the air, her mouth open, and her eyes flashing through combination after combination of colors.

"What's wrong with Lucy?" Aiden asked.

"The stained glass?" Teagan guessed. In Mag Mell the sprites had communicated by means of colored light. Lucy must have thought that the whole building was shouting at her. She zipped to the nearest window, her eyes flashing purple and red.

"Is she agreeing with the window, or arguing with it?" Mamieo asked. Teagan could only shrug. Whichever it was, Lucy was certainly very excited.

Lennie had settled into his usual pew near the back of the church while Mrs. Santini was kneeling at the altar. The second statue of the bilocating saint, Drogo the petitioner—his face grim and his eyes closed—stood mutely beside her.

"Sit by Lennie, okay, Tea?" Aiden said. "That way I can see you."

"Okay."

Lucy stayed in the sanctuary, continuing her discussion with the windows as Mr. Wylltson went to help Aiden change into his choir cassock and surplice before they went to the choir loft.

Teagan showed Roisin how to genuflect, then ushered her and Grendal to the wall end of the pew behind Lennie, where the cat would be out from underfoot. Finn let Mamieo step into the pew next, then followed her. Mrs. Santini came back to sit with Lennie, beaming at Mamieo.

"You got Abby here, Ida! And Aileen's sister. It's a miracle—" Her mouth dropped open, and Teagan turned to follow her gaze.

Leo, Angel, Donnie, and Rafe had arrived. The older boys wore dress slacks, shirts, and ties, but Rafe, the youngest, had a dress code of his own: a dark blue pinstriped suit and pricey Italian shoes.

"Hey, Aunt Sophia," Leo whispered as he smiled at Mrs. Santini. They slid into the pews around Teagan, bumping fists with Finn and nodding at Mamieo. "Hey, Lennie. How you doing?"

"Good," Lennie said a little too loudly. "Little guy's going to sing."

"Yeah? Well, we'll listen real good." Leo turned to Teagan. "So, we got a message from Abby saying to be here. Your friend need his truck back?"

"Not yet." Teagan took Raynor's list of parts from her pocket "But he's looking for these things." Leo glanced over it and handed the paper to Angel.

"Maybe we can help. What's wrong with Abby? She's lighting candles."

Teagan frowned and looked toward the altar. Abby *was* lighting a candle. The last time Abby had done that, it had been because she'd dreamed the goblins were coming. And she'd been right.

"Got to be man trouble," Donnie decided. "You know who he is, Tea?"

"She hasn't said anything about a guy."

"You four look after our Crabby, do you?" Finn asked.

"Crabby." Rafe grinned. "That's funny."

"Sure, we look out for her," Angel said. "She's like the sister we never wanted."

"But got anyway," Donnie added. All four brothers looked serious as Abby stood and walked back toward them.

"You doing okay?" Donnie asked as she sat down. "There somebody you need us to talk to?"

"I can talk to people myself, Donatello. What do you think?"

"I *think* if anyone is giving you grief, *Crabigail,* you let us know. We'll take care of it."

Abby glared at him. "Don't call me that."

"Ditto with the Donatello," Donnie said.

"What?"

"Don't call *me* that."

"Whatever," Abby said. "Rafe, why are you dressed like that in church? You look like Ralph Macchio playing at being a mobster."

"Ralph who?"

"Macchio. The *original* Karate Kid. Am I the only one here with any culture? You're never going to know anything unless you watch the classics."

"I watch classics," Rafe said. "*The Godfather.* That's a classic."

"How about the job for Finn?" Abby asked Leo. "You got my text, right? He needs to be employed." She gave Finn a look, but he ignored her.

"Haven't had a chance to speak to Ettore yet," Leo said.

"He's out of town arranging a funeral." Mrs. Santini gave him a sharp look over her shoulder. "No funny business, Zia," Leo assured her. "The guy was already dead."

"Why Ettore?" Abby asked. "Why not Uncle Vito?"

"Shhh," Mamieo said as Father Gordon and the altar servers emerged from the sacristy. "We're starting."

Roisin sat very close to Teagan, following her moves exactly, and glancing around as if she were surprised that they were all kneeling or speaking at the same time. The second time Roisin started, Teagan realized that this was probably the largest group the girl had ever been in. Even so, Grendal got bored after the first few moments and jumped up into the niche at St. Francis's feet, curled up, and went to sleep. Teagan tried to focus on helping Roisin, but her eyes kept going to Finn. He was looking at Father Gordon, a very serious expression on his face.

When Aiden started to sing *Panis Angelicus,* Roisin jumped up, and Teagan had to pull her down again. Lennie craned his neck to look at the choir loft above the door. He waved, and Teagan was pleased to see that Aiden remembered to *not* wave back.

Mrs. Santini pressed her hand to her large bosom. Teagan was sure from Father Gordon's beaming face that every word and inflection of her brother's Latin was perfect. Even Grendal lifted his head to listen. But the world didn't twist or tilt. Whatever magic Aiden had managed last night was gone.

"See?" Abby whispered after the last amen. "*That's* how Italians do it!"

Teagan didn't even bother pointing out that Aiden was Irish

and Welsh. She was more worried about the fact that old Mrs. Murphy was clearly watching Lucy zip from window to window. Teagan was afraid she might stand up and point or shout, but she just watched the sprite through the entire service. When Father Gordon and the altar servers finally walked down the aisle toward the doors of the church, Lennie jumped up to go find Aiden.

"I asked Uncle Ettore"—Leo said, taking up the conversation exactly where they had left it before Mass began—"because his new wife works in personnel."

"At the school district?"

"No, at the racetrack. Of course at the school district."

Mrs. Santini turned around. "Ettore got a new wife?"

"They got married in Vegas while he was on business out there," Leo said. "I thought everybody knew."

Teagan left the Gaglianos and Mrs. Santini to their family talk. She went to find Aiden, Lennie, and Mr. Wylltson while Mamieo walked Roisin and Grendal out of the church.

Her dad was easy enough to spot. Three single ladies had cornered him the moment he came down from the choir loft, but he was edging toward the door. Aiden and Lennie weren't with him. She wouldn't have thought to look for them in the confessional if Lucy hadn't been fluttering above it like a distressed butterfly. The sprite seemed exhausted from her conversations with the stained glass.

"Is Lennie walking home with us, too?" Aiden asked when Teagan shooed them out. "Because we were making plans."

"Yes, he is."

"What's Finn doing?" Lennie asked. "Doesn't he know we can go home now?"

Teagan turned to look. Finn was kneeling on the rail before the stand of votive candles, where Abby had knelt before Mass began. Old Mrs. Murphy, the last person in church, was watching him, her hands clasped before her lips, her head bowed just a little.

"Finn's a saint," Aiden explained. "He *has* to do that stuff."

Teagan had to admit that he did look a little like a saint with his head bowed and the candlelight all around him; an Irish gypsy saint who had tucked his bandanna in his back pocket in an attempt to look respectable.

"You two go out to the steps and wait with Mamieo," Teagan said. "I'll bring Finn."

When Teagan reached the front of the church, Mrs. Murphy smiled knowingly at her.

"Good luck keeping that one," she said, giving Teagan's arm a motherly pat.

"What do you mean?" Teagan asked, but the old lady just shook her head and walked away. Teagan stepped up to the rail.

"I've said three prayers this morning," Finn said as she knelt beside him. "It's more words than I've spoken in a church since my own *máthair* died. I prayed that you find a way to help your apes, that the *aingeal* keep our Aiden safe, and"—he turned his head and looked down into her eyes—"that the Almighty make me into the man your da expects me to be."

NINE

THEY met Mamieo coming in the door as they walked out. She gave them a keen look. "So that's what you're up to, is it?" Teagan felt her cheeks flush. "John Wylltson sent me to find you."

"We weren't up to anything, Mamieo," Finn said, tying his bandanna back on.

"Everyone's waiting for you," Mamieo said. They were gathered under Drogo the gardener, but they didn't look worried about Teagan or Finn. They were listening to Mrs. Santini.

"Oh-ho." Finn nodded. "Will you look who came down where I can reach him?" Maggot Cat was sitting on top of a delivery van on the other side of the street, with his hind legs splayed and his head hanging. "I'll be right back, Tea."

Teagan caught Finn's arm. "He's not hurting anyone right now."

"And if I deal with him he won't hurt anyone later, either."

"Leave the creature be, boyo," Mamieo said.

"What?" Finn turned to Mamieo in disbelief. "You're telling me to let a goblin go?"

"Leave it be," Mamieo repeated. "I spent the whole night complaining to the Almighty that you'd dragged a damned *lhiannon-sídhe* home with you; you and that *aingeal*."

"And what did the Almighty say?"

"He said, '*Watch your language, Ida.*' And after I'd apologized for my Irish tongue, he asked, '*Why don't you go right down and kill the creature now?*'"

"'I couldn't do it now, and you well know it,' I told him. 'Not after I've seen that he loves the girl as strong and right as I loved my Rory.'

"'*Would you have killed him the day he lied to Roisin, before his love grew strong and right?*' the Almighty asked. 'I don't *think* I would,' I says. 'Not if I knew what was growing in him.'

"'*Then how about the day before he met the girl?*' the Almighty asked. '*Before he ever loved at all?*'"

Mamieo was quiet, considering the *cat-sídhe*.

"And what did you say, Mamieo?" Teagan asked at last.

"I told Him I'd get back to Him. It's something I have to think on."

"I should deal with that *cat-sídhe* now and you can think about it later," Finn said. The van driver made his argument moot by pulling away from the curb, Maggot Cat still perched, like a fuzzy party hat, on the rooftop.

"I already cooked," Mrs. Santini was insisting as they joined the group waiting beside Drogo the gardener.

"There are seven of us now, Sophia," Mr. Wylltson said. "Are you sure?"

"Sure I'm sure. Aiden asked me to make spaghetti last night. He said he would sing for me. How could I say no?"

"And so it begins," Mr. Wylltson said, starting down the steps toward the car.

"What begins?" Aiden asked.

"The fine Wylltson tradition of singing for your supper. I would never have survived college if I hadn't had a song in my heart and a willingness to share it with young ladies of great refinement and culinary skill."

"And what did my Aileen have to say about that?" Mamieo asked. Teagan moved a little closer so she could hear the answer.

"She tamed me with one glance of her fine Irish eyes."

"Like Max and the Wild Things," Aiden said knowingly. "Did you roar a lot before she got there?"

"You know, I believe I did." Mr. Wylltson winked at Tea. "But your mom knew just the trick for hushing me."

"What was it?" Aiden asked.

"I'll tell you when you're a lot older." Mr. Wylltson folded himself into the passenger seat of Mrs. Santini's tiny car. "I'll see you at home."

"See you at home!" Aiden took Roisin by one hand and Lennie by the other and started skipping toward the Wylltson house. He looked like Christopher Robin towing along a large, pimpled Pooh Bear and a trendy, modern Disney princess. Grendal walked behind them.

"It's time we had a talk." Abby glanced sideways at Finn.

"You and me?" Finn looked surprised. "What would we have to talk about?"

"Goblins." She gave Teagan a look that said, *See? I'm trying.*

"We don't get civilians involved."

"Why?" Abby asked. "Because the booger men might get us?"

"Boogey men," Teagan corrected.

"Whatever," Abby said. "I've had Tea's back since she was, like, five years old."

"You have no idea what you're dealing with, Gabby. You can't even see most of the creatures."

"Like I'm safer *not* knowing? I know I'm living with an invisible cat and a fairy, right?"

"She has a point," Mamieo said. "She is in the middle of it."

Finn shook his head. "*She* doesn't have to be. She could go back to her Italian mama."

Abby stepped in front of Finn, and they all stopped walking.

"Italians don't leave friends when they're in trouble. And what that angel said sounded like trouble."

"You did say talk in daylight," Teagan reminded him.

"And walk while you talk," Mamieo said. "Because Aiden's getting too far ahead of us."

Abby moved aside, and they started walking again.

"All right," Finn said. "It was too easy. What we did in Mag Mell was too easy."

"It wasn't easy," Teagan said. "We nearly died. All of us."

Finn just shook his head.

"I've dealt with goblins all my life, haven't I? There's no 'nearly' about them. They're wicked cruel, wicked fast, and smart enough to think one step ahead of you. Remember how they took your *máthair*, Tea? No hesitation. No warning. And the Highborn are the worst of them."

"Highborn," Abby said. "Like Kyle."

"Yes."

"Because I could totally see him."

"You're missing the point."

"You're missing *my* point, Dumpster boy. *I can see them*, right? If I can see them, I can deal with them."

"No, Gabby. The Highborn Sídhe are deadly. You heard Thomas talking about the 'games' they play. This"—he traced the scar along his jaw—"was a Highborn. Just one, come to this world to play at the clubs. I met him by accident, and I almost didn't live through it. They're hunters, and they don't generally hunt alone. Mamieo says my grandfather Rory was smarter than me. Faster than me."

"That's true." Mamieo sighed. "Rory was the finest of men." Teagan glanced at Finn, but he didn't seem offended.

"They came hunting him on the moors, that's the thing," Finn said. "And he didn't live through it."

"Which is why you need my help."

Finn stopped walking again. "I don't need your help."

"You just said you did."

"I'm the Mac Cumhaill—"

"Who totally needs help." Abby picked a piece of lint from the sleeve of her tweed jacket.

"I don't."

"Uh-huh."

"Crap. Will you stop talking, woman? I don't want you involved in this mess. You'll get yourself killed." Finn ran his hand through his hair. "I can't send you home, but I'm sure as hell not going shopping with you. I'm walking with the boyo," he said, and stalked away.

"Shopping?" Abby looked after him. "Random. You know what I think? I think he needs to develop some conversational skills."

Mr. Wylltson was sitting with Thomas on the porch steps when they arrived, a copy of Shakespeare's *Hamlet* open between them. Teagan was glad to see the happy, passionate look on her father's face, the one he wore when he was having a particularly good literary discussion. Thomas looked just as happy—until Roisin brushed past him, stepping daintily over the book, and went into the house without speaking.

Mr. Wylltson glanced at Finn, who just shook his head. Even Mamieo looked a little sorry for the Highborn.

Aiden smiled. "Can I go to Lennie's house to get some stuff?" He glanced sideways at Thomas. "Lennie and me have a top-secret plan."

"Is it illegal?" Mr. Wylltson asked.

"Nope," Lennie said, "It's—" Aiden elbowed him, and he looked confused.

"All right." Mr. Wylltson nodded, and Aiden and Lennie ran across the street.

Thomas was staring at the door.

"You didn't by any chance inspire the upstart crow?" Mr. Wylltson picked up the book.

"Ravens and crows are different creatures," Thomas said absently, still looking after Roisin.

"Who's this upstart, then?" Finn asked, seeing what Mr. Wylltson was doing.

"It's another name for Shakespeare," Mr. Wylltson said when Thomas didn't answer. "It comes from the greatest literary snark of all time. A writer named Robert Greene, jealous of Shakespeare's growing popularity, wrote, 'for there is an upstart Crow, beautified with our feathers, that with his Tyger's hart wrapt in a Player's hyde, supposes he is as well able to bombast out a blanke verse as the best of you.' Of course you had nothing to do with the bard. *Lhiannon-sídhe* don't inspire English poets."

"That's true." Thomas finally looked away from the door through which Roisin had vanished. "But Shakespeare was Irish."

"Do you have any idea what they're talking about, Tea?" Abby asked.

"No one knows for certain who Shakespeare was," Teagan explained. "People have different theories."

"Of course they do," Mamieo said. "But in Ireland it's well known that he was ours. You'll learn more of Hamlet at Munster in Éire than at all your universities put together. It's an Irish tale through and through."

Mr. Wylltson shook his head. "William of Stratford wasn't Irish."

"I wouldn't know about William of Stratford," Thomas said. "But I do know that this"—he held up the book—"was written by William Nugent, the second son of the baron of Delvin, also known as William Shakespeare."

"Elizabeth Hickey was right!" Mr. Wylltson said. "I always suspected there was something to her theory."

"The Nugents were Milesian to the core," Thomas said, a little life coming back into his voice. "Musicians, churchmen, scientists, and writers, well acquainted with Irish rebellion and English law. Some were so thoroughly acquainted with the law that they were hanged by the neck until dead."

"You can't get more Irish than that," Mamieo said approvingly.

"So you did bedevil the man, then?" Finn asked, settling onto a step on the other side of Thomas.

"We tried. But every time we'd almost have him, he'd write a Falstaff, Dogberry, or Don Armado into a scene. Humor is impossible to work with."

Teagan saw the look on Abby's face and pulled her inside.

"You guys need an intervention," Abby said. "Seriously. Someone to come in and just throw out all the books. Can I use the computer?"

"Let me check and see if Molly replied to me about my history notes first. Then it's all yours."

Aiden and Lennie had come back from the Santinis' with a box, and were tiptoeing through the living room, apparently pretending to be invisible. They saw Teagan looking at them and sprinted for the kitchen.

"What was that all about?" Teagan said.

"I don't want to know." Abby leaned over her shoulder to peer at the computer screen. "Is that an e-mail about Jing Khan?"

"Molly can't take notes for me," Teagan said as she read it. "She's picking up some foreign exchange students from their orientation breakfast. She says she can pick me up at the zoo, though, on her way back. Jing's going to take notes for both of us, and hand them over in fifth period."

"The Mighty Khan? You think you'll even be able to read them?"

"Jing's grades are as good as mine—in history, anyway."

"But not so much in math."

"Since when have you cared about Jing's grades?"

"Since he's the captain of the soccer team, and Donnie's making book."

"He's taking wagers on our soccer team?"

Abby shrugged. "Jing's grades fall and he's out of there, right? And the team is nothing without the Mighty Khan. Do you ever wonder what they were thinking?"

"The Turtles? Constantly."

"No, Jing's parents. I mean, the guy's got a brain. What if he wants to be president or something someday? What kind of name is Jing Khan?"

"He'd have to give up soccer to become president. Politics is time-consuming."

"Yeah." Abby smiled. "He'd never do that, right?"

TEN

FINN came in the front door. "Mrs. Santini is looking for Lennie and Aiden," he said. "Her silverware's gone missing. I saw them come in . . ."

"They were headed toward the kitchen," Teagan said, getting up. "They can't have gone far."

They found the boys in the backyard. They had a cardboard box set up against the far wall and Mrs. Santini's silverware was scattered on the ground around it: forks, spoons, and table knives.

"What's this, then?" Finn asked.

"We're practicing," Aiden explained. "In case the bad guys come. Dad said I couldn't use real knives."

"So you're going to throw spoons at them? What were you thinking, Lennie?" Abby said. "Was this your top-secret plan?"

"Nope," Lennie said. "This was just an idea."

"Actually, it's not a bad idea, Gabby. Do you have an extra spoon, boyo?"

Aiden handed one to him. Finn balanced it on his finger thoughtfully, then tossed it in the air, caught it, and flicked it toward the box, his hand moving almost too fast to follow. The spoon stuck, handle first, into the cardboard.

"Luck," Abby said.

"Really?" Finn gathered up another spoon and a fork, tossed them in the air, then grinned at her. "Tines." His hand blurred, and the fork stuck, tines deep in the box. "Handle." The spoon stuck handle first, just as deep into the cardboard.

"What's the trick?" Abby demanded.

"It's not a trick," Aiden said. "Finn's magic."

"No magic, boyo, just practice," Finn said, balancing yet another spoon on his finger. "You can feel the heft of it, the way it will fly. Then you"—he threw again, and the handle punctured the box—"*think* it into the cardboard. Want to try it, Tea?"

"She won't be any good at it," Aiden said.

"It's physics." Teagan picked up a fork. "I should be able to learn it." She threw it, and it slapped sideways on the box and fell to the ground.

"The trick is feeling the balance so you know when to let go," Finn said.

Teagan tried again. This time the fork hit tines first, but not hard enough to stick.

"That's it!" Finn said. "Your hand learns the thing, you see."

"So, if she's ever attacked in a restaurant, she'll be safe." Abby shook her head.

"Only if she throws harder. You've got to mean it with all your heart, girl." Lennie and Aiden picked up the silverware. Finn was showing them the difference between the balance of a fork and a table knife when Mr. Wylltson came out the back door.

"Mrs. Santini is looking for her silverware—" Mr. Wylltson said, just as Finn sank another table knife in the box. "Oh, there it is. May I try?"

Teagan finally got a fork to stick, but Mr. Wylltson hadn't even managed to hit the box when Mamieo came out the back door.

"What on earth is going on here?" she said, just as he let one fly. "The whole lot of you should know better. You gather every piece of that up. And count the forks. I think John Paul flung that last one over the back wall."

They collected the silverware and Teagan made sure Aiden washed it before they carried it back to Mrs. Santini, then helped her carry a vat of spaghetti, a basket of homemade breadsticks, and a huge green salad back to the Wylltsons'.

They set up card tables so everyone could sit, and Mamieo put Teagan, Abby, and Roisin to work setting them.

"Did you put garlic in the spaghetti?" Aiden asked.

Mrs. Santini squeezed his cheeks together. "Extra garlic, just for you!"

"Thank ooo," he said through puckered lips.

"Where are the candles?" Lennie asked.

"I forgot them," Mrs. Santini said. "I'll be right back!"

She returned with two candles stuck in the tops of wine bottles, and tall cups to hold the breadsticks on each table.

"What's Aiden up to?" Abby asked.

"I'm not sure." Teagan frowned. The room looked . . . romantic.

"It's the top-secret plan," Lennie said.

"Okay," Aiden said, surveying the room. "I'm ready to sing."

"An Italian song, remember," Mrs. Santini said.

"Yep," Aiden told her.

Teagan looked at the tables, the candle, the spaghetti, the breadsticks standing upright in the cup on the table, and suddenly it clicked.

"Oh, no, he's not."

"Oh, yes, he is, and it's perfect. Just like it was in the movie." Abby covered her smile with her hand.

Aiden cleared his throat and began to sing.

It was "Bella Notte," from *Lady and the Tramp*. Sung perfectly. In soprano.

Teagan felt herself leaning toward Finn. Aiden's voice was doing it again—not shifting things, exactly, but definitely filling the room with magic. It was as if invisible feathers fell around them, soft as whispers, bright as snow.

Roisin turned to look at Thomas over Aiden's head.

When Aiden stopped singing, Roisin leaned down and kissed his cheek . . . then walked over to Thomas. He held out one arm, and she wrapped her arms around him and buried her face in his shirt. Thomas closed his eyes and put his arms around her slowly, as if he couldn't quite believe he was holding her, and started speaking softly to her in Irish.

"Rats," Aiden said.

Mr. Wylltson patted his shoulder. "'Bella Notte' is a little out of your range, son."

Aiden looked up at him. "Do you think garlic will help?" His voice was tight with tears.

"I know it will," Mr. Wylltson said. "But it will take ten or fifteen years."

"Oh, they're a cute couple," Mrs. Santini whispered loudly. "Too bad. I think Leo was looking at her. Come on, Aiden. You sit by me."

"He's going to be trouble when he's eighteen, you know?" Abby said.

Teagan sighed. "He's trouble now."

By the time they had finished saying grace, everyone but Aiden was laughing and passing food between the tables; Mrs. Santini was shouting across the room at Lennie about his table manners; Grendal was eating meatballs under the table; and Lucy hovered consolingly over Aiden's head, flashing red and yellow messages to him.

Mamieo laughed so hard at something John Wylltson said that she almost fell out of her chair, and Abby had to bring her a glass of water while Finn ran upstairs to get her a heart pill.

Teagan walked over to Thomas's table while Finn was gone. Thomas was showing Roisin how to twirl spaghetti on a fork. He looked up at Teagan, his face a mix of joy and . . . *regret.* Why was there a shadow of regret?

"You're inspiring Aiden, aren't you?" Teagan said softly. "There was magic in his voice when he sang over me. And again tonight. But not at church this morning. Not when you weren't there."

"I can't help it," Thomas said. "But it will never work against anyone in this household. I've promised."

Roisin said something in Irish. Thomas nodded. "She says

she's sorry she's breaking his heart. But she's several centuries too old for him."

Finn had come back with Mamieo's pill. Teagan smiled at Roisin, then went back to her place.

They'd had spaghetti the first time Finn had eaten with them. With her mom. When things had been normal. Finn leaned close to Teagan.

"What are you thinking?"

"That mom would have loved this," Teagan said. *This is normal now,* she thought. *Normal includes Grendal and Lucy, Thomas and Roisin. A little brother who's magic . . . and Finn. And it is very, very good.*

Teagan came awake suddenly, cold with sweat. She had dreamed she was being hunted by creatures with bloody muzzles and ember-bright eyes while voices spoke words she didn't understand. She'd had the dream before, on the night that Finn had led the goblins away. The night before her mother had collapsed and died.

It was different this time—the yowling had followed her out of the dream. She thought at first that there were alley cats fighting in the street until she heard the words tangled in the yowls. *Cat-sídhe* were outside, crying out for death and marrowbones.

Teee-ghaaaan.

That wasn't a *cat-sídhe* voice. And it was closer than the street. Much closer. Teagan tried to sit up, and her fear turned to panic. Her muscles wouldn't obey her.

She opened her mouth to warn Abby, but no sound came out.

Her heart was pounding so hard she was sure it was shaking the bed. And then there was a weight on her chest, pressing down, threatening to crush the air from her.

Teee-ghannn, let me in.

As suddenly as it had come, the pressure was gone. She sat bolt upright, gasping for breath. Abby was snoring softly in the moonlight, the crucifix still clutched in her hands.

A nightmare. It was just a nightmare. Teagan forced herself to get up and look out the window to prove it.

There was something dark and man-size standing on the porch roof looking at her window. Her stomach knotted as she remembered the shadow that touched her face in Mag Mell. It had reached through her skin and bones, brushing her mind.

The man-shape moved, and Teagan realized that it wasn't a shadow—shadows don't cast shadows of their own. It had a gaunt human face with cavernous eyes, but it moved incredibly quickly. A ninja, she thought irrationally. A *dead* ninja . . . because this creature wasn't alive; she was sure of it. It had no electric halo, no tickle of life about it.

Teee-ghannn, let me in.

"No."

"Tea?" Abby sat up. "What's wrong?"

The creature reached toward the window, entreating.

"No," Teagan said more loudly.

It turned, and suddenly she could hear it scratching along the wall, its nails—or claws—against the siding.

"What's that?" Abby asked.

"It's headed for Aiden's room!" Teagan said as she bolted for the door. *God, please don't let it in. Please don't let it touch Aiden.* She stumbled on the pants Abby had left on the floor, staggered, then ran down the hall, throwing open the door to Aiden's room.

"What the crap?" Finn pushed himself up on his elbow, but she jumped over him. The creature was already at the window, its pale hands pressed against the glass, sliding it up.

Teagan slammed the window down again, but she couldn't push it far enough to lock it. Then Finn was behind her, his hands beside hers, holding the window down.

Aiden screamed.

"I got you, Choirboy." Abby had followed Teagan. She scooped Aiden into her arms, and he hid his face in her neck. "I got you."

"The latch is broken," Teagan said. The pale face outside the window was crying, its mouth hideously open, its thin, clawed fingers scraping at the glass, trying to pull the window up. Lucy smashed against it on the inside, trying to get at the creature. Her knife was out, and her eyes flashed deadly red.

Then Thomas came out of nowhere. He reached past them, jamming Aiden's light saber like a charley bar between the upper frame and the top of the lower window.

"That should do it," he said.

Finn wrapped his arms around Teagan and pulled her away from the window. The blue light from the blade lit the creature's blank, almost featureless face.

"We're being attacked by the thing out of *The Scream*?" Abby said. "Seriously?"

"Is that one of your movies?" Finn asked.

"It's a painting. By Edvard Munch. Wait. *I can see it.* Why can I see it? Is it, like, a Highborn?"

"It's a *sluagh,*" Finn said. "A harbinger of death, like the *bean-sídhe. Sluagh* sense when a soul is leaving its body. They come for the souls of people who die abandoned and all alone."

"But I can see it," Abby insisted. "And it isn't a Highborn or an angel."

"Of course you can," Finn said flatly. "That thing was once a Fir Bolg."

The creature opened its mouth and keened once more, then turned and slid off the roof.

"Are the rest of the windows locked?"

"The downstairs windows are always locked."

"So whose soul did it come for?" Abby asked. "Who's dying?"

"Mamieo!" Teagan and Finn said at the same time. But they found Mamieo and Mr. Wylltson in the hall, coming to see why Aiden had screamed, and Roisin and Grendal in the kitchen eating ice cream and potato chips.

"Maybe it got a wrong address." Abby was still hugging Aiden. "That could happen, right?"

ELEVEN

"WHAT were you doing here, you bastard?" Finn said softly. He was standing on the sidewalk in front of the house, looking up, as if the *sluagh* might still be clinging under the eaves in the morning light. "No one's dying, and no one's alone. This home should be safe from the likes of you."

Teagan stood beside him, but she had no idea what she was looking for. Abby had gone to school already. Mamieo was getting ready to walk to the elementary school with Aiden. Finn and Teagan would walk halfway with them, to the stop where Tea caught the bus to work. Mr. Wylltson and Thomas were in the kitchen arguing about the literary influences of Shakespeare, while Roisin and Grendal had a late breakfast. No one had slept much the night before.

"I can't believe it was a Fir Bolg," Teagan said.

"It wasn't," Finn said. "No more than Fear Doirich is an *aingeal*. Any creature can walk away from what it was meant to be."

"Did it come out of Mag Mell?"

"No," Finn said. "The *sluagh* live here, in the sewers. It most likely came up through that"—he pointed at a storm drain in the street—"and went back down it as well."

Aiden stepped out the door clutching the old purse he had confiscated from the dress-up trunk so he could have a kit like Finn's.

In the ten minutes since Teagan had brushed his hair, Lucy had managed to re-weave half of her nest, twining in a lovely strip of aluminum foil and bits of colored paper. Aiden saw Teagan eyeing it.

"Gotta go," he said, and tried to duck past her.

"Aiden!" Teagan caught his shirttail. "You can't go to school with a sprite's nest in your hair."

"It's Lucy's *house*." Aiden clutched his kit in one hand and tried to protect his hair from Teagan with the other. "She likes it!" The sprite buzzed angrily as Teagan started picking her decorations out of Aiden's curls.

"We don't get civilians involved, remember, boyo?" Finn said. "Even if Lucy is living in your hair, we can't let civilians know."

"Civilians like my teacher?"

"Exactly."

"But not like Abby?"

Finn grimaced. "Apparently Gabby has enlisted."

"Good," Aiden said. "Ouch, Tea. You're pulling!"

"Hold still, then." Teagan worked at a string the sprite had tied into her nest.

Mamieo came out, her own purse in her hand. She'd used a dab of her glamour powder—just enough to make her look like a movie star. An old movie star, all shimmer and dazzle on top of her wrinkles.

"What's wrong with the girlie?" she asked.

"Teagan is messing up her nest," Aiden said.

"I think I can help." Finn knelt down and opened his kit, and Aiden immediately stopped squirming and squatted down to watch. The only thing more interesting to Aiden than Finn's kit was the knife he carried, and Mr. Wylltson had been very clear with Aiden about not touching that.

Teagan watched as Finn moved neatly folded socks, an empty water bottle, his roll of duct tape, and a camp cup aside. Not one ounce of wasted weight, and every item something he might need if he had to move fast.

Aiden's kit was a work in progress. When Teagan had checked earlier, it had Scotch tape instead of duct tape, M&M's for Lucy, a pair of socks, and two Lego men.

"Do you keep your knife in there, too?" Aiden leaned over the bag.

"No," Finn said. "A knife's no good if it's tucked away where you can't get to it."

"You didn't put your pocketknife back in your kit, did you?" Teagan asked. She had confiscated it before breakfast.

Aiden clutched his purse. "No."

"Here we go," Finn said, pulling a tweed cap from the bottom of his bag and glancing at Mamieo. The old woman pressed her lips together, then nodded.

"It's a Donegal tweed, boyo," Finn said, "and it belonged to my grandpa Rory. Mamieo gave it to me when I was about your age."

"A Mac Cumhaill hat," Aiden whispered in awe.

"That it is." Finn shooed Lucy away and settled the cap on Aiden's head. He leaned back to examine it, then pulled it off to the side. "That's how we wear them." Lucy chittered angrily, her eyes flashing purple and red. "Settle down, bug. The boyo wants to wear it whether you like it or no."

The sprite grabbed the bill of the cap and tried to flip it off Aiden's head.

"Stop it, Lucy." Aiden put his hand on top of it to hold it down. "I want it." She landed on the hat and glared at Finn.

"His teacher won't let him wear that in class," Teagan said. "No hats."

Mamieo twinkled at her. "They'll all be wearing hats by the end of the day, if necessary."

"Mamieo can be most persuasive." Finn smiled.

And so can you, Teagan thought. Finn didn't need the glamour dust of Mag Mell, though. His smile was enough to befuddle.

"That settles it, then." Mamieo adjusted Aiden's cap one more time. "We'd best be going. I want to get there early enough to talk to the pratie's teacher about the hat." They started down the sidewalk, with Finn and Aiden in the lead and Teagan and Mamieo following behind.

"If you don't keep your knife in your bag, where do you keep it?" Aiden asked, taking Finn's hand.

"Here or there, depending," Finn said. "It's no good if I can't reach it, is it?"

Aiden nodded. "Did you fight goblins when you were my age?"

"Na," Finn said. "My da took care of them."

"Like Mamieo's going to take care of me?"

"Just like," Finn agreed. "So you do what she tells you."

"I'm going to go in here, Aiden," Teagan said when they reached the coffee shop on the corner. He held his kit behind him and nodded.

"But before I do, let's have a bag check. Come on." She knelt on the sidewalk next to him.

Aiden sighed and opened his purse.

"What's this?" She pulled out a butter knife.

"Dad said I could use table knives."

"On cabbage."

"I *need* it, Tea," Aiden said. "In case the bad guys come."

"Leave the buttering of bad guys to me, pratie." Mamieo took the knife from Teagan and dropped it in her own purse.

"I don't want to go back to school," Aiden said. "I want to go back to Mag Mell. Lucy and Roisin want to go, too. It's not good for them here."

Teagan glanced up at Aiden. "You don't want to go back there."

"Yes, I do," Aiden insisted. "And I'll take care of Roisin and Lucy!"

Teagan almost missed the pair of steel forceps that had worked their way to the bottom of the bag.

"Don't take my scissors, too!" Aiden said as she pulled them out.

"These aren't scissors." Teagan put them into her backpack. "They're my lab forceps. You use them for holding things, like tweezers."

"They're pointy."

"But they're not good for cutting. I'll get you some real scissors after school, okay?"

"With points?"

"No points." Teagan handed the purse back. "Be good for Mamieo."

Aiden took Mamieo's hand and swung his purse in the other as they went down the street.

"You think Lucy will cause problems?" Teagan asked.

"Of course. But the biggest problem will be that purse. We really need to get him something more manly. He's going to get beaten up for carrying that thing."

"That hat wasn't in your kit before. I know—I helped you rearrange it before we went into Mag Mell."

Finn grinned. "I got it from Mamieo. But I wanted the boyo to keep it on his head, and it's all in the presentation." He opened the door of the shop for her. The Black Feather smelled enticingly of coffee, spices, and books. Just walking past could wake her up most mornings. This morning it was going to take more than the aroma of freshly ground coffee, though.

"You want some java or chai?" Teagan asked.

"Na. Never got used to the stuff. You like this place," Finn said as they stepped inside and walked to the counter.

"I love it. I remember sitting in that chair"—she pointed at the huge black armchair by the side window—"sharing a peppermint hot chocolate with my mom. It was snowing outside, and I picked all the peppermint candy off the top of the whipped cream while she wrapped a present for Dad. It must have been the Christmas I was four."

"You've lived here that long?"

"All my life." Teagan ordered a chai latte, then turned to Finn. "Are you sure you don't want anything?"

"I'm sure."

"Are you hiring?" Teagan asked the barista when she handed her the cup.

"Maybe. I can get you an application."

Finn studied the stuffed and mounted raven whose wings spread over the pastry counter while Teagan took the application from the barista and slipped it into her backpack.

"You're not thinking—"

"Oh, but I am," Teagan said. "Thomas can't just sit around the house. If he's going to be in this corner of the multiverse, he needs a job. And they do poetry slams here every Friday."

"The man *tortured* poets," Finn said as they left the shop.

"Have you ever sat through a poetry slam?" Teagan asked.

"Can't say that I have."

"Dad would consider it payback."

"You've lived in the same house all your life," Finn mused as they walked down the street. "I can't imagine it."

It was past rush hour, and they were the only ones waiting at the bus stop. Teagan sat down, and Finn settled himself on the bench almost a foot away. She could still feel the hum of life in him, a magnetic pull.

"So . . . what did you and my dad talk about the other night?"

"I told the man I loved you, and he asked me questions I couldn't answer."

"About your future?"

"About you," Finn said. "About your hopes and dreams, and how I would fit into them. Your da is a thinking man, Tea, a planning man. I want to be like him. And I want to be sure you know me, and know what you're choosing."

"Tell me something about yourself, then."

Finn's eyes went to the storm drain on the far side of the street.

"The first time I saw a *sluagh* was the night my parents died." Finn glanced at her, uncertain. "It was a car accident, in the rain. The car rolled, and both of them were thrown out."

"Weren't they—"

"Wearing seat belts? They were. The straps had been cut almost clean through."

"*Cat-sídhe.*"

Finn nodded. "My belt was fine in the back seat. I wasn't hurt at all. Just hung upside down. I got loose, crawled out the window, and ran to my ma. I was holding her when I saw the *sluagh*'s arm come up out of the storm sewer. I knew what it meant. She was dying, and the creature had come to steal her soul. I screamed for my da. He'd always kept the goblins away, always taken care of us. But he didn't come. The car had rolled over him, you see, but I didn't know it till I ran to him.

"'Da, it's coming,' I told him, but he didn't move. His body was bent and broken. So I took my grandpa Rory's knife out of his boot and stood between my *máthair* and the creature as she whispered her last prayers. In the end, it came on, knife or no. It wanted her soul that bad."

"You killed it?"

"They're already dead," Finn said. "I tried to put an end to it, but it went back down the sewer."

"Your mother . . ."

"It didn't take her soul. But she was gone just the same."

"How old were you?"

"Eleven. Almost eleven. Old enough to know to hide my grandfather's knife before the cops arrived. They thought I'd done it anyway. Because of the cut seat belts, you see. They couldn't prove it, so I went to foster care instead of juvie. I went back for the knife after I ran away from my last foster home."

Finn went up the bus steps ahead of her. Teagan watched him pause for a second at the top and scan the faces of the passengers, then check the corners of the bus. Her dad was right. She didn't know much about Finn Mac Cumhaill at all.

TWELVE

THE bus was surprisingly full. Finn let Teagan take the only seat and stood beside her. She slipped her hand into his. Finn never looked down, but he held tight, all the way to the zoo.

"I've never been here before," he said as they got off the bus and crossed the street. He looked like *the Mac Cumhaill* again—cocky and confident. But Teagan was sure the hurt wasn't gone. He'd just tucked it away somewhere inside.

"You're kidding."

"No. I've never liked the idea of all the poor beasties locked up to be looked at."

"Neither do I." Teagan showed her badge at the gate and paid for Finn. "That's why I'm here. I want to get as many of them out of the cages as I can. I've been working toward being able to do that for years now." When they reached the lab, Teagan tapped in her key code.

"You're early." Agnes glanced up as they came in, and her mouth fell open. "Finn?"

"Do I know you?" Finn asked.

"I read about you on Tea's Facebook page," Agnes said. "Well. He's a sexy beast, Tea. I like his eyes."

"The sexy beast is standing right here," Finn said. "Where he can hear every word you're saying."

"Oops," Agnes said. "Forgot there's no mute button on reality. Nerd girls rarely have an opportunity to practice social skills in the physical presence of hotness. My bad."

"Finn, meet Agnes Benson, lab tech and veterinary student by profession, and crypto-creature debunker by choice."

"Debunker?"

"I convince idiots that they're idiots." Agnes pointed to her computer screen. Her webpage was up—the word *Crypto* in a red circle with a slash through it, and then *Zoologist*. "Preferably while I'm being paid to do something else."

"Anything new?" Teagan asked.

"This one's still driving me crazy. You remember the sanitation workers that had cell phone pictures of monster creatures? Looked like a mix between a grizzly bear and a hairless Doberman? Somebody posted this on YouTube." Agnes clicked on an embedded video. It was footage of a red '57 Chevy truck blasting past.

"Oh, my god, Bernie!" The owner of the cell phone was clearly from New York City. "What are those things? What are we seeing?"

"Dogs." Bernie had a New York accent as well. "Those things are dogs."

"Those are not dogs," the first voice said. "I know a dog when I see a dog."

Agnes froze the video and leaned forward. "But if you're not dogs, not bears, not robots, not computer generated, what the heck are you?"

"Robots?" Teagan repeated.

"I'm grasping at straws."

"They look like authentic hellhounds," Finn said seriously. "Creatures from another dimension." Teagan frowned, but he just shrugged.

"A cute accent, and a sense of humor," Agnes said. "Where did you find him?"

"It's a long story," Teagan said.

Finn leaned against the counter, his legs stretched out and his arms folded, watching over Agnes's shoulder as she brought up a new video. This one showed Brynhild from a different angle—straight on as she blew through a stoplight, the hell-hounds right behind her. There was even a flash of Thomas, Roisin, and Finn in the back of the truck, but Finn's face was turned toward the hounds.

"See those people in the truck bed? I think they're actors."

"Why?" Finn asked.

"Look at their body language. They're acting as if there really is something chasing the truck, and they're very good. I'll bet they're from a local theater group. If they are, I'll track them down. C'mon, c'mon." Agnes tapped her finger on the desktop. "I just need one clue."

"Is that a traffic light camera?" Teagan asked.

"It is," Agnes agreed. "Can you believe someone would go to the trouble of doctoring traffic light footage? And leaking it to

YouTube? Which proves that some city employees spend their lunch breaks chasing unicorns and farting glitter."

"I need to culture some pus," Teagan said, taking the pill bottle out of her backpack. Finn grimaced, and Agnes looked up.

"You have a patient with an abscess?"

"A cat."

"You'll find *Pasteurella multocida* or *Streptococcus*, then, and an old puncture wound from a dog or cat bite."

"Just want to make sure."

"You know where the equipment is." Agnes went back to the computer. "I'll keep Finn for you. You know how Dr. Max is about visitors in the lab."

Teagan looked at Finn, who was looking irritated about the *cat-sídhe* pus. "I'll be right back."

He nodded, and turned his attention to the computer screen again.

Teagan checked on the patients in the next room before she stepped into the lab. A parma wallaby, orphaned when it was not quite old enough to care for itself, lay curled in a ball, sleeping the day away. If she hadn't had a sprite and a *cat-sídhe* living with her, Teagan would have taken the nocturnal baby home to care for it.

A golden-headed lion tamarin lay lethargically in a cage across the room. Dr. Max wasn't sure what was wrong with him yet.

Her own patient, a river otter that had tangled with a jogger's dog, was grooming himself in his isolation cage. Wild animals could bring diseases with them when they were brought to the clinic, so they were kept well separated from the other patients.

"Hey," Teagan said softly. The otter stood up and studied her, made a series of *eh-eh-eh* sounds followed by a high-pitched squeak, and then went back to his grooming. "Ready to go back to the river, huh? Just a few more days in the cage, and you will."

In the lab, Teagan took an agar-ready petri dish and labeled it, then used a Q-tip to wipe the cat pus across it. She started to dispose of the rest of the pus, then glanced at the clock. She had time to make a slide.

Under the microscope, the little bead-chain bacteria did look like *Streptococcus.*

"Tea," Agnes called. "Are you done? You need to be at the primate house."

"Be right there." She cleaned the slide and went back to the office. Finn and Agnes had returned to the cell phone video of the Hellhound Incident.

"Why isn't it possible?" Finn asked.

"I'm not saying it's impossible," Agnes said. "I'm saying that there has never been any physical evidence. If something is real, it will leave evidence."

"Something we could touch, then?"

"Touch, taste, see, smell, or hear." Agnes spread her arms. "Our body is the scientific instrument we use to study the universe around us. That's all we have. Our brain and our five senses."

"Perhaps there are people with more than five senses," Finn said. "People who live with one foot in this world and one in another."

"People who see leprechauns?" Agnes teased. "With that accent, it almost works." He grinned, and Agnes turned red.

"Are you coming, Finn?" Teagan asked.

"I am."

"Bye!" Agnes waved with her fingers as he followed Teagan out the door.

"I thought we weren't supposed to involve civilians," Teagan said.

"You don't like me talking to other girls?"

"I don't like you grinning at them," Teagan admitted.

"Then tame me with your fine Irish eyes, girl."

"Humph."

"You have nothing to worry about. You've had my heart since . . ."

"When?"

"I was just trying to sort it," Finn said. "It could have been the time you explained how its cockles were related to a shellfish." He paused. "No, it was when you flat refused to kiss me—and me thinking I'd never see you again, risking my life to lead the goblins away into the night. It was heroic. And sad."

Teagan punched his arm.

"All right." He smiled. "It was the first time I set eyes on you. My heart stopped beating, and that's a fact."

"I know," Teagan said. "The first time I met you, it made me throw up."

Finn knit his brows. "I'll never get over how romantic you are. It's like you've stepped right out of one of those fairy movies Aiden's making Roisin watch."

"I just wish you wouldn't smile like *that* at other girls."

"I'm the Mac Cumhaill," Finn said. "They come running no matter how I smile. You should see what happens when I rescue a kitten."

"Let me rescue the kittens from now on."

"I'll leave the kittens to you, then. But I'd rather you not doctor the *cat-sídhe*."

Teagan thought for a moment, then asked, "Why did you pick up Thomas, in Mag Mell? Highborn have killed lots of your family. You could have left him to die."

"I'm not made that way," Finn said.

"Well, this is how I'm made, Finn. I have to figure out what's rotting the *cat-sídhe*'s bodies. Besides, if it's contagious, Grendal might get it."

"I hadn't considered that." They'd reached the ape habitat, and Finn pointed to a chimp on a platform in the outside exhibit. "Is that your Cindy?"

"No," Teagan said. "This is one of the nicest ape habitats at any zoo—three separate exhibits—but Cindy has her own enclosure at the back of the primate building." She pointed out the habitats as they walked: the Kovler Gorilla Bamboo Forest, the Strangler Fig Forest, and the Dry Riverbed Valley. In the last, two chimps were playing chase.

"The creatures are bigger than I thought," Finn said.

"A male can weigh over one hundred fifty pounds. They are very strong, and very dangerous. They could tear a human apart."

"Not cute and cuddly, then." Finn frowned. "The nets keep the apes in?"

"And the moats."

"Still, it's a pretty nice place to live. If you can stand people staring at you all day. Why isn't Cindy in this one?"

"Cindy and Oscar have a special habitat because they're here for language research. Cindy was raised by humans, and when she came to the zoo, she had no idea how to socialize with other chimps. That's part of what I was hired to teach her, so that she could meet Oscar."

"You taught her how to be a chimp."

"How to socialize with other chimps." Teagan caught sight of an old couple out of the corner of her eye. They were holding hands beside a street lamp. She dropped her eyes so they wouldn't think she was staring. "When Oscar came, I was worried because Cindy had never gotten along with any other apes. He hasn't been here long, but it was love at first sight."

"Like you and me. What are you peeking at, girl?" Finn turned to look toward the elderly couple.

"Those two," Teagan said. "They followed me last week."

"The cute old couple?"

"Yes. And they're not cute. I think they're . . . hungry. I asked Mameio about them. She said she'd never heard of such creatures."

The octogenarians were shuffling toward them now. Smiling.

"They don't look menacing." Finn's eyes narrowed. "They look familiar."

"Not menacing?" Teagan took his hand. She pulled him down the walkway, almost running.

Finn looked over his shoulder. "What the crap?"

Teagan looked back. The octogenarians weren't keeping up. They were gaining. Even though their shuffle didn't look any faster, they were gaining.

"Run," Teagan said. She ran as fast as she could down the walk and around the corner.

They made it to the private door of the primate research area before Teagan whirled around. The last time the old people had chased her, she'd crossed a street and then they were gone. This time she saw it happen. They didn't *poof!* disappear. They faded from solid to translucent to . . . nothing.

"What the crap?" Finn said again. "Are they ghosties?"

"I don't know. This is the second time I've seen them."

"But they did you no harm?"

"They didn't catch me." Teagan took a deep breath and closed her eyes.

"What are you doing?"

"Focusing. I've got a job to do." She took two more deep breaths and shook off the chill that had settled over her, then let go of Finn's hand and keyed in the code. *Focus on the here and now,* she told herself. *Not the crazy multiverse.* She pulled open the door and ushered Finn in through the back entrance, into her normal world again.

The research area was not open to the public. Cindy and Oscar's enclosure had a Plexiglas wall with a desk on one side where observers could sit and take notes, but Teagan walked past it to the second viewing area. She hated watching the chimps through Plexiglas. Here, the main part of the habitat was separated from Teagan by bars and a guardrail longer than a chimpanzee's arm, so that no one could step within reach of the animals. There was a stand of bamboo in the back, and a small room where Cindy used to hide before Oscar showed her how to build a nest in the tree.

Oscar only looked up from the orange he was eating, but Cindy came over to the bars.

"Finn Mac Cumhaill," Teagan said, "meet my other family, Cindy and Oscar."

"Gabby's side? I can see a resemblance."

Cindy was studying Finn. *Cindy's boy,* Teagan signed in ASL, pointing toward Oscar. *Teagan's boy.* She pointed toward Finn. Cindy touched her fingers to her lips, then her cheek. *Kiss.* She pointed to Finn.

"What did she say?" Finn asked.

"Girl talk. She gave me something to think about." Cindy touched her fingers to her lips and then to her cheek again, then went over to Oscar and gave him a kiss on his cheek.

"The monkey told you to kiss me," Finn said, smiling. "That's what she said, isn't it?"

"She's not a monkey, she's an ape." Cindy started searching through Oscar's hair.

"And now what's she doing?"

"Trying to set a good example. She thinks I should check you for fleas."

"The social grooming will have to wait." Dr. Max had come in behind them. "Finn Mac Cumhaill, I presume? I'm Dr. Maxwell Walden."

"I'm guessing I'm the only person on the planet without a Facebook account," Finn said, shaking his hand.

"Pretty much." The look Dr. Max gave Finn was not exactly

warm. "Ms. Wylltson has a bright future ahead of her in the field of veterinary medicine or in animal cognition. Or both, if she doesn't allow herself to be distracted."

"Animal cognition?" Finn asked.

"Cognition is how we know what we know. Awareness, perception, reasoning, judgment. And empathy—that's a big one. Most creatures naturally empathize with others of their own kind. Ms. Wylltson has the ability to empathize with creatures that are completely different from her. And what's more astonishing is that they empathize with her. Empathy is the root of all communication. Sometimes I can't decide whether we should be studying the animals she works with, or studying her."

"He's exaggerating," Teagan said. "I just . . . pay attention."

"I am not exaggerating," Dr. Max insisted. "She's able to make a connection with animals like no one I have ever seen. And that's what she's here to do today. Make a connection. Help these politicians understand that Cindy and Oscar are more than simply animals. And maybe get the funds cut for a certain research center in Texas."

"And why's that important?"

"Labs that follow the rules are bad enough," Teagan said. "But this lab doesn't even bother. An orangutan was necropsied there last year. That's what the paperwork said, anyway. It was actually a vivisection."

"Necropsied? Vivisection?"

"A necropsy is an animal autopsy," Dr. Max said. "It happens after an animal is dead. In this case, they cut him open and pulled his heart out while it was still beating. That's vivisection."

"They cut him open while the living heart still beat inside him?"

"It was beating until they took it out," Teagan said. "It's illegal, but that didn't stop them."

"Politicians like the ones visiting today can get these labs defunded, or even shut down." Dr. Max stopped speaking abruptly and adjusted his necktie as Agnes appeared in the doorway, a group of men and women in business suits behind her.

"If you wouldn't mind"—Dr. Max made a shooing motion toward Finn—"we need to look completely professional here. No distractions."

"I understand," Finn said. "I'll just . . . wander about until you're done then, Tea. Maybe have a look about for . . . our old friends."

Teagan spent the next hour helping the senator and her committee communicate with the chimps. Cindy even brought out her baby doll to show them. Dr. Max explained the type of independent thinking that was going on as Cindy and Oscar talked with Teagan. Cindy was eager to play, using phrases she had constructed herself and expressing concepts as complex as those of a five-year-old child. Teagan did her best to draw them out and have fun. By the end of the hour, every committee member was smiling, and when Cindy blew the senator kisses, the woman blew kisses back.

After they left, Teagan stopped by the office to pick up her backpack and realized that she hadn't arranged a meeting place with Finn, and he didn't have a cell phone. She wandered through the African animal displays, and finally found him in the Kovler Lion House watching the Amur tiger.

"I couldn't find your ghosties," Finn said, and nodded toward the tiger. "She's impressive, though. The sign says she's got hooks on her tongue that can rip the skin from flesh and the flesh from bone."

"Have you been sitting here the whole time?"

"I wandered around a bit before I found her."

"Were you looking for her?"

"I was. Your da told me you got upset because he called you Tiger. I was checking for a resemblance."

"That's ridiculous."

The tiger yawned, showing her enormous teeth. Teagan fought a yawn of her own, and lost. Finn looked from her to the tiger, and raised one eyebrow.

"No similarity at all," he said.

"It's an automatically released archaic motor pattern," Teagan said. "Everyone knows yawns are contagious. And I was upset because he *used* to call me Rosebud, not Tiger. Come on. I've got to get out to the gate to meet Molly."

"Skinner's sending a therapist for Aiden because he's *different*. But you're as different as Aiden, in your own way," Finn said as they walked.

"My differences fit in better. And I know what to do with them. Aiden hasn't figured it out yet. So, you've seen what I'm working for, why I want to go to school. How will that fit into *your* dreams?"

"I fit you into my dreams every night, girl."

"I *meant* your plans for the future."

"I've never had plans for the future," Finn said softly. "I thought I knew what was going to happen. I'd fight goblins until they killed me. But I'm working on plans now. I'm planning on keeping you alive." He hesitated. "I don't feel comfortable letting you go off on your own to school."

"You're not going to be able to stay with me twenty-four/seven. Security won't let you wander the school grounds."

"I'll wait for you *outside* the school, then."

"No." Teagan stopped walking. "I know things are different now. I know there are all kinds of dangerous creatures out there. But I have a life, and I'm not going to change it completely because of the goblins. If I do that, they'll have won."

"But—"

"And *you're* going to have a life, too. Something more than following me around. You trust Mamieo to be able to take care of herself, right?"

"I do. But nobody's tough enough to fight everything."

"Then I'm going to do the best I can, just like you and Mamieo do. I'm going to school, and then I'm going to take the bus to the pet shop after school to pick up some food for Lucy. I'll see you at home."

Finn wrapped his arms around her, and rested his chin on top of her head.

"You're da's right," he said. "This is going to be complicated."

THIRTEEN

THEY had barely reached the street when a horn blared and Molly pulled up in her yellow Volkswagen. Someone had put black antennae on the roof, making it look like a jaundiced bedbug.

"Oh, no," Teagan said.

"What is it?" Finn asked.

"The Birthday Bug. Molly's mom is very big on birthdays. They decorate everything. Including people. If you think the *outside* is bad, wait until you see what's *inside.*"

Molly was wearing wraparound shades with yellow frames, and bug antennae, too. A brunette who looked too young to be in high school was sitting in the passenger seat. The brunette rolled down the window and bobbed her head to make her own pink antennae jiggle and the LEDs around the rose-colored rim of her shades flash.

"Whose birthday is it?" Teagan asked

"*My* birthday," the girl said, in a very cute French accent.

"This bug looks contagious," Finn said.

"*Oui.* Would you like to catch some?" She flashed the LEDs at him.

"I'm already caught."

"Are you sure you have room?" Teagan asked, eyeing the two girls in the back seat, who'd also been decorated.

"We can all get cozy. Back seat, Isabeau," Molly said.

Isabeau got out, and Teagan decided she was old enough for high school after all. Her . . . attributes hadn't been as obvious when she was sitting down, but her low-cut mini-dress and knee boots didn't hide any of them. She pulled the seat forward, then tipped her face up at Finn, jiggling more than just her antennae when she did.

"Get in back with us," she said. "Come on. We won't bite."

"I'll take the bus," Finn said. "It'll be safer for us all. I've got some window repairs to do at home." Isabeau shrugged and climbed into the back seat, and Teagan got in the front. Finn made sure her feet were in, then shut the door and leaned on the window frame.

"I'll see you at home, then, Tiger."

"Rosebud."

"Be careful. Keep your eyes open."

"I will."

"Why do you 'ave to keep your eyes open?" Isabeau asked as they pulled away. "Do you have a stalker?"

"Nothing like that." Teagan fastened her seat belt.

"Sakiko, Katie," Molly said, "meet Teagan. Sakiko is from Tokyo, and Katie's from London. You've met Isabeau."

"From *Marseille,*" Isabeau said.

Teagan turned to greet the other exchange students. "Hi." Sakiko was a plump little girl who looked uncomfortable in the middle of the seat. Katie, though . . . Except for the ridiculous shades she was wearing, Katie was model-perfect.

As perfect as Kyle.

Teagan turned back around, but the hair on the back of her neck was prickling. "How long have you girls been in the states?" she asked.

"Isabeau got here on Friday, and both Katie and Sakiko came in on Saturday," Molly answered for them. "Today was their orientation breakfast. You want some birthday gear?" She held out shades and pair of purple antennae.

"You should take them," Isabeau said. "They would—how do you say? *Improve the look?*"

"She means your outlook," Molly said quickly. "'Rose-colored glasses,' correct, Isabeau?"

"Correct." Isabeau giggled.

"Actually," Teagan said, "I would like a pair. But . . . could you trade with me, Katie? I don't like purple."

"No," Katie said. Her voice was deep for a girl, almost husky.

"Yes, trade!" Isabeau snatched the glasses from Katie's face.

"Give them back!" Katie grabbed them away from her, but not before Teagan saw that the girl had eyes, not pools of darkness where eyeballs should have been. She didn't look wicked cruel, wicked fast, or wicked smart—just angry. She shoved the glasses on again, and turned to stare out the window.

"Never mind," Teagan said, and took the purple shades and antennae from Molly.

"Did you hear that Mrs. Rapp had an accident?" Molly asked. "She slipped on a bar of soap in the bathtub. Jing told me about it when I called to ask him to take notes for us. He heard it from his dad."

Isabeau giggled again.

"It's not funny." Molly pushed up her sunglasses to look at her in the mirror. "Over seventy percent of all home accidents occur in the bathroom."

"Sorry," Isabeau said. "But Jing *is* a funny name."

"Oh." Molly nodded. "I thought you were laughing at Mrs. Rapp. She's in a lot of pain." Molly glanced at Teagan. "And she's not going to be alone. Mr. Diaz is teaching our AP Psychology class until we get a sub."

"Ouch," Teagan said. Mr. Diaz was a retirement check waiting to happen. Her phone buzzed and she pulled it out of her pocket.

"Tea." Abby's voice crackled into static, then came back. "Are you on your way? 'Cause we've got something for your . . . friend behind the library. We're in the parking lot."

"We're almost there," Teagan said. "I'll see you in a few."

"Hey, isn't that Abby and her mobster-wannabe cousin?" Molly said as they pulled into the lot. Today, Rafe was wearing a suit and a fedora. He appeared to be ignoring Abby as she yelled at him.

"Mobster?" Isabeau leaned forward. "Like ze Soprano?"

"More like the Godfather," Teagan said. "If they ever remake those films, Rafe is going to be first in line for the part of Michael Corleone."

"*Oh, my godz,*" Isabeau gasped. "'Eee's *adorable!*"

"Is he a sophomore?" It was the first thing Sakiko had said.

Teagan glanced at her in surprise. The Japanese girl had almost no accent at all.

"Freshman," Molly said.

"Just barely," Teagan added. The object on the asphalt between Abby and Rafe appeared to be the source of Abby's excitement. At least it didn't have any obvious arms, legs, or fangs.

Molly rolled down her window. "Hey, move that thing so I can use the parking space, okay?" Abby and Rafe both just looked at her.

"I'll get it." Teagan climbed out of the car. The thing on the ground was definitely mechanical, and coated with ancient-looking grease and grime.

"What is this?" she asked.

"You asked for parts," Rafe said. "So Leo sends parts. He's appreciating the use of the truck, if you know what I mean. Broads like it."

"Broads?" Abby put two fingers to her temples. "Do not tell me that word came out of your mouth, Raphael. I swear, you are giving me a migraine."

Rafe shrugged at Teagan. "Abby says to leave it out here, but I said no way. It's rare, right? There might not be another one in the state."

"Didn't one of you bring it here?" Teagan asked.

"Leo dropped it off," Abby said. "He said it was for you."

"I can't carry it around." Rafe frowned. "This is my second-best suit. I've got to keep it clean for work."

"Like the corpses are going to care?" Abby shook her head. Rafe had inherited Abby's old job at the funeral home.

"She won't touch it, either," Rafe said to Teagan.

"I got work after school, too. You think people want a grease monkey painting their toenails?"

Molly honked the horn, and Teagan carefully picked up the piece of machinery, doing her best to keep the grease off *her* clothes. She stepped out of the parking space, and the Birthday Bug pulled in.

"Tell Leo 'thank you,'" Teagan said, trying to figure out what part of the motorcycle it was. "Raynor will appreciate it. I think."

"Leo says it's not as bad as it looks," Rafe assured her. "And about the job—"

Katie climbed out of the car, followed by Sakiko.

"Hello," Rafe said. "Like I was saying, Leo says—"

Isabeau slid out and tugged on her skirt, which had ridden up a little.

Rafe did a double-take. "Did I say hello?"

"*Oui,*" she said.

"I did? Well, I meant hel–*lo*. You ladies need someone to show you around the school? 'Cause I'm"—he brushed an imaginary speck of dust off his lapel—"available."

"I'm Isabeau." She dimpled at him. "What's your name, please?"

"Rafe."

"Raphael," Abby said. "One of the famous Turtle Brothers."

"Leonardo, Michelangelo, Donatello, and Raphael?" Sakiko asked.

"Of course not," Rafe said. "Who would name their kids

after a dumb cartoon? Unless, you . . . uh"—he peeked sideways at Isabeau—"like the Teenage Mutant Ninja Turtles?"

"'Eeero's in a 'alf-shell! *Oui!*"

"Really?" Rafe's voice broke. He cleared his throat and pitched it lower. "I mean, really? So did my mother. She made us take martial arts classes and all that. Put a pair of *sai* in my hands and I'll go totally Turtle on you."

"I'm taking them to the office." Molly took Isabeau's elbow and started to pull her away. "See you in class, Tea."

"Wait," Rafe called after them, then turned back to Teagan. "Tea, I was supposed to tell you . . ." He looked after the girls again. "Never mind. I'll catch you later!" He had to run to catch up with Isabeau.

"You going to miss any of this when you graduate?" Abby asked.

"Not at all," Teagan said. "You?"

Abby hesitated.

"Abigail Gagliano, is there something you haven't told me?"

"Yeah," Abby said. "That you're not leaving that thing in my locker."

"*Our* locker. Have you had lunch? Because I'm starving."

"No. But I've got to go by the media center. I got a note about an overdue book."

"You checked out a book?"

"My freshman year. See what kind of trouble books cause? They're not going to let me graduate unless I pay for it or bring it back."

"Okay. I have to stop by the office. I'll meet you at the cafeteria in ten."

Teagan considered a detour to the ladies' room to clean up the part, but the grease and grime had congealed into a seemingly permanent matrix around it, like the shell of a geode, and she was afraid if she added a solvent—even water—the entire contraption would fall apart. She settled for wrapping it in pages of the school newspaper before she went to the office.

The guy behind the desk stood up when Teagan came in. "What's in the package, beautiful? Anything fragile, liquid, hazardous, or perishable?"

"No." Student aides in the office were always a pain. "I need a tardy slip."

He pushed a clipboard at her, and Teagan wrote down the time and why she was late. He handed her a yellow slip of paper with his name and phone number on it.

"A tardy slip," Teagan said, pushing it back at him. She was definitely not going to miss high school.

He shrugged and gave her another piece of paper.

"Thanks."

She put the tardy slip in her pocket and carried the motorcycle part to the cafeteria.

Abby was standing at the end of the salad bar, sorting through the black buckets of flatware. She held up a fork with something green dried like webbing between the tines. "This place is so unsanitary. They just leave these forks and spoons sitting here, gathering any crap that falls on them."

"Find me a clean one, too," Teagan said.

"Are you going to carry that thing around with you all day?" Abby asked after she'd found two forks that passed inspection.

"It's either that or put it in our locker," Teagan reminded her.

"In that case, let me get your salad for you." Abby pushed one tray and loaded up two plates of salad while Teagan trailed behind her.

"What was the book?" Teagan asked. "The one you checked out."

"Romeo and Juliet."

"Romeo and Juliet?"

"It's complicated. I was a freshman, right? My brain was unsettled, but I got over it."

"Why didn't you just bring the book back?"

"I threw it in the river."

"Why?"

"Are we going to eat or talk? We've got, like, five minutes." They found seats at an empty table, and Abby looked around and lowered her voice. "Is Finn going to chase down that *thing* today?"

"He thinks it went down the storm drain, but he's fixing the latch on Aiden's window and putting charley bars on every window in the house."

"Did you guys talk? Like *talk*, talk?"

"Yes," Teagan said.

"And?"

"And why did you throw *Romeo and Juliet* in the river? And how come I never heard about it?"

"Because you were an *infant*."

"I'm not an infant now."

Abby pushed a piece of lettuce back and forth across her plate. "I don't want to talk about it."

"It's still bothering you," Teagan said as the bell rang.

"I'm over it," Abby said. "I just had to pay for the stupid book, all right?"

FOURTEEN

"SO," Jing said as he put the homework notes on Teagan's desk, "who's this Finn Mac Cumhaill? He's not in this school. I checked the enrollment lists."

"Jing, you're going to get expelled the next time they catch you in the computers," Molly said.

"Finn's my adopted cousin," Teagan explained. "He's not from around here."

Rafe came in the door, followed by Isabeau. She was still wearing her birthday baubles.

"You're not in this class," Molly said. "Either of you."

"I should be in P.E." Rafe smoothed his lapel, then settled into the desk beside Teagan. Isabeau sat down behind him. "But I don't like taking off the suit, you know what I'm saying? It wrinkles in the locker. Where are you supposed to be, Isabeau?"

She checked her schedule. "Science. Where they dissect piggsies?" She shook her head. "I don't think I should go."

"You can't skip classes," Molly told her. "As a foreign exchange student, you represent your whole country!"

"Relax, Mollster," Rafe said. "She's not going to get busted on her first day. I just hadn't finished talking to Tea when you dragged the ladies away." He looked around. "This classroom is half empty, anyway."

"Word got out that Diaz is baby-sitting us until they can find a sub," Jing said.

"And who are you?" Isabeau asked, smiling up at Jing.

"The Mighty Khan," Rafe said. "*Jing* Khan, captain of the soccer team. They've never lost a game."

"And never will," Jing said. "Losing is not in my vocabulary. How's your cousin?"

"You mean Abigail?" Rafe shrugged. "Why would you care?"

"We've been together since ninth grade," Jing said. "I care."

"In some of the same classes, maybe."

"That's together." Jing pressed his hand to his heart. "I've been waiting for the lady to look my way."

"And dating the whole cheer team while you waited."

"Killing time till she is mine. Besides, it was their idea."

"No offense," Rafe began. "Truly. But Abby's mom is old-fashioned, see? She's never going to let her date a guy who's not Italian."

"You mean she doesn't approve of very tall, very dark, and very handsome?"

"A little too tall, a little too dark for an Italian," Rafe said. "You know what I'm saying?"

"Ouch. At least I'll always have handsome."

"I hear you can convert," Teagan offered.

Jing smiled. "If Abby's interested, I will." He glanced toward the door as Mr. Diaz came through it, and Isabeau started to get up.

"Sit tight, sweet face," Rafe murmured, pulling her back into the chair. "If we leave now, we're busted."

"I'm passing out a seating chart, people," Mr. Diaz said. "Just write your name on your seat. And don't think I'm not checking it."

"He's not checking it," Jing said.

Rafe put his name down, and ran his finger across it.

"Bada-bing, I'm a senior." He passed the chart to Isabeau. "Want to grade up?"

"Do you ever follow the rules?" Molly hissed. "You're corrupting the morals of an exchange student."

"Chill out." Rafe tipped his chair back. "Like I said, I needed to talk to Teagan. I'm here to pass on some information, you know? And it don't look like Mr. Diaz cares." Mr. Diaz had leaned back and closed his eyes.

"So you talked to your uncle about the job?" Teagan asked as she signed the attendance sheet.

"Ettore talked to Vito, and Vito said no dice. Everybody working here's union, and you don't mess with union jobs."

"So—"

"Unless they *want* to leave, they're not going anywhere."

"I see," Teagan said.

"Okay." Molly made a shooing motion. "You passed on your information. Are you going yet?"

"I kind of like it here." Rafe nodded toward Mr. Diaz, who hadn't moved. "It's restful."

"Uncle Vito," Isabeau said. "Sounds like zee real Mob."

"Sure, sweet face." He did his best De Niro imitation. "It's a Family thing, ya know what I'm sayin'? Tea's friend needs a job, so's I'll just toss da lunch lady inta da river wid a pair of cement overshoes. Bada-bing, job opening."

"That's not funny," Teagan said. "Mrs. Meredith is a nice lady."

"It's funny," Jing said. Molly glared at him. "For a freshman," Jing added. "He wouldn't need cement, though. Just a couple of her meatloaves."

"New loafers!" Isabeau quipped.

"See?" Rafe beamed. "That's what I'm talking about. Humor, Tea-ster. Lighten up."

"I've got some notes to copy." Teagan turned away, leaving Rafe and Isabeau to their flirting. She had finished half of them when the bell rang.

"I'm not going to survive this," Molly said as they walked to their next class. "Isabeau's host family fell through, so she's staying with us. She's sleeping in my bedroom, Tea. And she talks. All. Of. The. Time. How am I supposed to study?" She glanced back down the hallway when they reached their next class. "She's not following us, is she?"

"I don't think so." Teagan tucked the newsprint parcel under her arm and adjusted the strap of her backpack.

"Good. I never thought I'd say this, but Calculus will be like heaven. No talking. Nothing but the sweet clicking of calculators."

It was quiet, at least. Teagan finished her assignment and copied another half a page of Jing's notes before the class was over.

"You want a ride?" Molly asked as soon as the bell rang.

"No," Tea said. "I need to stop for some crickets and mealworms."

"Oh, joy. Katie and Sakiko's host families are picking them up. That means I'll have Isabeau all to myself."

As she left the school grounds, Teagan decided that if she was bringing food for Lucy, she should probably bring something for Grendal as well. She walked to the Mickey D's across the street and bought a cheeseburger to go. She shoved it into her backpack on top of her books, tucked the motorcycle part under her arm, and ran to the bus stop.

She got off the bus in front of St. Drogo's and walked the two blocks to the pet shop, then decided to drop the package off at the park before she went home. Finn and Raynor were sitting at the picnic table when she got there.

"We've been discussing the *sluagh*," Finn said. "The fact that the creature's coming around is unnatural, but Raynor thinks it might have been attracted by the scent of Lucy or Grendal. They smell of Mag Mell."

"Can dead things be curious?" Teagan asked.

"They can be hungry," Raynor said. "There are similarities. What's this?" he asked when Teagan handed him the newsprint-wrapped bundle.

"A token of Leo's esteem," Teagan said. "He thinks Brynhild's good for picking up girls."

"He'd better not put a necker knob on my steering wheel," Raynor said.

Something *shifted* against the pyracantha bushes behind Raynor, and Teagan jumped.

"Relax," Raynor told her. "He's a friend."

"Joe, Teagan; Teagan, Joe," Finn said as Raynor started unwrapping the layers of newspaper. "I was just telling Joe about you, Tea. He's here to help keep the little beasties from escaping Mag Mell."

Joe stepped around Raynor, and Teagan almost gasped. It was as if part of a painting had suddenly stepped off the canvas, and managed to do it without leaving a hole where it had been. Joe blended in completely when he stood against the vegetation. It wasn't until he moved between Teagan and the red bricks of the library that she could see him plainly.

He was about seven feet tall, and wore a shabby coat that looked as if it might be made of bark. Yellow owl-eyes blinked at her from between his bushy brows and long gray beard. There was something incredibly *familiar* about him.

"My mother painted someone very like you," Teagan said. "Are you . . . the Green Man?" She knew he wasn't, even as she said it. Joe's eyes were larger than the eyes of the Green Man in her mother's painting, and his gray hair and beard hung more like Spanish moss than leaves.

"That would have been my brother," Joe said. "The good-looking one of the family. Always peeping his pretty face out of the greenery, posing for sculptors and artists."

"Family? Are there two Green Men?"

"There are nine, but we drifted apart about two hundred million years ago." He elbowed Raynor, who was studying the lump he had unwrapped. "Get it? Drifted apart!"

"Wait . . . Pangaea?" Teagan asked. "Didn't the supercontinent start to drift apart two hundred million years ago?"

"I told you the girl has a brain," Finn said. "She's impressive."

Joe breathed deeply. "She smells like good dirt, too! Earthy, with a hint of hoppers and crawlies."

"Mealworms and crickets in my pocket," Teagan explained. "I'm taking them home for a sprite. So there's a Green Man on each continent? That would only be seven."

"Continents are temporary," Joe said. "Things shift. We are nine, but right now, one brother sleeps under ice, and one sleeps under the sea. They are dreaming of good seeds, waiting until the world changes again. Forests are complex, complicated things—a few million years is sometimes not enough to get proper planning and preparation done. When new continents rise, my brothers will wake. Their plans will be in place, and their work will begin."

"What is that thing, anyway?" Finn nodded toward Raynor's greasy gift.

"I don't know," Teagan said.

"Something for that abomination he's hiding, from the smell of it." Joe wrinkled his nose. "I had hoped that you'd get over machines when the steam age ended, Raynor."

"Have some respect for your elders. We've earned the right to a little fun now and then." He scraped some grime off the hunk of metal. "It's a carburetor."

"Elders?" Teagan asked.

"I may be older than the continent," Joe said, "but I'm no more than a sprout to Raynor."

Raynor adjusted his glasses to get a better view, and pried something loose. "She doesn't need all of that information."

"Raynor has trust issues with Highborn," Joe said in what Teagan could only assume he meant to be a whisper. "He's been burned before."

"We've discussed it," Raynor said.

"Thomas said Raynor was the guardian angel to Irish saints since before there was an Ireland," Teagan said. "What was before Ireland?"

"Yggdrasil, for one. She's older even than Mag Mell, though they're both from the first creation." He leaned toward Teagan. "Don't let Raynor bother you. He's afraid you're going to get Finn into more trouble than he can handle. We were just discussing it."

"How would I do that?"

"Joe," Finn interrupted, "weren't you about to talk to some trees?" Joe nodded. He knelt, put his palm down on the dirt, and pressed. His hand sank in as if the soil were just muddy water, and he moved it back and forth in a stirring motion.

"If I can find a wakeful root, I can join the conversation."

"Trees talk through their roots?" Teagan asked.

"Through the fungi," Joe said. "Their roots are connected by threads of mycorrhizal fungi."

"I haven't studied plants," Teagan said, squatting down beside him. Finn stood over them.

"Fungi aren't plants," Joe explained. "Plants create their own food from light and air, like I do. Fungi must consume something that was once or is still living, like you do. But they're not truly animals, either." He hesitated, as if he had found something, then shook his head and reached deeper into the ground.

"Mycorrhizal threads grow right into the cells of plant

roots. Through them, the whole forest is connected. At one time, my forest stretched from the Great Lakes to the Everglades, from the coast to the plains . . . a single root mat of connections. The conversations were . . . wonderful. Now it's chopped to bits by roads"—he glared at the carburetor Raynor had set on the picnic table—"and towns, and the good dirt is ripped up by plows. The root mat I'd worked on for millions of years is gone. The trees and plants are isolated."

"Times change," Raynor said.

"And they will change again." Joe was almost shoulder deep in the ground now. "Ah! Here we go. The old willow." He closed his eyes. "Interesting. Some of his root hairs are grafted to root hairs from Mag Mell. And there are many voices. This little piece of green is all connecting through the willow, Raynor."

"You mean the whole park?"

"Yes."

"Then tell the willow to stop." Raynor set the carburetor down.

"He couldn't if he wanted to," Joe said. "It's Mag Mell who's bonding to him. There's something in this creation she needs."

"What?" Finn asked.

"Aiden," Joe said. "That's your brother, isn't it, Teagan? Finn was telling me all about your family. I'd like to meet him."

"Tell Mag Mell to toss Fear Doirich out here where I can get him," Raynor said. "And then Aiden can visit."

"Might," Teagan corrected quickly. "*Might* visit." Fear Doirich wasn't the only scary thing in Mag Mell. Joe pulled his arm out of the ground and brushed off bits of soil that clung to it.

"You know she's not strong enough to do that. She wasn't strong enough the day he led the Sídhe in. It's not as if she wants Fear there, or welcomed him."

"So," Finn said. "The big monkey bats that you said were trying to come out this morning—"

"Were looking for Aiden. Mag Mell needs him back. Something very bad is going on in there, Raynor."

FIFTEEN

"WE probably didn't need to run the whole way," Finn said when Teagan stopped to catch her breath before she went up the steps of the house.

"Big monkey bats," Teagan said. "Raynor said *big* ones were trying to get out, not little swat-bats."

"They're just flying monkeys," Finn said. "I saw worse things at your zoo."

"You've never read *The Wonderful Wizard of Oz*, have you?"

"I haven't."

"Have you seen the movie?"

"No."

"There were some really scary flying monkeys in Oz. They carried Dorothy—the heroine—and her friends away."

"And?"

"I had nightmares for weeks after I saw that movie."

"You had nightmares about monkeys? You?"

"They were *really* scary monkeys. They had . . . vests. And hats."

"Pfft." Finn wasn't even trying to hold back his laughter. "You faced hellhounds, and you think that movie monkeys are scary?"

"You thought my dad was scary."

"That's a different thing," Finn said, opening the door for her. "Your da *is* scary. Mamieo is watching over the boyo. She wouldn't let a bat-monkey flap away with him, not even a large one. Even if one got past Raynor, which it didn't."

"That we know of—" Teagan stopped.

Aiden, Lennie, and a total stranger were in the middle of the living room. Their palms and feet were on the ground, and their rumps in the air, as if they were doing the camel walk. All three of them turned their heads to look as Teagan and Finn came in the door.

"That's my sister," Aiden said. "And *the Mac Cumhaill.*" The woman smiled.

"Hello. I'm Zoë Giordano. Call me Zoë."

The dance therapist.

"Your brother was just telling me about Elvis."

"He was?"

"Yep," Aiden said. "The King."

Zoë straightened up and reached both hands high over her head, and both Aiden and Lennie followed suit. She was wearing a tie-dyed full-body leotard with an orange peasant skirt over it, and her curly black hair, streaked with gray, hung to her shoulders.

"We're doing a few stretches before we get started. Would you care to join us?"

"No, thank you." Teagan motioned toward the kitchen. "We've got to . . . take care of something." Like feeding the sprite that for some reason was not hiding in Aiden's hair. "Is Dad home, Aiden?"

"Everybody's home," Aiden said. "Except Abby. They're in the kitchen *pretending* not to listen to us."

"Could you just"—Zoë wrinkled her nose—"shut the door as you go through? I hate disturbing your whole family like this."

"Come on back, Tea," Mr. Wylltson called. Mr. Wylltson and Mamieo were sitting at the table with cups of tea. Finn nudged Teagan and pointed.

Thomas sat on a chair in the corner where her mother's easel had once stood, reading one of Aileen's books to Roisin, translating the words into old Irish as they went. Grendal was sitting like a child in his lap.

"Go ahead and shut the door, Rosebud," Mr. Wylltson said. Teagan pulled it shut behind them.

"Aiden's *talking* to someone who's practically a stranger?" Teagan asked.

"Started right up the moment she came through the door. I expect it was Ms. Skinner's recommendation that did it."

"Recommendation?" Finn pulled out a chair and sat down. "I thought Skinner couldn't stand the woman."

"Exactly," Mr. Wylltson said. "What more of a recommendation would he need?"

"Where's Lucy?" Teagan asked.

Mamieo pointed at a corner of the ceiling. "Collecting spider webs. She's been about it all day."

"Lucy!" Teagan called. "Look what I've got." She pulled out the bag of crickets. The sprite zipped down in front of her. Teagan took a cricket from the bag, and Lucy's eyes flashed shocking pink. She snatched the insect, ripped off its hind legs, and started eating it head first.

"Fascinating." Mr. Wylltson leaned closer. "And disgusting."

"You can see her, then?" Finn asked.

"No. It's like the cricket is being shredded, and disappearing one bite at a time."

"She was really hungry," Teagan said, picking up the cricket legs. Lucy looked up from her meal long enough to chitter at her.

"You can't keep them," Teagan scolded. "They'd only end up in Aiden's hair." The sprite finished the head, then peeled off the chitinous parts—the wings and shell—before she ate the rest. Teagan decided to wait to clean up until after Lucy had finished.

"I brought you something, too, Grendal." She fished the cheeseburger out of her backpack. Grendal jumped out of Thomas's lap as soon as he saw it and came across the floor, climbed up a chair, and hopped onto the table. Teagan held it out to him, and he took it slowly, as if she were offering him great wealth.

"Thank you," he said, and bowed. He took the cheeseburger, reverently folded the paper back, and took a tiny nibble. "Ah," he said, then nibbled a little more.

"Now you've done it," Finn said.

"What?"

"He's sounding like Maggot Cat's little friend, isn't he? It's probably the cheeseburgers that caused the *cat-sídhe* rot."

Mr. Wylltson got up and took a box of cornstarch from the cabinet. He poured some in his hand, and leaned down.

"Dad," Teagan said. "Don't—" He blew the fine powder over the table. Grendal saw it coming and jumped to the floor, but Lucy wasn't watching. The cornstarch fell like snow, but it didn't settle on the sprite. It vibrated around her like dust dancing on a speaker.

"She exists as energy!" Mr. Wylltson said. The sprite's eyes flashed red and purple as she lifted into the air, the cornstarch cloud orbiting around her.

"Cover your nose," Teagan warned. "She pulls nose hair when she's angry." Mr. Wylltson cupped his hands over his face.

"I apologize, Lucy," he said. "It's just hard to treat someone you can't see as a person. I wasn't thinking." The sprite lit on his hand and tried to pull his fingers away from his face. "Hmmm. I can feel her as well."

Grendal settled into nibbling his cheeseburger again, making mewling noises at it.

The kitchen door flew open, and Abby stormed straight to the sink.

"I'm going to kill him." She turned on the faucet.

"Who?" Finn asked. "I'd like to meet the man before he dies."

"Jing. You know what he does, Tea? He brings the whole soccer team into the shop to have their toenails painted."

"Jinghez Khan paints his toenails?" Mr. Wylltson still had

his hands cupped over his face, but Teagan could tell by his voice he was smiling.

"I thought his name was Jing," Teagan said.

"Jinghez," Mr. Wylltson corrected. "It was on his library card application when he was five. It's one of the alternate spellings of Genghis."

"He doesn't want anybody to know that," Abby said. "He's just Jing now."

"Oho." Finn rocked his chair back on two legs. "But *you* knew it, didn't you?"

"So? I've known him for years."

"Gabigail and Jinghez Khan. I suppose he has plenty of this *testosterone* you were telling the boyo about?"

"They do call him the Mighty Khan," Teagan said. Abby turned brick red. She rolled up her sleeves, turned, and started scrubbing her hands vigorously.

"And this Jinghez paints his toenails?" Mamieo shook her head. "It's unnatural."

"They wanted wolverines on their big toes for luck, right? It's the school mascot."

"So, why do you want to kill him?" Mr. Wylltson asked. "If you like the young man—"

"*They came in right after practice.* What, do they think I like sweaty toe jam?" She finished scrubbing, reached to turn off the faucet, and froze. Lucy was hovering right in front of her.

"Oh. My. God. Is that Lucy? She's, like . . . a disturbance in the Force!"

"Dad dusted her with cornstarch," Teagan explained. "She's

not a happy sprite." Lucy turned and dove through the stream of running water, splashing it out on the counter. Some of the white powder orbiting her was washed away in the stream.

"She's washing it off," Abby said. "That's so cute."

Lucy did a flip turn and dove through again and again, until every bit of powder was gone, then sat on the countertop and buzzed like a beetle until she was dry. When she was done, she settled on the table with her back turned pointedly toward John Wylltson.

"Is it safe to take my hands down now?" Mr. Wylltson asked.

"It is," Mamieo said. "The bug is giving you the cold shoulder."

"Do we have ice cream?" Abby asked. "Because I seriously need some spumoni."

While Abby rooted in the freezer, Teagan offered Lucy a mealworm. It quickly went the way of the cricket, and then Lucy lifted into the air, her eyes flashing purple as she hovered in front of Teagan.

"What are you up to, bug?" Finn asked. Lucy leaned forward like a tiny Tinker Bell and touched her face to the tip of Teagan's nose.

"Ew," Finn said. "That creature's been eating insects."

Lucy settled back onto the table and helped herself to another mealworm.

Teagan had completely forgotten about Thomas sitting in the corner until the Highborn started laughing.

"What's funny?" Finn asked.

"This place shouldn't be called the Wylltsons'," Thomas said.

"It should be called the Widdershins'. Everything here is backwards. A sprite and a *cat-sídhe*"—he waved at Lucy and Grendal—"eating together. They're deadly enemies. And Finn, the purest Fir Bolg blood left in this world, made to mend and tend. But what do you do? Fight!"

"That's what Doirich's curse does, then, isn't it?" The corners of Mamieo's mouth turned down. "Forces the boyo to be something no Fir Bolg should be."

"We might speak a bit more softly." Mr. Wylltson motioned toward the living room.

Teagan pulled a chair over by the door and sat down. "I'll keep an ear on them, Dad. They can't hear us over that music."

"I'd be a lover, not a fighter, if I could," Finn said. "But it was never up to me."

"Curses and covenants I can understand," Thomas said. "But not *the Mac Cumhaill* living in a Highborn's nest. Teagan, you are at least part Highborn—made to rule and reign, gather destroyers and bend them to your will. And what do you do? Tend beasts. It's completely un-Highborn. Unless . . . there was Moll, Mab's daughter with one of Fionn's men."

Roisin looked up and frowned at the mention of Mab's name, but then Grendal mewed at her and she went back to looking at pictures in the book Thomas had handed her.

"I never heard Mab had a child with one of the Fianna," Mamieo said.

"Goblin girls find warriors irresistible."

"Which Fianna would do such a thing?" Mamieo asked.

"Caílte Mac Rónáin."

"The hound master? No!"

"Yes. He had a fling with the Queen of the Sídhe. Fear wasn't very happy about it, either."

"Hound master?" Teagan asked, putting the rest of the crickets and mealworms in a plastic container so she could refrigerate them.

"Not the godless beasties that chased you, girl," Mamieo assured her. "Caílte's hounds were the Cú Faoil. They fought beside Fionn's men."

"Irish wolfhounds," Mr. Wylltson said. "Julius Caesar wrote about them in his *Commentaries on the Gallic War.* They could snap the neck of a wolf the way a terrier snaps the neck of a rat."

"They're poor imitations that carry the name today," Mamieo said. "Little cousins of the real thing. Caílte's hounds were battle dogs, the size of ponies. Smart enough to think it through if you set them to a task, and faithful enough to get it done no matter how long it took. Caílte Mac Rónáin was the fastest runner of the Fianna, and if he hadn't been, he couldn't have run with the Cú Faoil." She glared at Thomas. "Now, what's this fabrication about the man?"

"It's no fabrication," Thomas insisted. "Caílte was fast, but he didn't run from Mab. She bore a daughter by him, and sent the child out as a changeling."

"Like a cuckoo laying its eggs in another bird's nest." Mamieo snorted. "That's no kind of *máthair.*"

"She's Mab," Thomas said. "Did you expect her to nurse it? She left the girl with a family not far from the hill where she'd met Caílte."

"What happened to Moll then?" Mamieo asked.

Thomas dragged his chair to the table and lowered his voice.

"When she was twelve, Mab called the soul out of her, so that her earthly mother thought that she had died. They put her in a coffin and buried her in the churchyard. That night, the phookas dug her up and carried her to Mag Mell for her trial."

"So, what happens at these trials?" Abby asked as she filled a bowl with ice cream.

"They looked into her to see if she was worthy to be woken," Thomas said.

"Woken?"

"Highborn blood lies dormant in the half blooded creatures Mab sends out," Thomas said. "Until something stirs it."

"Caílte's girl is living as one of the wicked goblins?" Mamieo said. "I don't believe a word of it."

"Moll was physically the living image of Mab," Thomas said. "But inside she was . . . defective. She had too much of her father in her to ever become Sídhe. Mab forced her back into the coffin and ordered it put it back in the churchyard they'd found it in."

"She buried her daughter alive?" Finn asked.

"Shhh!" Teagan waved. The music in the living room had stopped. She had just started to push the door open when it started again. "Never mind. Just a CD change."

"*Tried* to bury her daughter alive," Thomas said. "But Fear was furious about Mab's affair with Caílte. He wanted to make her suffer for it. He told the pallbearers to give the child to the first person they met, and instructed the phookas to protect her all her life. He forced Mab to watch her own image grow old and die."

"A wee coffin! It's Moll Anthony of Kildare!" Mamieo set her teacup down. "Her that died twice! I know the next part of the story well, though I've never heard the beginning. So Moll Anthony was Caílte's child, then, was she? But she didn't live in the time of the Fianna."

"Time runs differently in Mag Mell," Thomas said.

Teagan nodded. The last time they'd traveled to Mag Mell, they'd been there for a day, while only hours passed in Chicago. In her mother's books it worked the other way as well—someone might spend a week in Mag Mell and return to find a century gone.

Mr. Wylltson frowned. "Am I unfamiliar with the story of Moll Anthony? Or is it one I have forgotten?"

"The Anthonys lived by the old Hill of Allen, where the Fianna, including Caílte Mac Rónáin, had their home in ages past," Mamieo said. "Little Jamie Anthony was walking one day when he came upon a funeral—six strong men carrying a wee coffin. They followed him to his own doorstep.

"The boyo ran inside to tell his *máthair*, and when they came out, the men had gone, leaving the coffin behind. The woman heard a tapping inside, and fearing someone had shut a child up in the box, she opened it. There was the girl, alive and breathing. The family took her in, and when they were of age, Jamie married her."

"I thought Irish stories didn't have happy endings," Abby said. "Didn't you tell me that, Tea?"

"Happy for whom?" Thomas asked. "One day, when she was at the market, who should walk in but her earthly *máthair,* the woman who had seen her daughter buried at twelve years of age? 'It's me, Mother,' Moll says, and shows a strawberry birthmark to prove it."

"That's creepy." Abby scraped the last bit of ice cream out of her bowl. "But it's still a happy ending."

"They say Moll had the healing touch with animals of all kinds." Mamieo poured herself another cup of tea, and offered some to Mr. Wylltson, but he shook his head.

"Mab won't hear her mentioned," Thomas said. "The rumor is that if the affinity for animals didn't come from Mab as well as Caílte, Caílte's blood would not have been strong enough to pass it on. If you have the same 'defect' Moll did, Teagan, that would be proof that it came through the blood of Mab's family." He smiled. "She would hate that."

"So, it's like a goblin birth defect?" Abby asked. "And Tea got it from one of those regressive genes?"

"I believe you mean recessive, Abigail," Mr. Wylltson said.

"Whatever. It's on both sides of your family, right?"

"May we join the party?"

Teagan nearly fell out of her chair. The music in the other room was still playing, and she hadn't noticed the door open. But Zoë Giordano was standing right beside her.

"I want to show her Mom's books," Aiden said.

"If you wouldn't mind?" Zoë looked at John Paul Wylltson.

"Of course not. I'm very proud of my wife's work."

Aiden pulled Zoë over to Roisin.

"This is my aunt Rosin. She's in Mom's books. I'll show you." Zoë sat down on the floor next to Roisin, and Aiden crawled into her lap. He turned to the page of *Loveleaves and Woodwender* where a little girl in white danced in front of a house made of trees.

"That's where Mom and Roisin lived. It's in Mag Mell."

Roisin looked at the dance therapist, her face very still.

"It's okay, Roisin," Aiden said. "She's huggable." Roisin leaned against Zoë, and the older woman put an arm around her.

"You have an interesting family, John Wylltson," Zoë said. "Aileen's death must have been very hard on all of you."

"I dreamed about Mom, Zoë," Aiden said, reaching up and twining his fingers in her hair.

"You did?"

"She was playing chess with the bad guys," Aiden said. "But she didn't win."

Everyone in the room was frozen, just watching them.

"Are you certain?" Zoë said. "Sometimes winning doesn't look like you think it will."

"But does winning have a happy ending?"

"Yes," Zoë said. "I think it does."

"Mom said Irish stories never have happy endings."

Zoë picked up another one of Aileen Wylltson's books.

"What about her books? Do they have happy endings?"

"Yes."

"Then maybe her heart knew something that her head didn't. I believe in happy endings."

Roisin got up. Teagan was surprised to see that there were tears on her cheeks. She wiped them away with the palms of her hands, went to the maid's stairs, and smiled at Zoë before she disappeared up them.

"I . . ." Mr. Wylltson's eyes had the cloudy look they got when he was trying to access his lost memories.

"Will you have some tea?" Mamieo asked Zoë.

"No, thank you," Zoë said, smiling. "I have another client waiting." She stood up. "I'll be back next Monday, all right, Aiden?"

"Yep," Aiden said. "I'll sing while you dance."

"I'd like that!"

Finn showed her to the door.

"Do you suppose she's Irish, then?" Mamieo asked when she was gone.

"With a name like Giordano?" Abby said. "I don't think so."

"But she fits right in, doesn't she?" Thomas picked up the book Aiden had left on the floor. "She's completely widdershins, too."

"I like her," Aiden said. "Her dances untangle me."

"Too bad we can't all get untangled." Abby put her bowl in the sink, just as her phone chirped. She pulled it out of her pocket and turned it off. "Jing," she said. "I'm not taking calls from him. Or texts."

As Abby tried to leave the room, Teagan caught her elbow.

"You know he likes you, too," she whispered.

"Yeah."

"Does this have something to do with the book in the river?"

Abby sighed. *"For never was a story of more woe / Than this of Juliet and her Romeo."*

"Did you just quote *Shakespeare?!"* Teagan gasped.

"I know, right?" Abby rubbed her temples with two fingers. "I think I have a migraine coming on."

SIXTEEN

THANKS for loaning me your notes," Teagan said as Jing settled into the desk beside her, his cell phone in hand. *Jinghez "Romeo" Khan.* She had to hide her smile. How *was* he going to become president with a name like that?

"Not a problem," Jing said. "Word in the halls is we won't have Diaz today. They found a sub." He fiddled with his cell phone. "Abby wasn't at the pep rally this morning. And she isn't answering her phone."

"She has a migraine," Teagan said. "She said she was going to sleep it off."

"An honest-to-god migraine, or an avoid-the-jerk migraine?"

"Honest-to-god," Teagan said. "She was lying in a dark room with a cold pack on her head watching psychedelic pinwheels spin when I left for school."

"At your house?"

Teagan nodded.

"I hear she's been spending a lot of time at your place lately. So how come you never ask me over?"

"I don't play matchmaker," Teagan said. "I wouldn't be very

good at it. But Jing, about the toenails? Probably not a good idea to go to Smash Pad right after practice."

"Tell me something I don't know. I figured that out about ten seconds after my boys took their shoes off." He put his flip-flop-clad foot up on the desk. "That's a fine wolverine, though. I'm wearing these to show it off. We're going to win this game."

Cade, one of Jing's teammates, turned around in his seat and stretched.

"We always win, Khan."

Teagan and Molly both leaned closer to Jing's foot, examining Abby's artwork.

"It's got hearts for eyes," Molly said.

"What?"

"Your wolverine has little tiny hearts for eyes."

Jing leaned over to stare at his foot.

"Damn." He turned to Cade. "Take off your shoe, man."

Cade pulled off his shoe and sock.

"I can't look," Jing said. "Tell me—"

"No hearts," Molly said. "Look for yourself." Cade held his foot up for Jing to see.

"Damn," Jing said again, but he was smiling.

"What, is it shoes-off day around here?" Teagan looked up to see Rafe and Isabeau coming into the room. Today Isabeau wore a pair of hot-pink Gucci wraparound shades, a form-fitting pullover, a pair of skinny jeans, and pink flats. Abby would have approved. She would *not* have approved of the pink lipstick on Rafe's face, though.

"What are you two doing here again?" Molly demanded.

"We would never skip this class," Rafe told her. "It's the only one we have together."

"You're going to get kicked out as soon as the new substitute arrives."

"Not if I can talk her into letting us stay," Rafe said. "Live for the day, right? But don't worry, we'll sit all the way over here where we won't bother anyone." They took the desks closest to the door.

"The sub is late," Molly said. "That's not very professional—"

"Shhh, he's here," Rafe hissed, then whistled appreciatively as the teacher stepped into the room. The man hesitated for a moment, clearly for effect, and the hair on Teagan's neck stood up. She knew him.

Kyle's face looked older, but he was definitely Kyle. When she had first seen him, walking across her backyard, he'd been totally Abercrombie. Now he was *Esquire,* right down to his designer wraparound shades.

"Your look is catching on, Isabeau," Rafe said. "Maybe I should get some glasses, too."

Kyle reached up to touch his frames.

"Unfortunately, it's not a fashion statement. I have a *wicked* eye condition."

"Is it contagious?" Molly asked. "Because if it's something like pinkeye, you shouldn't be here."

"'Is it contagious?'" He turned, and Teagan could see herself reflected in the mirrored lenses. "Now, that's an interesting question, one we will explore further. But first, let me introduce myself. My name is Mr. Bullen." He walked up the aisle, stopped in front of Teagan's desk, leaned down, and licked her forehead.

Teagan jumped up, trying to wipe the saliva away with her hand . . . but her forehead was dry. *Kyle's saliva had sunk in, and she could feel it buzzing through her.* She shook her head, trying to clear the cottony, cloudy feeling in her brain, and sank back into her seat.

"Holy crap," Rafe said.

"What the hell was that?" Jing had come from behind his desk. "You don't just walk in here and touch our ladies."

"Keep your jersey on, jock," Mr. Bullen said. "I'm the teacher here. If I do something, it has an educational value."

"It's Jing, *suit,* and what's the educational value in sliming a student?" A few people snickered, but ducked their heads when Jing glared at them.

"Well, let's see if there's anyone here smart enough to figure it out." Mr. Bullen turned to the class. "Why do you think Ms. Wylltson reacted the way she did?"

Molly pulled her bottle of hand sanitizer out of her purse and offered it to Teagan, who squirted a glob in her hand and rubbed it on her forehead.

"You contaminated her with bodily fluids," Molly said, as if it really had been a class demonstration of some kind. "That's not acceptable in our society. So . . . you're making a comment about our social mores?"

"Contaminated." Mr. Bullen wiped the corner of his mouth with the tip of his pinky finger, as if making sure no saliva remained. "What's your name?"

"Molly Geltz."

The cloud had settled inside Teagan, and she could feel it spreading, flowing down through her body. *Don't panic,* she told herself.

Mr. Bullen ignored her. "Well, Molly *Geltz*. I'm sure all of your teachers enjoy having you in class. I am going to enjoy you more. I have your full and complete attention, don't I?"

"Yes," Molly said uncertainly.

"And the rest of you as well. Because Ms. Wylltson and I did something unconventional."

"You know him, Tea?" Jing asked.

"Of course we know one another." Kyle smiled. "This was all planned."

"Bullshit," Jing said. "Tea's a friend of mine, and she's not that good an actor. She's scared of you."

Getting civilians involved with the creatures is a very bad idea. It'll get them killed.

"It's fine, Jing. I'm good."

"You're sure?"

"I'm sure."

Jing sat, but he was still shaking his head.

All she had to do to send Kyle back to Mag Mell was stab him with a piece of iron. And thanks to Aiden, she had one with her. She pulled her backpack closer with her foot. Her steel forceps were still in there, and they probably had enough iron in them to do the job. But she had to have him alone in the room, because people could be injured when he exploded. Or worse, dragged to Mag Mell with him.

"Mrs. Rapp was kind enough to provide a lesson plan." Mr.

Bullen held up a piece of paper. He gave them their reading assignments, but Teagan could feel him staring at her as she pretended to read.

"Mr. Bullen," she managed when the bell rang, "I was wondering if I could speak to you alone?"

"I'd be delighted."

"I don't think that's a good idea, Tea." Jing was standing protectively behind her.

"I do know him, Jing. And we need to discuss something."

Jing shook his head. "Fine. Whatever." He left the room reluctantly.

Two girls from the class hung back, clearly wanting Kyle's attention.

"Mr. Bullen," one said, "could you help me with—"

Kyle didn't even look at her. "Get out," he interrupted. "I want to talk to Ms. Wylltson."

Both girls scurried for the door, and Teagan's knees started to shake. She was alone with the Highborn. She swallowed, forcing herself to stand still. He'd enjoy her fear if he could see it.

"You like the older face?" Kyle turned from side to side to give her a better view. "Glamour is wonderful stuff. A little pinch, a tiny twist, and people see what you want them to see."

"What did you do to me?" Teagan demanded.

"Let's just say we went viral."

"Viral?"

"Well, retroviral."

Teagan shook her head.

"Come on, smart girl. It's the twenty-first century, not the thirteenth. You've heard of gene therapy. A retrovirus integrates its own genetic material into the chromosome of the human cell, *changing* it. Not that you have ever been exactly *human*. But it's the same principle."

He circled her like a shark, and Teagan held still, fighting the urge to run. He had to be just a tad closer . . .

"I gave you a little boost. A bit of my own genetic material to set you straight and get rid of that defective Milesian crap." He stopped, and stood behind her.

"You're changing my DNA?"

"You'll be a whole new person. Happy birthday to you! Now—" He leaned toward her, and Teagan could feel his breath on her neck.

She stabbed back hard with the forceps, bracing herself for the shock wave. Kyle screamed, and she whirled away. The forceps were sticking out of his thigh.

"Shit. These are Armani." He jerked the forceps out, and blood spread across the front of his pants.

"You're here in the flesh!"

"Flesh." Kyle sniffed the bloody steel, and just for an instant, his jaw appeared longer, his forehead sloped back, and a long, pink tongue flicked past pointed teeth, licking the blood from the forceps. And then he was Kyle again.

"Makes things more interesting, don't you think?" He smiled at Teagan. "What? Did you glimpse the family resemblance just then, cousin? Did you see the *predator?*"

"Stop fooling around, Kyle." Isabeau came back through the

door, without Rafe and without her accent. "You chose wrong, *Tiger.* I'm the one who's walking without my flesh and bones." She pushed her sunglasses on top of her head. Her eyes were like tar pits.

Kyle pulled off his own shades. The skin around his eyes was reddened, and his upper lashes were missing. "I *said* it was a wicked eye condition, didn't I? The thing is, even glamour needs something to work with, and when someone duct tapes your eyeballs open, you lose lashes when you peel it off. It's payback time, cuz."

Teagan put her hand to her head. She still felt dizzy. "How did you get here?"

"The same way anybody would. Stepped into Ireland and caught a flight out of Dublin. There's an angel guarding the park, but that doesn't mean we have to stay away. It just means we have to come the long way round. There's just *so* much to see and do in Chicago."

"Feeling a little woozy, Tea?" Isabeau asked. "You won't be able to stay in this creation. Highborn don't like it here."

"My mother did."

"She hadn't been licked by Kyle, and cured of all that nasty Milesian in her." Isabeau turned to Kyle. "That was disgusting. You were supposed to kiss her."

"That *would* have been disgusting." Kyle's pink tongue flicked across his lips. "Licking wasn't so bad."

Isabeau came closer and touched Teagan's face.

"Any fever yet? You're taking this better than I thought you would. Maybe Fear was right about you. Speak of the devil."

She pressed her hand against her chest. "I've been carrying a message for you."

She leaned close to Teagan and opened her mouth. It wasn't Isabeau's voice that came out. It was Fear Doirich's voice. His carrion-tinted breath wrapped around Teagan, bringing back all the horror of the dead garden in Mag Mell.

"I am your god, goblin child. Come to me."

"Have you been watching *The Exorcist*?" Kyle asked when she shut her mouth.

Isabeau shook herself, then spat in the corner.

"Shut up, Kyle. That tasted nasty. And I've had to hold it in since we left Mag Mell."

"I'm not ever going back there," Teagan said.

"Of course you are. And, you'll have to bring Aiden. Fear is waiting to welcome you with open arms. But he *will* need a sacrifice."

"I'm not—"

"You have a couple days to decide, of course," Isabeau said. "We don't want to travel while you're sick. The change *can* cause nausea and vomiting. I don't want to be on a plane next to that."

"A plane?"

"There is an unpleasant angel guarding the only gate near here," Kyle said. "We'll go back the way we came. If you don't come with us, and bring Aiden, we're going to kill your father and play games with all of your friends. Facebook is *wonderful*, isn't it? We know just who they are."

"Please tell the Mac Cumhaill we're here." Isabeau twirled a dark curl of hair around her finger. "Tell him I'm waiting for him. That will be fun."

"*Oh, my god!*" A girl from the next class had just come through the door. "You're bleeding!"

"'*Oh, my god,*'" Mr. Bullen mimicked. "High schools are such violent places these days."

Isabeau flipped her shades down.

"It's 'orreeble!"

Kyle forced the bloody forceps into Teagan's hand and limped toward the door. "I need to go clean up. Shit. Triple shit. My shoe is full of blood. Tomorrow, Ms. Wylltson!" He squished away down the hall.

"Tomorrow," Isabeau said, and followed him.

Teagan stepped out of the classroom, her head spinning. She took a few steps, then leaned against the wall, trying not to throw up. *The change can cause nausea and vomiting.*

She had get help, to tell someone Kyle and Isabeau were here. She pulled out her phone and dialed her home number. She almost wept with relief when Mamieo picked up.

"Mamieo!"

"What is it, girl?"

"I . . ."

Teagan shook her head. Something was off. Some piece didn't fit, didn't make sense, and she couldn't think clearly enough to figure out what it was. But if she told Finn, he would try to fight them. And he would be killed, because he would be alone. Raynor couldn't leave the gate to help.

". . . I'm not feeling well, so I'm coming home early. I just thought I'd let you know." Teagan hung up, walked out of the school to the street, and took the first bus home.

When she stepped through the door, her father was reading a newspaper in the living room while Aiden built a house for Lucy in the front alcove.

"Are you all right?" Mr. Wylltson asked. "Mamieo said you weren't feeling well."

"I'm just woozy. Where is everybody?"

"Finn went to the Black Feather with Thomas and Roisin," Aiden said, adding another block to his construction. "He's going to help me build a better house when he gets back."

"Thomas is going to get a job," Mr. Wylltson explained.

"Abby?"

"She's still upstairs."

Teagan could hear Mamieo's teakettle singing in the kitchen. They were all safe. For now.

Teagan licked her dry lips. She was incredibly thirsty. She went to the kitchen for a glass of water.

"There you are," Mamieo said. "You sit right down. I started the kettle as soon as you called, and the tea is about done. You're flushed, and that's a fact." Teagan sat at the table while Mamieo fussed over her.

Her head was spinning, making the room tilt. Teagan gripped the edge of the table, afraid she would fall off her chair. *Gene therapy. Fear Doirich sent for me.* She was trying to put the two ideas together in her head . . . but . . . She drew in a shaky breath. He'd wanted a child to replace the son whom Fionn Mac Cumhaill—the first Mac Cumhaill—had killed. A powerful child—her child, with the blood of her Milesian grandfather, Highborn grandmother, and his own angel blood mixed in its veins.

But if her DNA changed . . . why would he still want her? The pieces didn't fit together.

She drank the tea Mamieo gave her, a strong, sweet peppermint, then went to her computer, fighting a wave of nausea. *The twenty-first century, not the thirteenth.* Goblins on the World Wide Web. She brought up her Facebook page and deleted it, then went through every social site she could think of, deleting every trace of friendship, every connection that the goblins could track through cyberspace.

Abby came downstairs, looking pale and worn out, and settled beside Teagan.

"No more pinwheels," she said, before Teagan asked. "So, did you talk to Jing? 'Cause he's been trying to call me all afternoon."

"Yes," Teagan said. "He wants to come over and see you." That should keep Abby from taking his calls for a while longer. Because if she took one of his calls, he'd probably tell her about the crazy teacher who'd licked Teagan. The teacher Teagan had stayed after class to speak to. The one she'd stabbed. It had to be all over the school by now.

The front door opened before Abby could answer, and Finn, Roisin, and Thomas came in. Thomas was carrying a plastic bag and a paper cup. Roisin had a cup in her hand as well.

"You're home early, beautiful," Finn said when he saw Teagan.

Mr. Wylltson lowered his newspaper and raised an eyebrow.

"It's the truth, John Wylltson," Finn said. "Your daughter's beautiful."

"I don't suppose I can argue with good taste." Mr. Wylltson folded the paper. "How did it go at the Black Feather?"

"There was the small issue of a social security number," Thomas said. "It seems I can't work without one."

"Houston, we have a problem." Mr. Wylltson set his newspaper down. "I hadn't considered that. You and Roisin are technically illegal aliens."

Thomas held up the bag. "Brownies and mocha, as requested by Abby."

"Mocha." Roisin nodded. "Yum!"

"I told you, right?" Abby said. "Come into the kitchen. You think potato chips are good with ice cream, wait till you try this." Abby took the bag and headed for the freezer. Thomas followed Roisin and Abby from the room.

Finn turned back to Teagan. "Your cheeks are a bit rosy, girl." He started toward her, but Aiden jumped up and caught his hand.

"You said you'd help me build a house for Lucy."

Finn winked at Tea and sat down to help Aiden with his construction. Mr. Wylltson went back to his paper.

Good, Teagan thought. She didn't want either of them to hear the questions she had to ask Thomas. Sooner or later they were going to start putting things together. And if she didn't have a plan by then, some of them might die.

She found Thomas, Grendal, and Roisin watching Abby scoop ice cream into bowls while Mamieo refilled her teapot.

"You want ice cream, Tea?" Abby asked.

"No, thanks. Thomas, the other day you said that 'we all go slumming sometimes.' Does Kyle?"

"Yes," Thomas said. "He went out to Whitechapel the last time."

"Whitechapel?" Abby stopped in mid-scoop. "Like, East London Whitechapel?"

"Fear sent him after a girl named Mary. The Sídhe had tried to take her when she was a child in Limerick."

"She had Fir Bolg blood in her, no doubt," Mamieo said, setting a cup in front of Teagan.

"Her father had more than a little Fir Bolg in him," Thomas admitted. "It manifested in his ability as a tinker. He worked at an iron foundry, making knives for the Travelers out of bits and pieces of scrap steel. Your Finn is carrying the last knife Mr. Kelly ever made. Anyway, he realized the goblins were after his little girl and took the family away. The *cat-sídhe* found her years later living in Whitechapel, and Fear Doirich sent Kyle after her."

"Mary Kelly?" Abby licked an ice cream drip off her finger. "Oh, my god. I saw this on *History's Greatest Mysteries*."

"What?" Teagan asked.

"Jack the Ripper," Abby said. "He's saying Kyle is Jack the Ripper. I talked to him, Tea! Outside your house that time, remember?"

"He called himself Jack?" Thomas frowned. "That seems a little lowbrow for Kyle."

"He didn't call himself that. Someone just came up with it. No one knew his real name. Don't you get TV in Mag Mell?

There's been like a million shows about him. He was this well-dressed guy. He murdered prostitutes in Whitechapel . . . and then just disappeared. So, Kyle killed all of those girls? All eleven?"

"I know he killed five. He talked about it when he came back."

"The canonical five," Abby said, shoving a bowl of ice cream and brownies toward Roisin. "The ones who were gutted. So what about the others?"

"We inspire, remember? Kyle killed five, and those he inspired killed the rest."

"So why'd he take their organs out?" Abby asked. "Some people thought he was some sort of doctor because he took livers and stuff."

"It's his nature," Thomas said. "Kyle is a monster. Incomplete shifters are often . . . different. Even by goblin standards."

"Incomplete?" Teagan asked.

"They can't manage a complete shift. Just bits and pieces of one because their blood is too mixed." Thomas grimaced. "They end up looking like phookas."

In her mind's eye Teagan saw the long pink tongue licking blood from the forceps; the sharp canines. This was worse than any goblin story she had ever imagined. This should not be.

"Was there a Mr. Bullen in the program?" Teagan asked Abby.

"No . . . wait! There was this journalist guy back when it was all happening. He kept bringing up the Ripper stuff because he didn't want the story to end. I think his name was Bullen."

Abby put the lid back on the ice cream bucket. "Don't worry. If Jack the Ripper shows up around here, I'll call somebody."

Teagan laid her head on Abby's shoulder. *Oh, Abby,* she wished she could say. *He's here, he's here, he's here. And I have to figure out what to do about it.*

"Hey." Abby pressed her hand against Teagan's forehead just as Finn came into the kitchen. "You're burning up. You got a bug or something, Tea? You should go to bed."

"I thought you looked a little rosy." Finn pressed his hand to her forehead where Abby's had been, and the electricity arching between them gave her shivers that turned into tooth-rattling chills.

She clamped her jaw shut so no one would notice.

"I'm feeding her peppermint tea," Mamieo said. "With a bit of red clover mixed in."

"I'll make you some of the soup my *máthair* used to—" Finn began.

"No." Teagan stood up a little too quickly and had to catch his arm for support. She let go and stepped away. "I'll just go lie down. Really."

SEVENTEEN

TEAGAN took the pillow off of her head. She'd tossed and turned after Abby and Roisin had come to bed, achy and uncomfortable in any position. Her whole body hurt. Finally she'd taken her pillow and a blanket downstairs so she wouldn't disturb the others. Now the house had been quiet for at least an hour, everyone else sleeping in their respective rooms.

"Think," she said aloud. She needed Raynor to deal with Kyle, but as long as Mag Mell held the gate open, Raynor had to stay in the park. The shadows pouring out into Chicago would be at least as bad as two Highborn Sídhe. What could she do without the angel?

Tell Finn and Mamieo. Which was exactly what Isabeau asked her to do. They wanted to deal with Finn while Raynor wasn't around.

Tell Dad. He'd call the police. And tell them what?

Let Abby call one of her uncles and tell him Jack the Ripper was teaching at her school.

Teagan shook her head, and it felt like her brain was

sloshing back and forth inside her skull. She must be getting delirious. She closed her eyes and willed her body to fight whatever was happening to her. *Just fight.* But she couldn't.

She was drifting into sleep when the heaviness settled over her. The *sluagh* was back. She was dying.

No, Teagan thought. *If I die, there will be nothing to stop Kyle and Isabeau. I won't.*

She struggled against the pressure, but it crushed the breath from her. Her head was turned away from the alcove window, but she could see the shadow of the *sluagh* on the wall. He was just outside.

Teagan, let me—

"No!" She jerked herself upright with all her might, and found she was sitting up, panting. She stood and looked out the window. The voice had broken off in midsentence, and she was afraid that Finn was outside with the creature.

It wasn't Finn who'd distracted the *sluagh,* though. It was Maggot Cat. The *cat-sídhe* was staggering down the middle of the street. The *sluagh* moved, spiderlike, across the sidewalk toward it. Maggot Cat turned and ran.

Teagan turned to call for Finn . . . and then stopped. There was a body on the couch. Her body. Its chest was rising and falling—she wasn't dead. *I'm a bilocate, like Kyle.* She reached down and touched her forehead. It was burning hot. She wasn't through the sickness, then. But she'd already changed enough to step out of her flesh and bones.

She went to the bathroom and forced herself to look in the mirror. Her eyes weren't black and oily, or solid from lid to lid.

The iris was bigger, though. And golden. She'd seen eyes almost like this before. On the Amur tiger at the zoo. But the tiger's eyes didn't flicker and shift with inner light. They weren't molten gold.

"In what distant deeps or skies," she whispered, *"Burnt the fire of thine eyes?"*

She didn't even realize she was naked until she reached up to touch her reflection in the glass. Apparently clothes were not part of the deal when a bilocate stepped out of her body. She froze, listening for any movement in the old house. Nothing. She was alone in the night.

Teagan studied her reflection. She didn't feel any different inside . . . if you didn't count the energy pounding through her. It had swept every cobweb from her brain. And suddenly she knew what to do. Knew it all, in one flash, without having to puzzle over it or put the pieces together.

Fear Doirich had summoned her. Well, she'd go to him. She'd go walking without her flesh on, like Kyle had been doing when he'd pulled her father to Mag Mell. She'd go to Fear Doirich and drag him out by his hair. Because no matter what they had done to her, she wasn't going to let him mess with her family. Not anymore.

She could give him to Raynor, and after the angel had taken care of the master of the shadows, he would be free to go after Kyle and Isabeau. All she had to do was convince Mag Mell to let her bring iron in . . . and she knew how to do that.

She was going to need to move her flesh-and-blood body to the park. It wouldn't do to drag Fear Doirich out of Mag Mell and have him land in the Wylltsons' living room. She'd leave her body sleeping in the park . . . if she could figure out how to get back inside it.

She went back to the couch, concentrating on her plan, fixing it in her mind in case the fever tried to steal it, and lay down on top of her body. It felt like she was lying on a hot, bumpy mattress . . . but nothing happened. She wiggled. Still nothing.

She relaxed, and focused on being heavy . . . and the warmth spread through her as she sank in. She felt a moment of panic as her face went under, as if she was suffocating in the sticky wetness . . . and then she could feel the heat and ache of the fever. She was in her body again. And it didn't feel very good. She forced herself to sit up slowly, making sure her body came with her.

Her school bag was still where she'd dropped it by the front door. She took the books out, went to the kitchen, and got some bottled water. Her forceps were still in the bag, stained with Kyle's blood. She washed them off and put them back in, then added two granola bars. *Socks*. Finn had told her never to travel without socks, and he'd been right. And clothes. She wasn't going to hunt the Dark Man through Mag Mell naked and barefoot. She looked up at the ceiling. She couldn't risk waking Roisin, Grendal, or Abby. But there were clean socks in the basement laundry room, waiting to be put away. And a pile of dirty laundry as well.

She went down the stairs carefully, not looking at the paintings. She needed no reminders of what was waiting for her in Mag Mell. She didn't bother to sort for pairs, just grabbed handfuls of her socks, Abby's socks, any socks, and stuffed them into the backpack. She found a pair of her jeans and one of Abby's shirts in the dirty laundry and put them in, too. Her mother's old jogging shoes were still in the coat closet in the living room. Teagan went silently back upstairs for them.

She sat on the floor to put the shoes on.

Her head was pounding, and her heart beating too hard. She had to go now, before she lost her courage, or before her fevered body gave out. She hesitated by the front door. The *sluagh* was out there somewhere. There was a chance it wouldn't notice her if she went out the back, through the gate, and into the alley. It was the same way Finn had led the goblins away before her mother died. She went through the kitchen and out the door, walked across the yard, and opened the gate. She glanced back—there was a dim light in Mamieo's window, and above that, something on the roof. Something spiderlike.

Teagan slipped through the gate, not bothering to close it behind her, and started down the alley. She'd gone half a block when the *sluagh* dropped beside her.

"I'm not dying," Teagan said.

"You are," the *sluagh* said in a voice that sounded like air escaping a corpse. "You're coming all apart." It opened its mouth wider and wider. Teagan turned and ran, jumping over trash and trying to avoid the deepest shadows. She sprinted out onto the empty street. Almost empty.

The old couple stood beneath the streetlight. Teagan saw just a flash of a wrinkled hand lifted in a wave as she wheeled and dashed for the library. If she could get to Raynor, it wouldn't matter what was after her. *If* she could get to Raynor. There were footsteps on the asphalt behind her, matching her own, and then gaining.

She was almost to the park when something caught her arm, and she screamed. A hand clamped over her mouth, and she was looking up at Finn.

"Shhh. Are you trying to wake the whole neighborhood? What are you doing out here, girl? We sent you to bed because you were sick!"

"Where's the *sluagh*?" Teagan asked. "It was right behind me."

"Your ghosties had it." Finn looked back. "They'd dragged it back into the alley. The old woman had it by the foot, and the old man was whaling away at it with his stick. I'd have stopped to help, but they seemed to have it in hand. Who *are* they?"

"I don't know."

"And what are you doing running down the street in nothing but your nightclothes?" Finn took her backpack, then pulled his hoodie off and put it over her head. Teagan shoved her arms through the sleeves. They hung over her hands, and the bottom of the sweatshirt almost reached her knees, but it was warm.

"You'll freeze," she told Finn.

"I'm freezing already." He put the backpack on. "So let's go home."

"I'm going to see Raynor."

"In the middle of the night, with a *sluagh* chasing you, and ghosties chasing it?"

"Yes." Teagan wished she could slip out of her fevered body

and think clearly enough to keep Finn out of this: "Give me my backpack."

"I'll come along with you."

"No. We're breaking up." It sounded ridiculous and childish, even to her. Especially standing there in his hoodie while he shivered in the cold.

"Right here in the middle of the street? With you staggering like you're drunk?"

"Yes," she said desperately. "So go home. I've got to go see Raynor."

She swayed, and he caught her and swung her up into his arms like a child.

"Right," Finn said. "We're broken up, then. Let's get you to that *aingeal*."

Raynor and Joe must have heard them coming, because they were standing at the gate, waiting. Joe was squatting down, like a stump that had transplanted itself onto the sidewalk. His huge yellow eyes blinked. A stump with an owl on top of it.

"She's burning up with fever." Finn carried her all the way to the picnic table before he set her down. "There's a *sluagh* hunting her. And a couple of ghosties."

"She's burning with more than that." The angel touched her head. "There's almost no Milesian left in her. How did this happen?"

"Kyle," Teagan said. "Kyle was at school today. He's walking in the flesh, and he's going to start killing people."

"Why didn't you tell me?" Finn asked.

"Because they wanted me to tell you. It was a trap."

"They?"

"He has a girl with him—Isabeau—she's living with Molly as a foreign exchange student. She's walking without her flesh."

"Isabeau? The girl with the big—"

"Yes."

"Crap." Finn ran his hand through his hair. "I put you in a car with the creature."

"I got in a car with the creature." Teagan shook her head. *Focus.* "That's not important anymore. Kyle did something to me." She felt Finn tense. "Something that's changing my DNA. I'm a bilocate, Raynor. Just like Kyle. I want you to put me to sleep like you did my dad. I'll go into Mag Mell, and I will bring the Dark Man out. But we've got to hurry. This body isn't doing too well."

"You're planning on exploding?" Finn's eyes widened. "Exploding like Kyle did when he pulled your da back to where his body lay sleeping?"

"Yes," Teagan said.

"It takes iron to send a Highborn's spirit home that way," Raynor said. "There's no iron in Mag Mell."

Teagan took the backpack from Finn. "That's why I need Joe." She turned to the tree man and pulled the forceps from her backpack. "I want Mag Mell to let me bring these in."

"Your big bloody tweezers?" Finn asked.

"They're not bloody." She held them up to make sure. "I washed them."

"She's gone mad, Raynor. Don't listen to her."

"I'm not insane. Just . . . *foggy*." Like her head was full of cotton. "These have a high iron content. They'll get the job done."

"Mag Mell's not going to let iron in," Joe said. "It's painful for her. Like poison."

"Chemotherapy's poison," Teagan countered. "But when people have cancer, they put up with it. Tell her that if I bring Fear Doirich out, Aiden can visit. She can get well again."

Joe nodded slowly. He knelt and pressed his hand deep into the soil.

"So we're going back into Mag Mell." Finn looked at the shimmer under the willow. "In the dead of night."

"*I'm* going back," Teagan said. "You're not coming with me. Joe, make sure Mag Mell knows I want to come by myself. If she lets anyone else in, I can't help her."

"She'll let you carry iron in," Joe said. "She'll make sure you're alone."

"Can Mag Mell do that?" Finn asked Raynor. "Can she keep me from going through the shimmer?"

The angel nodded.

"And"—Joe's owl eyes blinked—"she promised she wouldn't tell Fear Doirich you've come like she did last time. She says she didn't know Aiden then. She didn't understand."

"Tea, don't do this," Finn said.

"Will you put me to sleep, Raynor? *Please*."

"All right."

"No!" Finn said. "The girl can't go into Mag Mell alone. It's like hell in there. You know it is, Raynor. You walked there with Pádraig."

Raynor looked uncomfortable.

Teagan waved at the mechanical mess on the table.

"You said you needed the right tools for the job. *I'm* the right tool for this job, and you know it. Finn would have no way of getting out again if you let him come with me. Aiden won't be there to show him the way. There's only one way I'm coming out. And that's if I'm dragging Fear Doirich with me." She put her backpack on the picnic table and sat down on the bench. "Um . . . could you all please turn your backs?"

"Turn our backs?" Raynor asked. "Why?"

Teagan could feel the blush even through her fever. "When I step out of my body, my clothes don't come with me." She pulled the jeans and shirt out of the backpack. "I'll need to get dressed."

"Ah," Raynor said, and turned around. Joe took Finn's shoulder and turned him away as well.

Teagan lay down on the bench. "Do it now, please."

"Go to sleep, Teagan," the angel said. The world blinked out.

PART III: PHOOKA

EIGHTEEN

AND on, as quickly as that. She rolled over and sat up, scrambling for her clothes before she even looked to make sure their backs were still turned.

"Okay," she said. "I'm decent."

Finn turned around, and she met his eyes.

"Holy crap." He took a step back, and looked away.

Of course. She had molten eyes. Tyger eyes. Things looked . . . different through them. Finn looked more *in focus.* Joe emitted a bioluminescent glow, but something behind her was much brighter. Teagan turned to see if the library had burst into flames. Raynor was outlined in a brilliant line of white light, and a fiery corona danced around him.

"Raynor"—Teagan put up her hand to shield her eyes—"what's behind you?"

"Behind him?" Finn said. "There's nothing behind him, girl."

"There is. It's like . . . totality in a solar eclipse," Teagan said. That's exactly what it was like—when you couldn't see the moon because the sun that usually gave it light was completely hidden behind it. In the moment of totality, all you could see was the burning atmosphere of the sun around a dark disk.

"I am a *caomhnóir aingeal,*" Raynor said. "I stand in the presence of the Creator of Creation." Teagan covered her ears at the sound of his voice. It was like thunder rolling through her.

"We should have warned her, Raynor." Joe took Teagan's arm. "You can't look at the fire of creation for very long. Your eyes will burn."

"That's why the shadows won't come out while you're here," Teagan said, turning her face away.

"That is why," Raynor whispered, and it was still like rolling thunder. "Bring Fear Doirich to me, Teagan Wylltson."

Teagan took her mom's jogging shoes off of her sleeping body and put them on, pried the forceps from her own hand, and picked up the backpack.

"You're better?" Finn asked. "You're feeling better?"

"The fever's in my flesh and blood."

Finn looked from her to the flesh-and-blood body lying on the bench. "Can she be killed, Raynor?" His voice was hoarse. "This part of her that's walking into Mag Mell?"

"She can be trapped, and then her body will wither away."

"Her body?" Finn was looking down at her sleeping face. "Will it be all right here?"

"I'm an *aingeal,*" Raynor said, "Not a doctor. But this fever—" He shook his head. "You will want to hurry, Teagan. If this body dies, you will have nothing to come back to."

"*Dies?*" Finn said. "I'm not allowing it. Put her back together, Raynor!"

"I couldn't if I wanted to," he replied. "Only Teagan can do that."

"Get back in your body, Tea. I'm calling Mamieo's doctor. We can go after Fear when you're better."

"It's not your choice, Finn," Teagan said. "It's mine. I want my life to be long. I want to spend it going to school and saving chimps and figuring out what to do about you. I want that so much. But if it *can't* be long, I'm going to do something that matters. I'm going to create a future for you and for Aiden."

"What are you talking about, girl?"

"If I bring Fear Doirich out, the curse on the Mac Cumhaills will be over. The goblins will stop hunting you. Aiden will be safe." She picked up her left hand, which had fallen from the bench and was hanging limply, and crossed it over the other hand, which was on her chest. *Great. Now I really look dead.* She poked her arm and it flopped down again. "Raynor's right. I have to hurry."

"No!" Finn started toward her.

"Joe." Raynor looked at the Green Man. "Could you?" Before Finn could react, Joe wrapped his massive arms around him. Finn kicked and struggled, but the tree man lifted him off the ground.

"I'll watch over your body," Raynor assured her. "I can't guarantee it will survive the fever, but I'll watch and guard you while you sleep. No evil will come near. And I'll be waiting here if you get back."

"*If* she gets back? What kind of crap is that, Raynor? Let me down!" Finn kicked hard at Joe, who turned and walked away with him.

"Tea!" Finn stopped kicking. Teagan walked over and stood

before him for just a moment. He didn't look away from her eyes this time.

"At least take my knife, girl. It's better than tweezers." She nodded and took the knife from his boot.

"Finn Mac Cumhaill," Teagan said, "I do love you."

"I'm taking this to mean we're not broken up, then. It was the fever speaking."

"No. It wasn't the fever. You want forever, and . . . I can't promise I won't change even more. But I'm going to take care of Fear Doirich before I do." She turned and started walking toward the old willow.

"Saying 'I love you' is no way to break up with a man!" Finn yelled behind her. Then ten thousand fingers played over her, and she felt a burning in the hand that held the knife. The light shifted . . . and she was standing alone in Mag Mell.

The breeze smelled of lavender, and a waxing silver moon, just past first quarter, hung in the sky. It looked closer than Teagan had ever seen it before, close enough that she was sure she could make out craters and mountainous ridges between the mares. The herds of woolly squirrelephants that kept trying to escape to reach Aiden were clearly not nocturnal. They hung from the undersides of branches like large shaggy pears. Here and there fireflies floated above the ferns. No, not fireflies, Teagan realized. These lights were more constant and pulsating, and they seemed to change color in waves. One floated past her face—it looked like an airborne baby jellyfish, with a four-leaf clover of light in its center.

Suddenly it exploded like a camera flash, the bright white

light burning an instant image onto Teagan's retinas—a swat-bat clinging to a tree trunk, his tongue extended like a frog's. He'd eaten the baby jellyfish.

The white flash that had been the doomed jelly's last, desperate warning had temporarily blinded her. She was alone in the dark of Mag Mell. If something was creeping up on her, she wouldn't be able to see it. Wouldn't be able to run.

Terror didn't feel any different in this body, Teagan discovered, even though she didn't have flesh to crawl or bones to rattle. It made it hard to breathe, hard to move.

She stood still, trying not to panic. Waiting for her night vision to return. It was almost completely back when a green light flashed behind her. She whirled just in time to see Finn dive headfirst past her. He rolled and bounced to his feet.

"I love you, too," he said. "Can I have my knife back?"

"Mag Mell said she wouldn't let you in!"

"She didn't. Joe did."

"He ripped a hole in the night."

"Just like his brother did when Mamieo stepped into Mag Mell to save your *máthair*. He said Mag Mell would stitch it right up again." He looked back the way he had come. "She did, didn't she? Quick as that."

"But Raynor—"

"Funny how those two disagree on so many things, isn't it? I'd say the tree man is more of the romantic type."

"Why didn't you just walk through? Why dive headfirst?"

"Raynor was chasing me." Finn pulled a leaf out of his hair. "I'd pretended to head for the park gate, while Joe got a good grip on the night. Raynor figured out what we were about at the last moment. That's one fast-moving *aingeal.* I thought I'd have to keep running to catch up with you, though."

"I couldn't see to go anywhere. Don't look directly at the floating lights. They explode when the swat-bats eat them." She handed him his knife, and he stuck it back in his boot.

"That's better. I felt a bit naked without it."

"You shouldn't have come." But she wasn't terrified anymore. Just very, very afraid.

"I couldn't help it. The whole 'breaking up' thing wasn't working for me. I do want forever. But I've told you before, the Mac Cumhaill never lives to be old and gray. I'm going to love you while I've got you. And that means taking care of you, girl."

"There's no way for you to go back. Aiden isn't here to show us the way out."

"Of course there's a way. I'll just have to be holding on to you when the time comes."

"I didn't want you to come. It's too dangerous."

"That's not your choice, Tea. It's mine."

"But . . . I'm devolving. Into something like Kyle."

"Prove it. What evil thing have you done?"

"I'm walking without my skin and bones!"

"That does concern me." He wrapped his arms around her. "But it doesn't prove that you're evil, does it?"

"No sparks," Teagan said.

"I noticed. And you're as cold as a fish. It's unsettling. But it will be all right."

"How do you know?"

"Look." He tipped her chin up, and pointed. "It's the silver moon, like in the boyo's song. *'She will be shining for you on your journey home.'* We'll get you back into your body, girl. In time to get you to the doctor. So, we'd better get moving. How were you planning to find Fear Doirich?"

"I hadn't figured that out yet," Teagan said, stepping away from him. "I thought I'd work it out as I went."

"We'd best start walking, then. We need to get you back together as soon as possible. Maybe we'll come on someone or something we can ask." As if on cue, they heard the baying of a distant pack of hunters. "There were Highborn running with the pack that chased us before," Finn said. "If we meet such creatures again, remember: no promises, and never tell a goblin your real name."

A jelly light flashed. This time, Teagan wasn't looking directly at it, and she saw the night-shine of a hundred little eyes turned toward them. Swat-bats, clinging to the bark of trees.

"Let's lose the names now," she said. "We don't know who might be listening in the dark."

"I'll call you Rosebud, then"—he took the backpack from her—"and you can call me . . . Sexy Beast. I like that."

"I'm not calling you Sexy Beast. I'll call you Mac. For Mac Cumhaill."

"It's the same difference, then, isn't it?" Finn slung the backpack over his shoulder. "The Mac Cumhaill *is* a sexy beast. By definition."

"You're trying to distract me, aren't you?"

"I am," Finn agreed. "Which way do you think we should go?"

"I'm not sure it matters," Teagan said. "Mag Mell's all *twisty* inside, isn't she? We'll just start walking and see where our feet take us."

"Tell me about what Kyle did to you," Finn said as they set off.

Mag Mell was just as maze-like but much less animated than she had been when Aiden was with them. Trees didn't move, and paths didn't open before them. They blundered through the brush until they found a game trail. As soon as Teagan could walk without tripping, she explained what had happened at school.

"So he put a bug in you that's changing your body," Finn said when she was finished.

"Making me less like Dad, or even Mom."

"More like your grand-*máthair* Maeve. She walked away from Fear Doirich because she loved Amergin, remember?"

"I don't—"

"Shhh." Finn pulled her into a darker shadow under a tree, his finger to her lips.

It took her a moment to sort out the sounds from the wind in the leaves. Wings. Big wings, coming closer. They didn't whistle like feathered bird wings. It was more like the sound of the wind on smooth sails . . . bat wings. Giant bat wings.

"Close your eyes, girl," Finn whispered. "They'll see them shining."

Teagan closed her eyes, and he pulled her close. The sound was above their tree now, and she was sure there was more than one creature. She could feel Finn's heart thumping and she wasn't the least bit afraid. Teagan held very still until long after the sounds of the wings had gone.

"Let go," she said at last.

"For now." Finn let her go. "But I'm not letting go of you ever again when we get out of here. Not ever."

They stepped back into the moonlight. Teagan scanned the sky, but the creatures were gone.

"What were they?" she asked.

"You don't want to know," Finn said. "But the good news is, they don't wear wee hats or vests."

They'd walked for more than an hour when she heard fiddle music, faint on the wind.

"That sounds familiar," Finn said. "We might as well visit the man. It's a place to start."

They made their way through thick, low brush until they found the fiddler's clearing. The fiddler himself was rooted in the center of the open space, his legs grown thick as tree trunks, his toes curling into the ground and holding him in place. He had his fiddle to his chin, and he was playing his sad music to the moonlight.

"Eógan," Teagan said, and he jerked, and the bow scraped across the strings like a scream. "That's your name, isn't it? You were Thomas's fiddler."

Eógan held perfectly still for a moment, then shook back his hair. He flinched when he saw Teagan's eyes and drew back as if he expected to be struck. Then he looked at Finn, and seemed to relax a little. His face was streaked with bird droppings, as if pigeons had been perching on his head. His eyes were very wide in the moonlight, and the whites around his irises almost glowed.

"I'm not going to hurt you," Teagan said. "Give me the backpack, Finn." She took out a water bottle and soaked one of her clean socks with it, then wiped at the droppings. He turned his head as if he could drink the liquid through the parched bark that covered his mouth.

She cleaned as much filth from his face as she could before she knelt down and wiped his feet with the wet rag. His toes writhed, and he strained as if he would pull them out of the soil. Teagan poured some water out on his feet, and Eógan closed his eyes and tipped his face up to the stars as the liquid sank into the ground.

"We need to find Fear Doirich," Teagan said to him. "Please help us."

Eógan opened his eyes. He looked at her for a long moment. If he couldn't understand anything else, at least the name Fear Doirich caused a flicker in his eyes. He lifted his fiddle and started to play something wild and frightening.

"That doesn't sound good," Finn said.

"I'm not like my brother," Teagan explained. "I can't understand your music."

"We can."

Teagan whirled toward the sound of the voice. The creature had the head of a goat, but from the neck down it was a stoop-shouldered human. His horns swept up and away from his forehead, twisting like those of a markhor. His eyes were slitted and bulging, his ears stuck out almost horizontally, and the shaggy beard that hung from his chin reached to his chest.

"You were warning them, tree-man?" Hearing a human voice when his animal mouth moved made Teagan feel slightly sick. Finn moved closer to her as five more creatures came out of the woods.

They looked like shape shifters who had stalled in process, leaving some with the legs of elk and others with the heads of dogs or boars. They were armed with stone knives and short spears. One had a strung short bow over his shoulder.

"What *are* you?" Finn asked.

"A little of this," the elk-head said.

"A little of that," a dog-head added.

"And all phooka." The goat-head laughed.

NINETEEN

THE terror was back.

The phookas smelled foully sweet and rancid, like dogs that had rolled in carrion. Two were almost naked, with nothing more than rags twisted around their waists, and all of them were smeared with dirt and old blood. But there were no Highborn with them.

"Why aren't you running?" the goat-head asked, moving closer.

"Why should she run from a mixed-up lot like you?" Finn asked, stepping between her and the goat-head. "She's Highborn, isn't she?"

Eógan tucked his fiddle under his chin and started to play again, very softly.

"Not her." The phooka pointed his short spear at Finn. "You. The meat."

"Come a little closer," Finn said, "and I'll show you."

A dog-head growled.

The fiddle played more insistently . . .

. . . and there was a voice in the music. Aiden's voice, trying to work its way past her fear.

Better be gone
So find your pocket watch
And all of your hope now . . .

Hush, Teagan told the voice. *I don't have a pocket watch. And things are about to get ugly here.* The goat-head focused on Finn, and the others spread out. Teagan had seen hyenas do the same thing. Preparing to attack. The voice in the music didn't hush.

Fair thee well 'cause we can tell
Nothing but courage will do . . .

Give me courage, then, Teagan prayed, forcing herself to step up beside Finn.

"This one is mine." She locked eyes with the phooka. "And I'm taking him with me." She hoped she wasn't shaking hard enough that they could see it.

"Where?" the phooka asked.

"Fear Doirich commanded me to come to him." She had to sound arrogant, as arrogant as Thomas had when he'd announced that he'd toppled kings. And she'd just have to hope that the phookas were goblins. Because if they didn't follow Fear Doirich, there was no reason for them to take her to him.

"What happened to your pet's hand?" Boar-Head pointed at Finn's bandage.

"I burnt it fighting something uglier than you," Finn said.

"Highborn"—a younger dog-headed man licked his chops—"where is your flesh sleeping? Is it near?" All of them looked very interested in her answer.

"No."

"Aileen's child," Boar-Head said. "I hunted the mother." Pink tongues flicked, and hooves, paws, and feet shuffled. Someone whined hungrily.

"Was she good?"

"The flesh was wasted. A Fir Bolg stole her. If the Dark Man called you, why didn't you bring your flesh?"

"There's a *caombnóir aingeal* guarding the way," Teagan said. The phookas looked at one another.

"*Caombnóir aingeal,*" they repeated several times.

"Take us to Fear Doirich," Teagan demanded.

"We can offer them to him for Samhain," Elk-Head said. "He might be pleased."

"The hunt, the hunt, the hunt!" It wasn't one voice that spoke, but a mixture of grunts and growls and longing.

"We'll take you," Goat-Head said. "If we get hungry on the way, we can eat the Fir Bolg." This met with general approval. Goat-Head poked at Finn with his short spear.

"Let's go, meat."

"Stop that," Teagan commanded. The phooka glared at her, but he lowered his spear a little as the other phookas surrounded them, urging them away from Eógan. Finn grabbed the backpack and slipped it on as they walked.

The fiddler's eyes were closed, his head tipped sideways as if he were listening. Before they were out of the clearing, the music grew louder—

Set your sails upon the hope
of June—

Teagan shut it out and tried to focus on the details that could keep them alive.

The phookas spread out as they entered the dark woods. They were clearly hunter-gatherers, stopping to eat at berry bushes and pick what looked like caterpillars from leaves as they passed. In places where the jellies hung thick enough to give light, Teagan could see movement in the trees beyond the five who surrounded them.

As they walked, a young phooka worked his way closer, dodging cuffs and blows from the older creatures. He was dressed in a rag, and his ribs and collarbones showed. If this were a pack of hyenas, he would be the one most likely to be made an outcast or eaten when food was short.

"Keep an eye on that one," Finn said. "He seems overly interested."

"Curious," Teagan said as the creature peeked around his larger companions. "The others are hungry or anxious, but he's curious." The young phooka saw her looking at him and ducked behind a fern.

"That's interesting." Finn motioned toward the grizzled dog-head, who had turned to watch their back trail and scent the wind. Teagan nodded. These phookas were watchful in a way that predators were not. They were showing not just the attention of those who hunted, but the caution of those who were hunted themselves.

"They're hunter-gatherers," Teagan said. "But something worse hunts them."

"Maybe so. There are no ladies with them. Wherever these boyos are going, they're expecting a fight."

The phookas stopped in a berry patch, picking the fruit they could reach and shoving it in their mouths. Finn nudged Teagan and nodded. The small phooka was making his way toward them, pretending to be interested in the berries. He edged cautiously past the goat-head.

He was the same size as Teagan. His ears were pointed and tufted like the ears of a red river hog, and stuck out straight from his head. His face was human, and almost handsome. No, handsome wasn't the word, Teagan decided. Beautiful, like the dryads in her mother's paintings. The hand that clutched his club was normal, but he raised his other hand to brush away a fly, and Teagan saw that it looked like a fleshy, flexible hoof. He studied them with frank curiosity.

"You're not from Mag Mell, are you?" Teagan asked. "Where did the phooka people come from?"

"Nowhere."

The goat-head turned around, berry juice staining his beard black in the moonlight. "God made us out of other things."

"You mean Fear Doirich?"

"Yes. God."

These phookas *were* goblins, then. They worshiped the Dark Man.

The boy nodded and held out his hoof hand. "God broke us."

The goat-head backhanded him, knocking him to the ground. He got up, shook his ears, and took his place as if being knocked down was simply expected. The grizzled dog-head raised his muzzle and scented the breeze again.

"We're followed."

"Now we run," Goat-Head said. "Keep up with us. If you keep up, we take you to Fear. If you do not, they will kill you."

Tea saw Finn's worried look, and she knew he was remembering that she'd had a hard time keeping up with him the last time they'd walked in Mag Mell. The phookas started to trot, and she and Finn fell in with them. Teagan waited for the burning to start in her lungs, or the ache in her side to come. But it didn't.

As long as they didn't speed up, so that her shorter legs were outdistanced, she was going to be able to keep up. For the first time since the phookas had arrived, her fear started easing. She pushed her legs faster, and there was no pain. She noticed the young phooka running ahead of her. He had to watch out not only for roots in the dark, but also for the other phookas, who seemed to delight in pushing or tripping him. Twice he hit the ground, only to roll, jump up, and start running again, a frightened and determined look on his face.

"I think they're trying to feed him to whatever is chasing us," Finn said the third time the young phooka went down. "They don't have to run faster than whatever it is behind us. Just faster than the little one."

The phooka scrambled to his feet and ran on, managing to avoid both roots and the other phookas for a few moments at least. Teagan realized that she was running better than she ever had before, leaping over fallen logs and weaving through the underbrush. She stretched her strides, pushing harder, and felt a runner's high starting to build.

"Doing all right?" Finn asked.

"I'm good." She was better than good. The phooka boy went down again ahead of them, shoved by the elk-head. Teagan slowed long enough to pull him to his feet, and when he was up she ran again, with Finn on one side and the young phooka on the other.

The feeling building inside her was more powerful than a runner's high. The phooka boy glanced at her and she could see it reflected on his face—a wild joy. *This is what it feels like to be a phooka running in Mag Mell.*

They passed through a clearing, and the goat-head, who was running ahead of her, turned to look, his eyes bright in the moonlight, his pupils dilated. He was feeling it, too, and he was . . . surprised. *This is not how it feels to be a phooka.*

This is how it feels to be a Highborn running toward a fight. We inspire. The phookas were picking up the joy from her. She wondered if this was what Aiden felt when he first sang to Mag Mell and the magic worked. Like nothing could hurt them, nothing could stop them.

Teagan whooped, and the pack took up the cry, baying as if they were on the trail of their prey rather than being hunted themselves.

TWENTY

FINN was running flat out to keep up now, not looking at her, just running. The phookas whooped and called to one another all around her, and the jelly lights scattered before them like schools of glowing fish swimming through the trees.

Teagan ran until she noticed that Finn was stumbling. She slowed to a walk, and the wild joy inside her settled into something more quiet. The pack slowed around her, apparently satisfied that they'd left whatever was hunting them behind.

Finn stumbled again.

"Are you all right?" Teagan asked.

Finn shrugged the backpack off and leaned over with his hands on his knees. "That's farther than I've ever run in my life. If I fall over, just sling me over your shoulder."

The young phooka she'd pulled to his feet stopped to watch. "If you fall down, we can eat you," he said. "Please fall down."

"I'd forgotten that bit." Finn straightened up. "I'll keep moving."

Teagan picked up the backpack, and Finn just nodded.

A dog-head slapped the young phooka in the back of the head and snarled as he walked by.

"Why don't they like you?" Teagan asked.

"I'm a man." The phooka waved at his boyish face. "So I . . . *think*."

"About what?"

He glanced sideways at her. "Broken things."

The dog-head looked back and growled, and the phooka boy ducked as if expecting to be hit again.

"You don't have to make friendly with the beasties, Rosebud," Finn said. "They *are* threatening to eat me."

Teagan started walking again, Finn on one side and the phooka boy on the other. Dawn was turning the world gray around them, the jelly lights sinking to the ground and blinking out as the creatures crept under leaves or into hollow logs. As the daylight grew, Teagan started to recognize her surroundings—deep pools lined with trees, their branches arched far out over the water. She saw a little frogman watching her from the pond's edge.

The phookas stopped moving and spread out under the trees.

The boy wagged his ears and went to join a group that was digging grubs.

"I wouldn't make friends with that creature," Finn said. "I don't think you can trust him. I know I can't."

"I'm just trying to understand them." She walked to the edge of a pool and looked in. Finn had told her they were all connected beneath the surface, the ground held up by a tangle of roots. The water was very clear and didn't grow darker as it went down. She could almost imagine another surface, under the sky of a different world below her, as if all the worlds of the multiverse were tangled together in the pools and connected by the roots of the mighty tree. She could see creatures swimming—golden fish near the surface, but larger, darker shapes too deep to make out as well. When Aiden sang in this wood, the little frogmen had come out of these pools, inspired to sing with him.

One of the dog-headed men farted loudly, and all of them laughed. She apparently inspired an entirely different kind of creature.

Finn walked up beside her.

"You're not tired?" he asked.

"No."

"Good. I don't like the way the creatures are looking at you this morning. *They're* not sure they like what happened last night."

Teagan peeked sideways at him, but Finn was watching the phookas, taking note of each one's position.

"They were keeping up with you, so I don't think outrunning them is an option. There are two ways out of here, if we have to go quick. Up a tree—the creatures aren't made for climbing—or down into a pond. The ones with horns and such won't be much for swimming."

"Neither are you," Teagan pointed out. When Ginny Greenteeth had pulled Aiden into one of the ponds, Finn had nearly drowned saving him.

"I'd say the trees, then. It looks like we could move from one to another."

"Didn't what happened last night . . . bother you?" Tegan asked.

"You mean the fact that you stopped to help the beastie? Na. I'm not the jealous type."

"Not that."

"Oh, you mean that you can outrun me? That is troublesome. Especially if you decide to run *from* me."

"I mean—the rest of it."

"The howling and such?" He considered for a moment. "Why did you stop when that creature fell?"

"Because he needed help," Teagan said.

"You're still my girl, then, aren't you? And after you helped him up—when you really started to inspire them—they didn't trip him anymore, did they? It's like what your da said about the Bard—he had a 'Tyger's hart wrapt in a Player's hyde.' You're just my Rosebud wrapped in a tiger's hide, that's all."

The tears on Teagan's face surprised her. What exactly could leak out of a soul? Not salt water. But still, they were tears.

"Why are you crying, girl?"

"Because Thomas was right. You are a saint. You shouldn't be able to love me when I inspire *phookas*. It's not natural."

"I've been thinking about it all night," Finn said.

"About being a saint?"

"About getting that heart back into its original hide so that I can prove that I'm no saint."

Teagan wondered if her body, sleeping in the park, was blushing.

He smiled. "It made it easier to run, having something to

look forward to. I'd tell you to inspire them to run some more if I thought I could keep up. We need to be done with this place. But *my* flesh and bones need a rest." Finn frowned suddenly and nodded toward the phookas, who had gathered near one of the pools. "What do you suppose is going on there?"

The goat-head had grabbed the phooka boy by the neck. He lifted him over his head and threw him into the pool. The young phooka bobbed on the surface for a moment, then disappeared. The rest of the phookas gathered around the pond, waiting. Teagan counted thirteen of them in the light.

The boy popped to the surface a moment later and tossed a flopping golden fish into the air. The dog-headed man caught it and started eating while the fish still flailed.

"Breakfast break, then," Finn said. "I'm picking that nice tree over there to sleep under." Teagan followed him to the tree. He sank down and leaned against the trunk.

"I've got granola bars in my backpack." She sat down beside him. "Would you like them? I'm not hungry, or thirsty. I don't think this body needs to eat or drink."

Finn ate the bars slowly, taking sips of water between bites.

"That's better," he said when he had finished. "Now if I can get some sleep before we start again, I might survive this. How are *you* feeling?"

"I'm all right," Teagan said.

"I mean . . . can you tell how your body is doing? Back in Chicago?"

"No," Teagan said. Would she even know if it stopped breathing? "I don't understand everything that's happening to me, Finn. But I know we're in an Irish story." Teagan watched the phooka boy tossing out more fish. "You've got to know there won't be a happy ending. Not with me turning into a . . ." She considered what term to use. Not goblin. She'd never worship the Dark Man. "Full-blooded Highborn. I'll settle for just you having a happy ending."

"I won't settle for it," Finn said. "It's both or nothing. Now, hush." He put his arm around her and pulled her closer.

"I thought you said this body was unsettling?"

"It is." He leaned his head against her shoulder. "Cold and unsettling, but softer than a tree trunk or a rock." There was no electricity when they touched, just radiant heat, as if she were cuddling a fire.

The phooka boy finally crawled out of the water with his own fish and walked over to sit beside them. He ripped its belly open and started eating the roe. He glanced at Teagan, scooped out a handful of roe and held it out toward her. Offering food was a universal sign of friendship.

"Thank you," Teagan said. The fish eggs were pond cool as they popped between her teeth. The boy's ear twitched, but he didn't look at her again. Goat-Head and the older dog-head were studying her, though.

Some of the phookas were stomping down grass and gathering leaves. It looked like they were building a large communal nest, yawning as they did so. They were nocturnal, then. It made sense, since they'd been moving all night. Goat-Head came over to her.

"Fear Doirich didn't call you," he said. The other phookas

had finished their nest. They came closer, ringing the tree. "We know the feel of the hunt. You came *hunting* our god."

The pond was too far away. They would have to go up the tree. But before she could wake Finn, the grizzled dog-head's nose twitched and his head snapped around.

"They're here." A huge, shaggy gray shape moved out of the underbrush.

It could only be a war dog, because it was exactly like Mamieo had described the Cú Faoil.

"Mac!" She shook Finn. He came groggily awake, and scrambled to his feet.

It would have been helpful if Thomas had mentioned that the war hounds are still here, Teagan thought, *still doing the job they were given in the time before time. Hunting goblins.*

"We fight here." The elder dog-headed man took his short spear from his belt.

Another Cú Faoil came out of the bushes, head low, stalking. And then another, and another.

"We die here," the elk-head said.

Goat-Head shouted as the Cú Faoil leaped, knocking him to the ground. Its fangs slashed, and blood misted Teagan as the phooka's scream turned to a gargle.

TWENTY-ONE

FINN caught Teagan around her hips and tossed her up to the branch above them. She grabbed on with both hands, swung her legs up, and wrapped them around the limb. Finn ran straight up the trunk of the tree and was on the branch with her before she could pull herself upright.

The phookas were dying. The goat-head's throat was gone, but his body still thrashed. The elk-head was fighting with his spear and his antlers, but even as Teagan watched, one Cú Faoil feigned a lunge to draw him out and another pulled him down. They were working together. Five war dogs taking down the whole pack of phookas, one by one. She'd seen films of arctic wolves working together as they hunted, but these creatures were fighting smarter than wolves. They were taking the best-armed first. The Cú Faoil had clearly studied this phooka pack long enough to know which ones were dangerous and what they were likely to do.

The phooka boy was right beneath her, his club in one hand, his back to the tree, ignored by the dogs for the moment.

"Hey," Teagan called. "Up here!"

Finn looked from her to the young phooka. "Oh, no."

"Yes." Teagan started to climb down from the tree, but Finn dropped past her.

"Up you go, beastie." He boosted the phooka up.

"Hurry a little," Teagan said. The Cú Faoil had pulled down all but two of the older phookas.

"I'm working on it."

The creature reached up with his fleshy hoof, and Teagan grabbed it. It was like holding a pig's trotter, still slick from the flesh of the fish he had been eating. She gripped as hard as she could and pulled him just high enough that he could grasp the branch with his human hand. He swung his legs up and wrapped them around the branch, like she had done, but he couldn't pull himself up.

Finn made it up the trunk again as the last phooka went down. He caught the phooka boy by the rags and heaved him up, just as a Cú Faoil leaped for him. The war dog's jaws snapped shut where the phooka had been a second earlier. The boy had his arms wrapped around Finn, and his eyes closed.

The Cú Faoil leaped again, but came inches short of the branch. The rest sat down amidst the blood and body parts, tongues lolling from the sides of their mouths, eyes on the three in the tree.

"They're thinking," Teagan said. "They're going to figure out how to get up here." One reared up on its hind legs, its front paws against the tree. Its head was at least seven feet off the ground.

"We should get a bit higher." Finn pried the phooka off and

put its hand on a branch above its head. "You hold on to that now." He stripped the bandage off his own hand and flexed the fingers.

"Is it healed?" Teagan reached for it, but he pulled away.

"It'll have to do."

The hair tufts on the ends of the phooka's ears were shaking. "Gil," he whispered. Teagan turned to him.

"Is that your name?"

His ear twitched. "Yes. I wanted to say it to someone. Before I die." He looked expectantly at Teagan and Finn, and she realized he was waiting for their names in return.

"We're not planning on dying." Finn stood up on the branch.

"I have something I need to do," Teagan said.

"Hunt god." Gil's ears drooped.

"The pool you were fishing in," Finn said. "It's connected to other pools, is it?"

"All of the pools, forever," Gil said.

"How brave are you, beastie?" Finn asked.

"Very brave?"

"Good. Because we're going to have to get to the next tree, and there'll be some jumping involved."

"Why?"

"Because that's the only way to get to that pool from this tree without waltzing through the Cú Faoil."

"Good." Teagan nodded. "Even if they can swim, their bodies aren't designed for diving. So we're going to dive deep."

"I can't climb out on limbs," Gil said.

Finn shrugged. "I can't swim, so we're even."

The phooka boy tottered, then sank down, his knees on each side of the limb, and his feet tucked up behind him, so they wouldn't dangle in front of the dogs' noses.

Teagan walked carefully out on the branch to the point from which they would have to jump. It was at least a five-foot leap to the next tree. The Cú Faoil followed beneath her, looking up expectantly. Gil was scooting along the branch after her, still not standing up, and Finn was right behind him.

"Can you make it, girl?" Finn asked.

"Do I have a choice?" Teagan launched herself across the gap, grabbing for the smaller branches above the one she wanted to land on. Her hand caught a branch, slipped, and then caught the one under it. The Cú Faoil leaped as well, jaws snapping inches below her feet.

"I can't jump." Gil held up his trotter. "I can't hold." Teagan reached up to the branch above her and braced her feet on the one below her.

"You don't have to catch the branch," she told Gil. "Just wrap your arms around me. Got it?"

"Stand up, beastie," Finn said. Gil shook his head.

Finn hauled him up with his good hand. The phooka shrieked as Finn tossed him. Teagan braced herself, but it still almost knocked her off the branch when he hit. And then his whole weight was hanging around her neck.

"Not so tight." Teagan managed to swing him over until he could get a hoof on the branch. "You're choking me."

Finn jumped across and landed easily beside them.

The Cú Faoil had figured out where they were going, and one splashed into the pool, but it didn't dive. It dog-paddled out to the middle, straining to keep its head above water.

"They will jump in after us," Gil said.

"Probably," Teagan agreed. "When you hit the water, dive as deep as you can. Finn can't swim, so we're going to have to help him stay under."

"I will hold him under." Gil flapped his ears happily. "Way down deep!"

"Thrilling," Finn said. The phooka dove, missing the paddling Cú Faoil and slicing cleanly into the water.

"You next," Teagan said, eyeing a war dog that had managed to leap to a lower tree branch and was scrambling with its hind legs trying to get up.

"I'm good," Finn said. "You just go ahead."

Teagan drew a deep breath and jumped feet first, folding her arms across her chest and aiming for a spot directly behind a Cú Faoil. The cool water was a shock when she hit it. Teeth slashed through the water, but too slowly. Then she was past, sinking deeper. When she started to rise again, she turned and opened her eyes. She saw Gil beside her, grinning widely. Light was all around them, coming from above and below, and massive roots surrounded them. Gil pushed her out of the way as Finn shot past, a completely panicked look on his face. Teagan caught the wrist of his burned hand as he started to bob back up, and Gil caught the other hand.

The phooka pointed a way through the roots, and Teagan nodded. Gil was a powerful swimmer, even holding on to Finn with one hand; he reached forward with his trotter, and moved his body like a dolphin.

There were pools of light and then darkness above and below them. The water that had gotten into her mouth when she first jumped in was fresh and sweet, and there was music all around her, like an Aeolian harp. The sound seemed to be coming from the great roots themselves. Whatever her new body was made of, it resonated with the music. It was better than food, better than water, better than sleep.

This song wasn't of Mag Mell, any more than the most massive of the roots reaching down around her were. Those roots were too mighty and the song too wild and joyful. It was the Song of Creation. Aiden's *cantus firmus*.

There were words, beautiful words that she couldn't quite make out. The more she focused on them, the more melodies she heard, mixing with them, harmonizing, then playing counterpoint. Aiden's song, the one she'd shut out when she walked away from the fiddler, was all around her. And then there was more than music—poetry and flashes of great masters' paintings. And Abby's paintings. Teagan laughed. She felt as if she were breathing art instead of air, and it was all she needed. She could swim forever, exploring each of the lights she saw around her.

She glanced over at Finn to see if he was seeing and hearing it as well. Apparently, he was not. His eyes had started to bulge.

Teagan waved at Gil and pointed up, and the phooka kicked for a dim green light. The surface of this pool was covered with giant lily pads, which stretched across it like curtains hiding the sky. Finn gasped and sputtered when his head broke the surface, then sucked in great gulps of air as they held him afloat.

"Did you hear it?" Teagan asked.

"I heard a mighty rushing in my ears as I was about to drown, if that's what you mean."

"Do you want us to pull you to the shore?"

"Give me a minute," Finn said, grabbing onto the edge of a lily pad. "I'll just wait here for a bit. Breathing air."

"Okay," Teagan said. The pull of the distant lights she had seen in the water was too much to resist. Were they pools as well? Above *and* below her? "Stay with him, Gil. I'll be right back." She turned and dove for the nearest puddle of light beneath her. The *cantus firmus* surrounded her again, filling her with almost unbearable joy until her head broke the surface under a blue sky. A spray of water hit her face, but her eyes didn't sting. She was in a pool, on a rocky lakeshore—looking up at a little girl.

Teagan opened her mouth to say "Don't be afraid," but it wasn't her own words that came out—it was the music of a harp.

"Mommy!" the girl shouted. "A mermaid! Her eyes are glowy, and she's singing!" Teagan grinned and dove again, following the roots and fish back the way she had come. Finn and Gil should have been just above or below her, but they weren't. She hung for a moment between the over and under lights—and then she saw Finn's legs treading water, almost too distant to make out. Mag Mell was just as tricky underwater as she was on solid land. Teagan swam hard, and bobbed up next to them.

"Where did you go?" Finn asked. "I was just about to ask the beastie to find you."

"I was exploring," Teagan said. "Apparently woods aren't the only way into Mag Mell."

"It's the world between worlds, with many a doorway if a creature knows how to find it," Finn said. "At least Mamieo says so. Can we get out of the water now? I'm turning into a prune."

TWENTY-TWO

FINN crawled out of the water and stretched out on the mossy bank.

"Girl," he said when she climbed up beside him, "look around. Are there any bloody big creatures preparing to eat us? Presently, I mean."

"No," Teagan said. "Let me see your hand."

"It's fine." He put his hands behind his head. "It's been a day and a night since I shut my eyes for more than a few minutes, and you've run the legs off me. I've got to sleep for an hour or two, or I'm not going much farther."

"I'll stand watch."

Finn nodded, and closed his eyes. Almost instantly his breathing changed, and Teagan knew he was asleep. Gil looked from him to Teagan, then curled up in a ball close to Finn and fell asleep as well. The phookas had been making one large nest. Teagan guessed that they probably slept in a heap for safety and warmth. Here in the deep, shady wood, it was chilly enough that the warmth of a nest would be welcome.

She trailed her hand in the water. The Song of Creation had

been powerful, joyful, and *right.* The kind of rightness that began to grow in Thomas when he first loved Roisin. The *rightness* that seemed to be at the very core of Finn.

"Each mortal thing does one thing and the same," Teagan whispered, remembering the poem in her mother's sketchbooks.

> *"Deals out that being indoors each one dwells;*
> *Selves—goes itself;* myself *it speaks and spells,*
> *Crying* Whát I do is me: for that I came."

Thomas was Highborn, and he could grow right. But . . . he was a *lhiannon-sídhe.* He came to inspire greatness in poetry and song. Not to hunt.

Teagan pulled her hand out of the water. The surface stilled, and she could see the reflection of her golden eyes. Not a mermaid. A rider on the storm. Born to . . . war.

The fierce joy of the hunt flashed through her like adrenaline, and she almost wanted to throw back her head and howl with the excitement of it.

"No," Teagan said aloud. "What I do is me. *I* came to help Cindy and Oscar. To rescue wounded river otters. To take care of Aiden. I will not become anything else." She turned away from the reflection of her golden tyger's eyes.

Gil had moved closer to Finn. The phooka boy was curled up against his back.

She headed off a fat black beetle that was crawling toward the sleepers, scooping it into her hand. She almost dropped it when it said, "Eeek!" and squeaked a string of sounds that she was sure were some kind of beetle speech. She carried it to a fallen log and set it down, and it scuttled away, tail held high like a stinkbug.

When she went back, Finn had turned over and put an arm around the phooka.

"Hey," she whispered. "I don't think that's who you think it is." The silly smile on Finn's face widened. She considered trying to move his arm, but that would probably just wake him up.

The sun was directly overhead when Gil stirred in his sleep. He tried to roll away, but Finn pulled him closer and nuzzled his ear. "Tea," Finn mumbled, then opened his eyes.

He screamed. Then Gil screamed, and then they were both scrambling to their feet.

Finn brushed at the front of his clothes as if the phooka had left residue. Which he probably had, even though Gil was relatively clean, for a phooka. "Why didn't you—?"

"You guys just looked so peaceful," Teagan said. "I didn't want to disturb you."

"Disturb me? I'm going to be disturbed the rest of my life. I was cuddling a phooka, girl. If Gabby ever hears about this—"

"She never will," Teagan said. Gil was looking back and forth between them in complete confusion, his ears down.

"Cultural differences," Teagan explained. "Phookas sleep in a common nest, don't they?"

"How else would you sleep?" Gil asked.

"It *was* a bit warmer," Finn admitted, and Gil's ears twitched. "I suppose we both slept better."

"You want fish?" Gil asked hopefully.

"Actually," Finn said, "I do."

For the first time, Teagan realized that they'd left her backpack beneath the tree where the Cú Faoil had attacked the phooka band. No more granola bars. Gil dove into the water and brought up a golden fish. Finn grimaced when the phooka boy handed him a piece of raw flesh, and Teagan laughed.

"What's funny?"

"I was just remembering a certain breakfast of bagels and cream cheese from a Dumpster."

"It's a different thing entirely," Finn said.

"Lots of people eat raw fish. It's called sashimi."

Teagan took a few bites to be polite, but let Gil and Finn eat most of it. Several of the big black beetles appeared to argue over the fish bones and guts. They were some kind of carrion beetle, then.

Gil picked one up and popped it in his mouth. The others, as if suddenly aware of the huge creatures watching them, scurried away, crying "Eeek! Eeek!" and stopping to argue every time they happened to bump into one another. Gil caught another and offered it to Teagan.

"Don't you eat that, girl," Finn said. "Or I swear I'm never kissing you, even when you're back in your body."

Gil shrugged. "I'd kiss you," he said.

Finn put his hand on the back of the phooka's neck and walked him a few steps away from Teagan. "No, no, you won't, beastie," he said, giving Gil a shake. "Snuggling up for warmth is one thing, but offering to kiss my girl is another. Do you have any idea which way Fear Doirich is from here?"

Gil pointed, licking the last of the beetle juice from his lips.

"That way?" Finn asked. "You're sure?"

"We always know where god is," the phooka said. "You have to pay attention. He might sneak up and *get* you."

"Not if we get him first," Teagan said. They heard the bay of a phooka pack, and Gil grinned.

"Ha," he said. "There will be very many phookas where we are going."

"Crap," Finn said. The baying was immediately followed by the call of the Cú Faoil.

"Crap." Gil sounded just like Finn.

"You don't suppose they're hunting each other?" Finn asked.

"Us," Gil said. "They're all hunting us."

"Let's go, then."

They ran until the dense wood changed into a forest of thin aspens. Teagan looked around worriedly. There were no trees big enough to climb, no pools to jump into.

It was clear from the hoots and howls that Gil was right—both packs were hunting them, but the Cú Faoil sounded as if they were going to reach them first. They could catch glimpses of the creatures behind them when they came to the mouth of a cave.

"In, in, in," Finn said, drawing his knife. "Maybe it'll lead somewhere. If not, at least they won't be able to come round behind us." Teagan ducked into the opening and put her hand over her head so that she didn't bump it on rocks as she walked farther into the cave. Finn stayed by the entrance, facing the Cú Faoil.

"It only goes back about fifty feet," Teagan called. "Then the ceiling's fallen in." By the time she got back to Finn and Gil, the Cú Faoil were sitting in a semicircle outside the mouth of the cave, their tongues hanging out.

They looked like they were waiting expectantly for someone to toss them a treat. Gil whimpered, and Teagan put her arm around him.

"All right, then," Finn said. He handed Teagan his knife.

"What are you doing?" she asked as Finn stripped off his shirt.

"I've been cuddling with their favorite kibble, haven't I, then?" He tossed the shirt to Teagan.

"I am the Mac Cumhaill," he said, stepping out with his arms spread and palms up. "I'm hoping that means something to you lot. I'm in deep cack if it doesn't."

"The *Mac Cumhaill,*" Gil whispered, his ears straight up.

"Shhh." Teagan held her breath. The Mac Cumhaill *was* a sexy beast. One that was about to get eaten.

Irish wolfhounds were sight hounds—they depended more on their eyes than on their noses. But they were still hounds. The leader sniffed Finn cautiously. It seemed to spend a little extra time where he'd cuddled Gil, but when it got to Finn's head and shoulders, the huge, shaggy tail started to sway. The Cú Faoil whined, the eager sound of a dog that's found a lost master. It lay down and rolled onto its back, exposing its stomach.

"They fought beside the Fir Bolg," Teagan said. "They recognize you!"

The other Cú Faoil pushed around Finn, nuzzling, whining, and wiggling like puppies. They were almost knocking him from his feet with their affection.

"You first, girl," Finn said, beckoning Teagan to come toward him once the war dogs had settled down a little.

"She's mine," Finn told the Cú Faoil as Teagan walked to him. "Do you understand?" They didn't wag, but they didn't attack her, either.

"Give me my shirt back, will you, girl? I'm embarrassing myself." She handed it to him, and he pulled it over his head.

"Now you, beastie," Finn said. "Come out." Gil had disappeared deeper into the cave.

"I'm not a beastie," he called. "I'm a man."

"Then step out here and prove it."

Gil's ears drooped like Wile E. Coyote's as he crept to the front of the cave. Teagan and Finn walked over to him. Finn took his hand and pulled him out into the sunlight. Instantly the Cú Faoil surrounded them, hackles raised.

"No," Finn said firmly. "He's mine, too." One Cú Faoil came forward anyway, rumbling deep in its throat.

"I said no." Finn slapped its nose hard and it slunk away, but not very far.

"I feel like meat," Gil squeaked.

"Now you know how I felt, running with your pack."

"But . . . you *are* meat."

Finn looked at Teagan and pointed at the phooka, clearly asking if he could let the Cú Faoil have him. She shook her head.

"Sorry, sorry, sorry." Gil wrapped his arms around his head.

"Don't worry," Teagan said. "He wouldn't feed you to the dogs."

"I'm pretty sure I would," Finn said. "*If* I were meat. Let's go find Doirich. This lot will be coming along."

TWENTY-THREE

THE Cú Faoil didn't stop for berries or caterpillars. The alpha male, who had shown his belly to Finn, and the female Teagan assumed was his mate, the one whose nose Finn had slapped, were vigilant and all business, on the hunt and constantly alert.

The four younger dogs were not so diligent. They chased woolly squirrelephants, who moved surprisingly fast when they had to, and snapped at flying beetles.

Teagan noticed the leaves woven into their shaggy hair before she saw the sprites peeking out from behind tree limbs and out of leafy bushes. They were cautious at first, but within an hour they seemed to decide that Finn, Teagan, and Gil were no threat. They came out of hiding and flitted busily around the Cú Faoil, twining flowers and leaves into their fur.

"That's got to be troubling for any self-respecting war dog," Finn said as two sprites wove tiny daisies into the alpha male's mane.

"Maybe not," Teagan said. "Those flowers could be a kind of fleabane."

One sprite held a Cú Faoil's ear upright while another leaned in and pulled out a surprisingly large insect and ate it.

"It's a symbiotic relationship," Teagan said. "Like tickbirds and rhinos."

"Birds and rhinos?"

"Tickbirds eat ticks off of rhinos' hides," Teagan explained. "They also raise an alarm if danger is coming. I could study this place forever."

Finn gave her a worried look and turned back toward Gil, who had fallen behind while they talked.

"How much farther it is to Fear Doirich?"

"Not far. Ai!" Gil jumped and whirled. The female Cú Faoil was looking pointedly away from him. "It *tasted* me!"

Finn frowned. "You'd best walk close. I don't know how hungry the creatures are."

"*They're* creatures." Gil's ears drooped. "But *I'm* a beastie."

"Creatures are the way they were intended to be," Finn said. "I don't know who made phookas, but . . ."

"You call me 'beastie' because I'm broken?" He held up his trotter and considered it. "God doesn't *want* phookas to have friends. That's why he broke us." He lowered his voice to a conspiratorial whisper. *"But god isn't listening."* He looked shyly at Finn. "I know you are the Mac Cumhaill."

"Let that slip, did I, beastie?" Finn sighed.

"Gil," Teagan said. "You *could* just call him *Gil* instead of beastie."

Finn frowned at her, and Teagan frowned back.

"You can call me Rosebud," Teagan told the phooka.

"Rosebud," Gil echoed happily. "And *Mac Cumhaill!*"

"No," Finn said. "Don't call me that. You can call me—"

"Sexy beast," Teagan said.

"Sexy *beastie?!*" Gil's eyes went wide.

Finn glared at Teagan again before he turned to the phooka. "*You* don't call me that, either."

"I thought you said you liked it," Teagan said innocently.

Finn stalked ahead of them. Teagan winked at Gil, then hurried to catch up with Finn.

"He's trying to be friends."

Finn glanced back at Gil and ran his hand through his hair. "He's a goblin."

"So was Thomas. At one time."

"Crap." He walked a few yards more, then looked back again. "*Crap.* Keep up, my man," he called. "Or the creatures will get you for sure."

"My *man?*" Gil's ears went straight up, and he almost skipped as he caught up to them.

"Why do you even care what 'meat' calls you?" Finn asked.

"If I wasn't hungry," Gil said, "I might be like you. That's why."

"No, you wouldn't," Finn said. "Because I make sense. It has nothing to do with being hungry."

"Why are you hunting god, Rosebud?" Gil asked.

"Because he breaks things," Teagan said. "And I'm going to stop him."

"Saa thought god would want you," Gil continued. "Sometimes god will do things for you if you give him presents."

"What sorts of things?" Finn asked.

"Miracles," Gil said. "Saa said sometimes god does miracles. He wanted a miracle."

"What kind of miracle?"

"I don't know," Gil admitted. "If you want a very big miracle, you have to give god something very big."

"Saa was the one with the goat-head?" Teagan asked. Gil nodded. "I'm sorry about what happened to them. I should have said it before."

Gill looked surprised. "I didn't care."

"I do," Teagan said. "They hadn't done us any harm."

"They would have," Gil assured her. "If god didn't want you. They'd have eaten him." He pointed at Finn. "We don't eat Highborn, unless god gives us permission."

A flock of brilliant blue birds exploded out of a bush by their feet, and one of the young Cú Faoil leaped, taking a bird in midair. It chewed happily when it landed, dripping blood and blue feathers from its jaws. The sprites went after the smaller feathers with glee, gathering them up and adding them to their weaving.

"I can understand you not caring for the others, Gil," Finn said. "They tried to feed you to the Cú Faoil, didn't they? Why did you stay with them, then?"

"A phooka must never walk by himself," Gil said at last. "If you have no pack, the others might think you look . . . tasty."

"That's disturbing," Finn said.

"Phookas are always hungry. They didn't eat me because I caught fish. You don't eat me because I can find god."

"We're not like that," Teagan said.

"No," Gil agreed. "Highborn aren't hungry. Highborn are liars. And they bend phookas, if they know their names."

The sun was sinking when the Cú Faoil started fading into the bushes. The old female went first, and one by one the pups followed her, until only the male was left, walking by Finn's side. Finn stopped and looked at him. The Cú Faoil sat down, and the corners of his mouth pulled back in a canine grin. Sprites hovered around him, watching Finn.

"You go on home to the family," Finn said. "I appreciate the escort, but I know you sent them off, and now I'm sending you. You can't go where we need to go." The Cú Faoil whined, but he didn't follow them as they walked on. He was still watching the last time Teagan looked back.

They'd walked for perhaps an hour and a half more when Gil said, "Here, here, here! This is where god lives."

They had been working their way up an incline, and when they emerged from the bushes, she could see the drop-off of a cliff ahead of them.

"He's not g—" Teagan stopped as she stepped to the edge. This wasn't the crumbling castle where they'd first met Fear Doirich. They were looking down on the stone walls of a city. Pennants flew from the battlements, and glass glittered in tower windows. But between the cliff and the city, as far to the right and left as she could see, were colorless tents, lean-to shelters, and ramshackle shacks that seemed to have been made from parts scavenged from a dump. She had seen something like this in news stories about borders and wars. A refugee camp.

And between the camp and the city wall were larger, more colorful tents and awnings, and the busy stalls of what Teagan assumed was a market of some kind.

"We can't just walk in there," Finn said.

Gil nodded. "Yes, you can. Phookas can't eat Highborn without permission. No one is allowed to eat meat that belongs to the Highborn."

"So I should pretend that Finn belongs to me?"

"Yes," Gil said. "Then they won't eat him."

"And you're sure Fear Doirich is in there somewhere?" Teagan asked.

Gil nodded. "God lives here."

"Then why'd we find him at that crappy ruined castle the last time?" Finn asked as Gil led them around a fallen tree to a narrow path.

"Mab lives here, too, doesn't she?" Teagan tripped over a rock but caught herself before she fell. The path down the side of the cliff was steeper than it looked from above.

"Yes," Gil said. "Mab, too."

"And what does that signify?" Finn asked.

"Fear Doirich was after me," Teagan explained. "According to Thomas, those two get jealous over their little affairs. Fear must have told Mag Mell to lead us there so Mab wouldn't know about me."

"I'm going to hit him again," Finn said.

"You *hit* god?"

"Would you stop calling him that?" Finn demanded. "He's nothing more than a fallen *aingeal*."

"But he can do miracles," Gil said.

They'd reached the edge of the camp. The phookas there looked at Finn with altogether too much interest.

"You go in front, Rosebud," Gil said. "I'll come behind."

The path led them past pits where animals had been slaughtered. Bone fires burned beside them, stinking of hides and hooves. Young phookas leaped around and over the fires, while others were screaming and fighting, rolling in the dirt.

The camp's inhabitants stopped to watch as they passed.

"Where are we headed, exactly?" Teagan asked.

"To the fair," Gil said.

"It's a fair? Not just a market?"

"Samhain Fair."

A haunch of something that looked far too human was roasting on a spit, sputtering fat into the fire.

"Hurry a little," Finn said, "if you don't mind. I don't like the way they're looking at me."

A massive bull-head stepped in front of them.

"Get out of my way," Teagan commanded, and the creature took a step back. She still had to brush against him to get past.

Teagan had gone to a medieval fair with Abby once, and this was surprisingly similar. There were booths selling food and jewelry and drinks. The Highborn here seemed just as fond of fashion as Kyle, Isabeau, and Roisin were—only their clothes were from every era imaginable. It was as if Abby's video collection had exploded, spilling incredibly beautiful people—straight from Wardrobe and Makeup—on location in a horror film.

Steampunk and Goth mixed with powdered Victorian. There were zoot suits, rolled-up jeans and white T-shirts from the fifties, and tight disco pants and ruffled shirts. Some of the Highborn were shadowed—literally, their footsteps dogged by shadow men who melted into the ground when they stopped walking, only to leap up again when they moved, matching them pace for pace. Others didn't have shadows dogging their steps; they had slaves. Fir Bolg slaves, walking behind them, eyes on the ground. Lowborn goblins, somehow damp as if they had just crept out of a bog, were almost as numerous as the Highborn.

Teagan shivered. They were getting too much attention. Her glowing golden eyes caused goblins to stop and stare, and Finn was getting a *lot* of admiring looks from females of all species.

She glanced over her shoulder and realized that Gil had stopped. The phooka boy was transfixed in front of a stall where a butcher was dismembering a bloody pig carcass. He was staring open-mouthed at a tray of pigs' feet on the counter in front of him. Swarms of flies buzzed around the meat.

More carcasses hung by their hind legs at the front of the shop. They were cocooned in cheesecloth, with just the tail showing to tell what the animal inside might have been. Teagan felt a wave of nausea when she realized that she was looking at a row of *cat-sídhe* tails.

"Come on, then." Finn put a hand on each of their shoulders and pulled them away. "No time for gawping."

A Highborn woman picking pieces of fried frog off a skewer looked Finn up and down. "God," she said appreciatively. "I haven't seen anything like *that* around here since we fought the

Fianna. He smells *wonderful.* Is he for sale?" Her friends turned to look as well.

"I'm keeping him," Teagan said before Finn could open his mouth. *Smell.* That's the first thing she'd noticed about Finn. He did smell wonderful. *Goblin girls find warriors irresistible.* That's what Thomas had said.

More Highborn women seemed to be gravitating toward them. She'd better get Finn out of here before he caused a riot. The woman in front of her dug a card from her purse and held it out.

"If you change your mind, contact me first. Seriously. I want him."

"I'll do that," Teagan said, taking the card.

"I'm ready to leave now," Finn said, after the woman had walked on. A male Highborn strolled by wearing an elaborately jeweled codpiece. He wagged it and smirked when he saw Teagan looking. The woman hanging on his arm smiled at Finn, then looked Teagan up and down, frowning slightly at her jeans and T-shirt.

"Grunge," Teagan said as she edged past them. "It's my thing."

"What's the fair for?" Finn asked Gil. "Or is it like this all the time?"

"Samhain is coming. *Everyone* gathers for the hunt."

"They'll hunt a girl through the woods." Finn looked grim.

"Yes." Gil wiped a bit of saliva that had started to slide down his chin. "A *tasty* girl."

"The phookas are going to eat her?" Teagan asked. She had

known they hunted children. They'd hunted her mother. She'd just never imagined the end of the hunt before.

Gil's ears drooped. "Not me. I'm not fast or strong. There will be nothing left when I get there," he said sadly. "Not even little bitty bones."

"Gil," Teagan said, "that's broken, do you understand? Hunting and eating children is the worst kind of broken."

His ears drooped further. "But I still want to."

"Gil." Teagan tried to put power into the name. *"Promise me you will not hunt any child, ever."*

The phooka boy's eyes narrowed, and he took a step back.

"That's not my real name," he said. "Only a stupid phooka would tell a Highborn his real name."

"I'm not like other Highborn."

"Yes, you are," Gil said. "You tried to *bend* me. Just now. I felt it!" He turned and disappeared into the crowd.

"Gil!" Teagan shouted. She tried to go after him, but the phooka had completely disappeared. "Where do we go now?"

"Head for the city." Finn eyed the crowd. "And keep moving."

They left the crowded market to walk the narrower alley behind the booths. Dirty phooka children and *cat-sídhe* fought over scraps of garbage.

"This place is Hell," Finn said, stepping over the rotting remains of a small animal. Teagan couldn't tell what it had been, much less what had happened to it. "It's no wonder Mag Mell wants to be rid of the lot of them. The crowds were better than this." They left the alley behind the booths and went back into the crowded street.

"Fear Doirich has to be in the city," Teagan said. "Gil did say to head that way."

"Don't look now, but Gil's following us."

"Maybe he doesn't know anyone here, either."

"He's up to no good," Finn said. "If he finds Doirich before we do—" They came around a row of stalls, and saw Zoë Giordano sitting on a crate, a phooka baby on her lap.

TWENTY-FOUR

A SOCIAL worker," Finn said. "We *are* in Hell. You see Skinner anywhere?"

"Zoë's a dance therapist," Teagan corrected.

"A civilian, still." Finn looked worried. "She must have wandered in like your da did the first time. Well, at least she won't remember it. If she manages to get out."

"Can we take her with us?"

"I don't see how." Finn frowned. "But I don't like leaving her here, either."

Zoë was still wearing clothes that she must have bought in the sixties, and, Teagan could see as she got closer, she had added long beaded earrings and a rainbow-colored peace sign on a silver chain.

"Everyone's ignoring her," Finn said. It was true. Highborn, lowborn, and phookas were walking all around her, but they would turn their heads away or look down at the last moment. "I think it's the clothes. Do you think they'd ignore me if I wore that getup?"

"No," Teagan assured him. "You'd still be cute."

Zoë looked up and smiled as they approached.

"You make house calls in Hell?" Finn asked.

"I don't have an office," Zoë reminded him. "Pretty eyes, Teagan. How's Aiden doing?"

"He's a little bit better," Teagan said, touching the baby's head. It was fuzzy as a puppy.

"Good." If Zoë realized they were having a conversation in the midst of a goblin fair she showed no sign of it. "And school?"

"Mamieo is going with him every day."

Zoë nodded. "He shouldn't have to walk alone." She leaned past Finn, and Teagan turned to see what she was looking at.

Gil was peeking at them from behind a goblin girl who was arguing with a bead vendor. Zoë crooked a finger at him in a "come here" motion, but the phooka ducked back behind a tent.

"What are you doing here, woman?" Finn asked.

"The same thing I was doing at the Wylltson house. Working."

Finn shook his head.

"And you walked right in? No one tried to stop you?"

Zoë looked surprised. "Of course not. I had an appointment!"

"Would you excuse us a moment?" Finn pulled Teagan a few feet away. "She thinks she's *working*. That's exactly what your da thought, too. That he was at his library, *working*."

"She doesn't seem as crazy as Dad did."

They both turned to look at Zoë, and she smiled and waved.

Finn smiled waved back. "She must have gone right past Raynor and come in through the park."

"He didn't say anything about her."

"She could have come in after we did, while he was minding your body, and still gotten here first. Mag Mell's that twisty, isn't she?"

"How are we going to get her out of here?"

"We can't, Rosebud," Finn said. "We've only got one way out ourselves, remember? But the goblins seem to be ignoring the woman. She might wander out on her own, like your da did the first time."

"I'm going to talk to her," Teagan said, starting back. "I need to make sure she's okay."

Zoë held the baby up, and Teagan took him. It was like cuddling Aiden when he was an infant, tiny and helpless. The phooka squirmed, and its blanket fell open. It had little flippers where its arms and legs should have been, and its head was far too large for its deformed body.

"He's broken." Zoë smoothed the baby's blanket over its flippers again, tucking it around him. "It just means he needs a little more love, doesn't it?"

Zoë's hand brushed against Teagan's, and Teagan blinked. The *cantus firmus.* She *felt* it when Zoë touched her as clearly as she had *heard* it in the pool by Yggdrasil's roots.

Zoë smoothed the baby's fuzzy hair.

"Comforting the broken is what you were created to do," Teagan said softly. Like Mamieo was made to mend and tend. Like Aiden was made to sing.

"I wouldn't say *that.*" Zoë smiled. "But I do know what you are talking about. I see it in clients I counsel all the time. They struggle along, trying to figure out their lives, and suddenly something *clicks.* They understand what they are meant for. Their hopes and dreams become . . . actions. They become real."

"Rosebud," Finn said, "give the wee beastie back. We've got places to be."

Zoë took the baby. "He's right."

Finn hesitated, even though moving on was his idea. Teagan was sure he was struggling over having to leave the dance therapist. "Is there anything we can do for you before we go?"

"Yes, there is." Zoë picked up a coin from the dust at her feet. "Do you see that little girl over there?" She pointed at the lowborn goblin haggling with the bead vendor. "She's been trying to get those green glass beads for an hour, but she doesn't have quite enough money. Slip this into her pocket. She'll find it."

"I don't think we can do that without her noticing," Teagan said.

"I can." Finn took the coin.

Teagan started to follow him, then turned back to Zoë. "Aiden says that your dances *untangle* him. He needs to see you on Monday. So . . . go out the way you came in, okay?"

"Don't worry." Zoë winked. "I never miss an appointment."

Teagan nodded and walked away.

Finn passed the lowborn goblin, stumbled, and bumped against her.

"Don't touch me, filthy Fir Bolg," she howled.

"Sorry." Finn smiled at her, and the goblin girl's mouth fell open. "Sorry," he said again as he backed away. The girl saw Teagan and her face fell.

"Oh," she said, and shoved her hands in her pockets. Her eyes lit up, and she pulled out the coin.

"You're a reverse pickpocket?" Teagan demanded as they walked on.

"I never stole a thing in my life," he insisted. "But that doesn't mean I don't know how to do a little sleight of hand, then, does it?"

"There's something strange about Zoë," Teagan said.

"It's *goodness,*" Finn decided. "Even if she is a little crazy. Goodness shows through more in places like this. It's unexpected. I pray to God she gets out of here, because I'm coming back for her if she doesn't."

Finally, they reached the city gates, carved wooden doors standing wide open as Highborn and phooka passed in and out.

As soon as they stepped through, Teagan noticed a difference. There were no lowborn on the streets. None. And the phookas here wore leather collars, as did most of the Fir Bolg slaves. Phookas and Fir Bolg walked in the dirt of the streets, while the Highborn kept to the boardwalks that lined them.

"Have you seen Gil?" Finn asked.

"Not since he peeked at Zoë."

"He's going to rat us out. Give us to Doirich." They watched the crowd for several minutes. When there was no sign of the phooka boy, they started walking again.

"It's so beautiful," Teagan said. "I'm surprised the Sídhe could build something like this."

"They'd be surprised as well." Finn touched a carved face on the side of a building. "This was the home of the Fir Bolg. This is where my family came from. If the damn goblins hadn't stolen stonemasons and carpenters, it would have fallen apart by now."

Teagan noticed several Highborn eyeing them. "Step into the street," she said.

Finn jumped down off the boardwalk. "What's going on?"

"Tell you in a minute." Teagan walked two blocks, away from the curious eyes, then turned, called Finn to her, and pretended to adjust his shirt. "Slaves don't walk on boardwalks."

The crowds grew thicker as they walked past shops . . . clothing shops. The displays in the windows could have been done in Chicago, and Teagan was sure the fashions she was seeing were straight off the runway. Smash Pad would fit right in. They could hear the roar of a crowd ahead.

"Sounds like a party," Finn said. "We might as well look."

Teagan followed the sounds to an open area where a ring had been set up and bleachers built around it. There was a post as thick as a telephone pole in the middle. A phooka with a massive bear's head stood, head down, panting beside it. Blood from gashes on his arms ran down and dripped from his fingertips. His thick leather collar was attached to a chain with the other end spiked to the post. A brindle hound—not a Cú Faoil, but a smaller, leaner hound the size of a boxer dog—lay dead on the ground at the phooka's feet, its head twisted at an odd angle. There were other phookas in cages to one side, awaiting their turns in the ring.

"Blood sport." Teagan felt sick. "Thomas said they played at phooka baiting."

A bell rang, and three more hounds bounded into the ring. Tea realized that the collar was there to protect the phooka's neck, so they couldn't kill him quickly. A Highborn stood up in the bleachers, shook himself, and stooped forward as his arms turned to legs and his face shifted into the face of a hyena. He leaped into the ring, circling the dogs and phooka for a moment, then dodged in. The phooka tried to fight them off with his fists, but the hyena twisted as it leaped and caught his ear. The phooka bellowed in pain. The hyena pulled him to his knees before the ear tore off, and the other hounds were on him.

The crowd gasped appreciatively and leaned forward in their seats. Most of their faces reflected the same hunger Teagan had seen on the Highborn's face before he transformed. A few transformed as he had and leaped into the ring to join the feast; others transformed incompletely, their faces changing, but their bodies remaining largely human. They were hardly different from the phooka they were feeding on. Teagan turned away as the phooka's screams were drowned out by Highborn cheers.

"It's disgusting," Finn whispered. "Mamieo would never have told me to let Maggot Cat go, not if she'd seen the like of this. Damned goblins are all alike."

"Let's get out of here," Teagan said.

"Wait." Finn turned her toward the stands and pointed.

Fear Doirich was sitting in his own box. He was dressed entirely in black velvet, a golden circlet on his brow and a scepter in his hand. There was no bright corona around the fallen angel like there had been around Raynor, just a curtain of darkness behind him. The woman sitting by his side looked so much like

Teagan's mother that Teagan almost cried out—only this woman was leaning forward, watching the dying phooka with a look of . . . *lust* on her face. Great-Aunt Mab, who ordered her own children buried alive.

The dark curtain rippled as if the wind had blown across it, and Teagan realized it wasn't a curtain at all. It was a solid wall of shadow men. She swallowed the bile that rose in her throat. Fear's breath had smelled of rotting flesh, and his touch . . .

"One way out, girl." Finn took her hand. "One way home. All you have to do is grab him and hold on."

Teagan looked down at Finn's fingers twined with her own.

"How can I hold the knife in one hand, grab him with the other, and still hold on to you?"

"You can't." Finn looked grim. "That's why I've got the knife. You just grab the thing, and I'll do what needs to be done. If we take him to Raynor, it will be over."

Suddenly there was a shout, and the crowd parted before a phooka—Gil. He fell on his knees in front of Fear, holding up his hand and trotter, his head bowed.

"Move." Finn started pushing his way through the crowd. "They'll be onto us. We can't let Fear open his mouth to sing."

"I know."

"Just grab him, and have done with it."

"I know, I know."

Gil was talking as fast as he could, and pointing back toward them with his trotter. Fear Doirich looked at Mab, and the Highborn Queen grabbed the phooka boy by the ear, and dragged him to his feet.

"I brought them to you," Gil squealed as Finn shoved through the last of the crowd. "Give me my miracle!"

"Miracle?" Fear asked.

"Make me a man!" Gil lifted his trotter. "Please unbreak me, god! Please unbreak me."

The Dark Man looked at them over Gil's head, and laughed. "Teagan," he said, and she could feel the magic in his voice. "And the Mac Cumhaill. What a surprise. How did you get here without my knowing? Come closer." Teagan could feel the magic in his voice.

"Finn," Teagan whispered as she stepped forward.

"I'm with you, girl," he whispered back. "You just say when."

Not yet. She wasn't quite close enough to the Dark Man. Mab was studying them, a quizzical look on her face. Her eyes flicked from Teagan to the knife in Finn's hand, and widened ever so slightly. *She knows,* Teagan thought. Mab had figured it out in less than a heartbeat.

I'm almost there. Teagan took another step. *Mab won't be able to stop me.* The euphoria of the hunt stirred inside her, burning away her terror as if it were mist. Fear Doirich was right in front of her. She had him.

The phookas in the cages started to rattle the bars as her excitement jumped to them. Even the Highborn were turning toward her now, their eyes wicked with blood lust. She was *inspiring* them all. Finn was right. Mamieo had never seen creatures like this. *Like her.*

"God," Gil squealed. "They're here to—"

"Shut up," Mab said, pulling a bronze knife from her belt and holding it to Gil's throat. "How dare you speak in the presence of your god, phooka!"

Gil clapped his human hand over his mouth.

Something was wrong. Teagan could feel it. If Aiden were here she was sure he would say that the wrong song was playing over her, something much, much worse than "Bad Moon Rising." She tried to push the excitement of the hunt down. *Why is Mab helping us? Focus. Focus on what is happening here.*

The Dark Man turned toward Mab. "What have you done?"

"Created a tool. And she's even better than I'd hoped she would be." Mab laughed as the Dark Man glanced back at Teagan. "I'll deal with the swine, girl," Mab said. "Do what you came for! *Quickly!*"

Gil squealed as Mab's blade started to slide across his throat.

"Now, Finn!" Teagan shouted, and lunged. Her hand grasped a long, hairy ear, and the whole world exploded in pain.

TWENTY-FIVE

TEAGAN could see the silver moon above her . . . and Raynor. His mouth was open, and his hand was raised as if he were talking to someone just out of sight, but he wasn't moving. Nothing was moving. The world was frozen like a single frame of a film clip. They had made it back to Chicago, in the mid-morning, from the look of the sun.

She felt her heart beat once, and it echoed through her like someone banging on the side of an empty oil drum. Twice. She could feel the blood rushing through her. On the fifth heartbeat, someone hit the play button and the world was moving again.

Finn knelt beside her.

He ran his finger down her cheek. "You're all right, then?"

Teagan closed her eyes and nodded. The electricity was back. Kyle's retrovirus hadn't burned *that* out of her.

"Your fever's gone."

"Yes," Teagan managed.

"Thank God." He pulled her to her knees and into his arms. She could feel *his* heart beating and the blood rushing through *his* veins. And then he kissed her. The current increased, and intensified into a white-hot flame, a welding arc, starting at his lips and sizzling through her. *Melting them together.*

"God, I love my body," Teagan said when she came up for air.

"Mr. Mac Cumhaill? Would you care to tell me what's going on here?"

Teagan froze. *"Dad?"* She scrambled to her feet. *Raynor had been talking to her dad?*

Abby was standing beside Mr. Wylltson, her arms crossed. They were both in their nightclothes and coats. If Raynor hadn't been beside them with a very unhappy look on his face, it would have looked like a chilly pajama party, bedroom slippers and all.

Finn stood up slowly. "I was thanking the Almighty for bringing us safe from hell, John Wylltson."

"If people thanked God like that at church, I'd go more," Abby said. "That was totally a ten, Tea. In case you were wondering."

Teagan knew she was blushing, and she couldn't help it.

"If you're done with your *prayers*," Raynor said, "could you explain why you brought a phooka out of Mag Mell?"

"Gil!" Teagan looked around. The little phooka was curled at Joe's feet, holding his hand to his neck.

"Who's Gil?" Abby asked.

"You won't be able to see him," Teagan said. "He's next to the holly tree."

Abby pulled a baggie from her pocket, took a handful of cornstarch out, and tossed it in the air.

"Got him," she said as the powder settled in its energy dance around the phooka. "What's wrong with him? He looks hurt."

"Mab cut his throat."

"Tried to cut his throat." It was the first thing Joe had said since they got back. "It's just a little scratch."

"So you brought him out instead of Doirich?" Raynor started pacing. "This is why I can't work with Highborn. They don't stick to the plan."

"Maybe they are made to improvise, Raynor," Mr. Wylltson said. "I've never known my daughter to make a foolish decision." He pulled Teagan into a hug. "Before now, that is. Raynor explained what was going on, Tea. But, don't you ever go off without telling me again. Ever. I don't care if I can't see the goblins. I'm your father. It's my job to take care of you."

"Why didn't you bring Doirich?" Raynor demanded again. "If you had, it would be over. All of this would be over."

"No." Teagan pushed away from her dad, trying hard not to let the tears burning her eyes spill. "It wouldn't. Mab has a plan, and taking Doirich would have fit right in with it. I think she's smarter than you are, Raynor. Smarter than I am, and just as evil as the Dark Man. She may have changed my DNA . . . changed *me.* But I won't let her use me."

"DNA doesn't make you who you are inside, Tea," Mr. Wylltson said. "That hasn't changed."

Teagan shook her head. He hadn't heard her howling with the phooka. Hadn't seen the blood lust she inspired in the Highborn's eyes.

Gil whimpered.

"Poor thing." Joe sat down and gathered the phooka onto his lap. Gil squeaked and closed his eyes. Teagan wasn't sure whether he was feigning death or had actually passed out from fright. Either way, the young phooka's body had gone limp.

"You're going to be okay," Teagan told him, just in case he was pretending. "Joe doesn't eat phookas. He makes his own food from sunlight."

"That's true," Joe told him. "I'll take care of you."

"Gil, on the other hand,"—Teagan sighed—"eats children. So whatever you do, don't let go of him, okay, Joe?"

"It eats kids?" Abby eyed the phooka. "You mean like Aiden?"

"I'm not planning on taking him home."

"By the way." Finn glanced at Abby. "Thanks for coming to take care of her. I owe you."

"You don't owe me." Abby glared at him. "She's my best friend, remember?"

"Wait," Teagan said. "What's going on?"

Abby waved at Joe. "This tree guy wakes me up by knocking on the window, right? He has to jump up and down so that I can see him."

Joe jumped in place to demonstrate. It did make him easier to see.

"He says that Finn asked him to come and get me—"

"You should have sent for me," Mr. Wylltson said.

"Sorry, John," Finn said. "I needed someone in a hurry, and didn't consider that you'd be able to run to the park."

"How *did* you get here?" Teagan asked.

"I borrowed Zia Sophia's Geo," Abby said. "I didn't believe the tree at first. But you'd come home sick from school, and now you were missing. Something happened at school, right? So I called Jing. He told me about the teacher licking you, and getting stabbed. Then Leo calls, right in the middle of our conversation. The cops came to their house and arrested Rafe."

"Rafe?"

"They found the lunch lady in the river, with her feet in cement."

"Oh, no," Teagan said. *Kyle and Isabeau hadn't waited a couple of days to start playing with her friends.*

"The cops said there were witnesses who heard Rafe talking about it at school."

Molly? Or Isabeau? Oh, God. Molly. Isabeau was sharing her room. If the Highborn had started killing . . .

"Leo had already called some people to get the lowdown. Mrs. Meredith was missing parts. When he said she was missing parts, everything just clicked together in my head, like one of Rafe's *bada-bing* things. You asking about Bullen; the teacher getting stabbed. Jack the freaking Ripper is teaching in our school, and you didn't tell me? What where you thinking, Tea?"

"Yes, what were you thinking?" her dad asked.

"That I could deal with it before any of you woke up," Teagan said.

"Just you and Dumpster boy?" Abby snorted. "The Turtles are on their way to school to deal with it."

"Abby, they can't. He's not human."

"We know. And guess what? We don't care what kind of unnatural he is. He messed with Rafe, right?" Abby's voice was shaking with anger. "He broke into my apartment and killed my fish."

"I still think we should call the police," Mr. Wylltson said. "Even though Raynor—"

"It's my job to deal with the likes of Kyle, John," Finn said. "Not the police. Not Gabby or her cousins, either. And if the creatures have started killing people, I need to be about it. Crap! My knife didn't make it out of Mag Mell!"

Teagan lifted one foot. Her mother's shoes hadn't come along, either. But bare feet and pajamas were the least of her problems.

If the goblins had started killing . . .

"Dad," Teagan asked, "where's Aiden?"

"I thought it would be best if he stayed home today, at least until we knew what was going on. Mamieo is looking after him."

Teagan bit her lip. Mamieo had been fighting goblins all her life. She would be careful. So why did she want to run home right now and make sure her brother was safe? She turned to Abby. "Why are the Turtles going to the school? It would be better to keep the other kids out of it."

Abby shrugged. "I told them to. It's the only place we can find him. Jing got into the district's computers for me. There's no information on Bullen there—no phone number, no home address. And he's only teaching one class. I figure the guy's not human, right? He could be hanging from the rafters someplace all night for all we know. But he'll be in class today, because he's after Tea."

Finn was looking at Abby as if she'd suddenly sprouted horns.

"What are you looking at?" Abby demanded. "You're the

one who sent the tree to find me. You expect I'd just sit here and worry?"

"What time is it?" Teagan asked.

"One."

"Class has already started."

"The Turtles are always late," Abby said. "But Jing won't let Bullen out of class until they get there."

"What did you tell him?" Teagan asked.

"That Kyle is Jack the Ripper. What do you think?"

Finn put both hands to his head.

"Jing was going to be in class anyways," Abby said. "I'm supposed to let him walk into that without knowing? I don't think so."

"He believed you?"

"He'll be careful," Abby said.

"Raynor." Joe was staring at the tree line. "You'd best look at this."

A roiling wall of shadow was bulging out of Mag Mell.

"I am assuming this means you made Doirich angry." Raynor took a step toward the wall of shadows.

It came completely out from under the trees into the bright sunlight, as tall as the willow and stretching across half of the park, a solid wall of darkness. No, not solid. Arms and legs and heads and hands twisted and churned in it, sometimes breaking out, only to be reabsorbed into the mass.

"Shit," Raynor said.

Mr. Wylltson frowned. "Are angels supposed to use that kind of language?"

"You'd use it, too, if you could see what I see."

"What is that thing?" Finn asked.

"Call it Legion," Raynor said. "For they are many."

"Demons," Mr. Wylltson said, turning toward the trees. "Like the shadow that killed my wife."

Raynor nodded. "They're going to try to get past me. I could use your help, John."

"*My* help?"

"Teagan told me you sang the shadows away in Mag Mell. I suspect these are hiding something. Something they hope will kill me so that they can come out after your children. If you stand in the doorway and sing—"

"Go," Mr. Wylltson said. "I'm right behind you."

Raynor started toward the darkness, growing brighter as he walked.

"Mr. Mac Cumhaill," Mr. Wylltson said, "thank you for going after my daughter. For bringing her home."

Finn nodded.

"And don't let anything happen to her."

"Yes, sir."

"Now you kids get out of here." John Wylltson's bedroom slippers slapped the frosty lawn as he started after Raynor.

When they reached the Geo in the library parking lot, Teagan crawled into the tiny space behind the seats, trying to focus on what might be happening at school instead of worrying about her dad and brother. Aiden was safe with Mamieo, and Thomas was there as well. . . . *Thomas*. She'd been sure Finn was right about him. But she wasn't sure about anything anymore. Not after what she'd seen in Mag Mell.

The tires squealed as they left the parking lot.

"If the cops stop us, we'll never get to the school, Gabby."

"When you have a car, Dumpster boy, you can drive."

"I need my shoes," Teagan blurted.

Abby glanced at her in the rearview mirror. "You want to check on Choirboy, right?"

"Please, Abby. I know we're in a hurry."

Abby did a U-turn.

Teagan jumped out of the Geo as soon as they reached her house. "Wait here," she said. "I'll be really quick."

Aiden and Mamieo were playing cards on the couch when she stepped through the door. Thomas, Roisin, and Grendal were watching. Aiden was more than all right—he was almost glowing with motes of Mamieo's glamour dust, which had escaped into the house. *It's the Milesian in him,* Mamieo had once said. The Milesian that had been burned out of her by Kyle's DNA.

"Tea!" Aiden shouted, dropping his cards and running to her, Lucy clinging to his hair. "I woke up in the dark and you were gone. So I sang for you."

"I know." She hugged him hard. "I heard you."

Thomas and Roisin stood up as well.

Thomas put his arm around Roisin. "You've been back to Mag Mell. You've seen our people. Seen what it's like."

"Yes," Teagan said. *Our people.*

"Finn." Mamieo's hand went to her chest. "My grandson. Is he—"

"Waiting for me in the car." Teagan ran up the stairs and grabbed her sneakers. She'd looked Thomas in the eye, and she still wasn't sure she trusted him. Not completely. Not after meeting the rest of the family. She didn't want to leave Aiden here without her or Finn, but it would be more dangerous to take him to the school to face Kyle.

When she went back down the stairs, they all started asking questions at once. She waved them off. "Aiden," she said when she reached the door, "sing for Dad. Sing your best song."

Teagan had to contort into a ridiculous pose to get her shoes on in the small space behind the seats, but she managed. She was tying the last lace when her phone vibrated in her pocket. She had completely forgotten about it. She pulled it out and flipped it open.

"Tea?" Agnes sounded like she'd been crying. "Are you in class?"

"Not yet. What's wrong?"

"They picked up Oscar this morning. They're taking him back. All the papers were in order. I did everything right. I don't understand how this could happen."

"I do," Teagan said. She couldn't watch over all of her friends. Some were going to die, unless she stopped the gob—her family. Unless she could stop her family.

"Dr. Max is making calls," Agnes was saying, "trying to sort it out. Wait—he's on the other line. Gotta go."

They made it to the school in less than twenty minutes. There were no police cars in the lot. Teagan took that for a good sign. The security guard didn't want to let them in the front doors, until Finn smiled at her.

"Go to the office and get passes," she called after them, but they were already running toward the classroom.

Isabeau was sitting at her desk. Molly's desk was empty. Kyle was standing at the board at the front of the room. He had written:

Sadism is all right in its place, but it should be directed to proper ends. —Sigmund Freud

And underneath that:

Sadism: the derivation of pleasure as a result of inflicting pain or watching pain inflicted on others.

The faces of the students in the room were tense, as if they had been arguing. Cade was sitting at a desk on one side of the center aisle, and Jing was sitting across the aisle from him. Whatever Abby had told them, it was enough to make them wary.

"There you are, Ms. Wylltson," Mr. Bullen said when Teagan stepped in. "I was beginning to think you weren't going to come—" His eyes slid past her to Finn. He snarled, but Isabeau just sat quietly, waiting to see what would happen.

"Where's Molly?" Teagan asked her.

"Gone," Isabeau said.

"We're here for Mr. Bullen," Teagan told her. "You can go back to Mag Mell, Isabeau."

"Or I can send you," Finn offered.

"I'm supposed to bring Tea with me," Isabeau said.

"I've already been," Teagan told her.

"Bad move," Kyle said. He took one step forward, jerked Cade out of his seat and slashed his stomach open, then shoved him at Teagan. He had no knife. He didn't need one, Teagan realized, as Cade's blood spread over her. He had claws.

Jing leaped to his feet. Kyle slashed at him, but Jing jumped back, and the claws caught only his jersey.

Kids were screaming and coming out from behind their desks, running for the door, but Teagan couldn't move without dropping Cade. She saw the pupils of his eyes widening as he went into shock, but he was too heavy for her to lower to the floor without dropping him. And then Abby was beside her, helping.

Kyle reached for Abby, but suddenly Finn was between them. His fist caught Kyle on the jaw and the Highborn staggered, then shook himself hard. When he stopped shaking, the glamour was gone. His forehead sloped over yellow-green eyes, and he had a half-human, half-animal muzzle. A shape shifter, but not a complete one.

Jing picked up a desk and threw it at him. Kyle ducked, and when he came up, Finn hit him again.

Someone had pulled an alarm—lockdown was sounded over the intercom, as if there were a shooter in the school. *Good. Everyone will be shut in their classrooms, away from danger.*

Kyle snarled at Finn, and then ran . . . up the wall. Abby crossed herself and shielded Cade with her body as she began to pray the rosary.

Kyle was crawling across the ceiling over Finn's head. Jing picked up another desk and threw it. His aim was better this time, and it knocked the Highborn from the ceiling. He fell on the other side of Finn and ran out the door. Finn was right behind him.

"Where's Leo?" Abby said, getting up. "I swear I'm going to kill him. I told him to be here. Don't worry, Tea. You take care of this guy. I'll find the Turtles."

"Cade?" Jing fell to his knees beside Teagan.

"He's in shock."

"Oh, man," Jing whispered, looking at the intestines that had spilled out over the floor. "Damn. Damn. Damn."

"He's not dead yet," Teagan said. "Call 911, and tell them he's been disemboweled. They can still help him. And don't touch"—she waved at the mess of intestines—"anything. Don't try to put it back; you'll only make it worse. Just make sure he lies still until they get here." Abby and Isabeau were both gone, along with the rest of the students who had been in the classroom. Teagan left Jing dialing his cell phone.

The hall was empty, all the classroom doors shut and locked. Finn had run through Cade's blood, and his tracks led toward the cafeteria. Teagan was almost there when someone screamed. She skidded through the doorway, and stopped.

Finn, Angel, Leo, and Donnie had Kyle surrounded. She didn't see Isabeau anywhere, but Abby was standing by the salad bar, her mouth open, and her hand up as if she could stop what was about to happen.

Someone hadn't made it into lockdown. Teagan didn't know the girl Kyle was holding off the floor by her hair. She was screaming and twisting, trying to get away. Kyle tickled her belly with his claws. "I've been waiting for you, Tea!"

Finn reached for his knife that wasn't there; Abby whirled and grabbed a whole bucket of flatware from the salad bar.

"Dumpster boy!" she shouted, and threw the whole thing at

Finn. The flatware spilled out of it as it tumbled. Finn snatched a spoon out of the air, and his hand flicked toward Kyle. The spoon seemed to blossom from the dent at the base of the Highborn's neck, even as the rest of the flatware rained to the floor.

Kyle let go of his hostage's hair to grab the spoon with both hands, but before he could pull it out, Angel had the girl, and then Leo was right against the Highborn's back. It was only when Kyle arched that Teagan realized that Leo had a knife in his hand. Kyle went down so violently that the knife was pulled from Leo's grip.

The girl he'd been holding ran screaming from the room.

Leo stepped back. "When you get to Hell, tell them Leo Gagliano sent you."

Teagan felt the tears welling in her eyes as she stared at Kyle's motionless form.

"Tea," Finn said as she walked past him. "Don't cry. Two worlds are better off without Kyle in them."

"Yeah, right," Abby said. "That's like telling her not to be Teagan Wylltson. You're welcome, by the way."

"For?" Finn asked.

"Passing the silverware? I told you I was psychic."

"What?"

"I said if we ever got attacked in a restaurant we'd be safe, right?"

"This is a cafeteria, Gabby. And you said if Tea was attacked, she'd be safe."

"So, she's safe."

Teagan shut out their bickering as she knelt beside Kyle. He turned his face toward her as the pool of dark blood spread around them. She could feel the life seeping out of him. He didn't have the strength to move again, but even through his beast-mask of a face, Teagan could see the fear. Kyle was afraid of dying. She couldn't pretend she wasn't glad his life was over. Glad he wouldn't hurt anyone else. But the fear in his eyes was unbearable.

Teagan took his hand, careful of the claws, and held it in her own, pressing her palm to his. Kyle's eyes widened in surprise.

Leo pulled a handkerchief from his pocket, took the spoon from Kyle's other hand, and wiped it down.

"What are you doing?" Finn asked.

"Prints," Leo said. "Any security cameras, Angel?"

"I'll have Jing take care of it," Abby said.

"Who's this Jing?" Leo asked.

"I'll introduce you sometime. Right now you should take Finn and get out of here. The cops will be here any minute."

Kyle's eyes clouded, and Teagan felt the last flicker of life drain away. *Like it had drained from her mother.* Aileen Wylltson had never opened her eyes as she lay dying. But her face had been . . . peaceful. Teagan's lips moved, silently forming her mother's poem:

> *Selves—goes itself;* myself *it speaks and spells,*
> *Crying* Whát I do is me: for that I came.

"You should get away from that thing, Tea," Leo said. "It's probably got diseases."

"Leave her alone, Leonardo," Abby said. "Tea does what she does."

Teagan closed her eyes. *Tea does what she does.*

I may be Highborn. But I am not *like my family.*

What I do is me: for this I came.

If I am any creature of yours, Almighty, she prayed, *help me speak and spell something other than this into creation. Give me the courage to live what I am.*

"Are you praying for him? That's rich."

Teagan looked up. Isabeau had come into the room.

"For myself," Teagan corrected.

Finn started toward Isabeau.

"Finn," Teagan said. "Wait. I want her to carry a message. Tell Mab I said no more."

"No more games?" Isabeau laughed. "Oh, there's plenty more coming. Have you heard about your little chimp friend yet?"

"I heard." Teagan pulled Leo's knife from Kyle's body. Leo reached for it, but she waved him away.

"What are you doing?" Abby asked.

"What I came for." Teagan stood up. "Tell Mab I won't allow her to hurt my family and friends."

"*You're* challenging Mab? By yourself?" Isabeau scoffed.

"She's not by herself, is she, goblin?" Finn said.

"You mess with her, you mess with us," Abby agreed.

Isabeau pushed her shades up on top of her head, and her oil-puddle eyes looked blankly at Teagan. "You know this means war."

"Then let there be war," Teagan said, and threw the knife like she meant it.

ABOUT THE AUTHOR

Kersten Hamilton is the author of *Tyger Tyger,* Book One of the Goblin Wars trilogy, as well as several picture books and many middle grade novels. She has worked as a ranch hand, a woodcutter, a lumberjack, a census taker, a wrangler for wilderness guides, and an archeological surveyor. Now, when she's not writing, she hunts dinosaurs in the deserts and badlands of New Mexico. For more about Kersten, please visit www.kerstenhamilton.com.